PRIVATE
DOWN UNDER

JAMES PATTERSON
& MICHAEL WHITE

PRIVATE
DOWN UNDER

CENTURY

Published by Century, 2013

2 4 6 8 10 9 7 5 3 1

First published in Australia in 2012 by Century Australia

First published in Great Britain in 2013 by
Century
Random House, 20 Vauxhall Bridge Road,
London SW1V 2SA

www.randomhouse.co.uk

Addresses for companies within The Random House Group Limited can be found at:
www.randomhouse.co.uk/offices.htm

The Random House Group Limited Reg. No. 954009

A CIP catalogue record for this book
is available from the British Library

Hardback ISBN 9781846058905
Trade paperback ISBN 9781846058912

The Random House Group Limited supports the Forest Stewardship Council®
(FSC®), the leading international forest-certification organisation. Our books
carrying the FSC label are printed on FSC®-certified paper. FSC is the only
forest-certification scheme supported by the leading environmental organisations,
including Greenpeace. Our paper procurement policy can be found at:
www.randomhouse.co.uk/environment

Printed and bound by CPI Group (UK) Ltd, Croydon, CR0 4YY

Prologue

I'D SEEN PICTURES of Justine Smith, Jack Morgan's No. 2 at Private LA, but she was far more beautiful in the flesh.

I stood at Sydney Airport International Arrivals and watched her waft out of customs with a trolley looking like she was ready for a model shoot – no clue she'd just been on a 14-hour flight. She was here to launch the latest branch of the Private franchise created by Jack Morgan in LA – a top-notch investigative agency for top-notch people.

I held back, let her family greet her first. There was her sister, Greta, and husband, my new buddy, Brett Thorogood, the Deputy Commissioner of New South Wales Police, their kids, Nikki, eight and Serge, ten. Then I stepped forward, shook her hand.

I'd parked my Ferrari 458 Spider in the pick-up zone. The Thorogoods headed off after we'd all synchronized watches for the launch party tonight and we were off, pulling out of the airport and onto the sun-drenched freeway.

None of us could have known what a fuck of a week we were about to have.

Chapter 1

HE CAN SEE nothing.

He can hear nothing.

He runs, gasping, hits a hard object – face first. His nose shatters, sending a cascade of agony through his head and down his spine. Falls back, slams to the floor. His head cracking on concrete. More pain.

He can see nothing.

He can hear nothing.

The sack hood over his head stinks of sweat and blood. He tries to loosen the ties, but it's no good.

He vomits, it hits the fabric, splashes on his face.

He thinks he'll choke and part of him doesn't care, wants it. But the survival genes kick in and he panics, pulls up, the spew running down his shirt front. He reaches out and touches the wall. Moves left as fast as he can. He feels the vibration of feet, people running toward him.

A burst of terrible agony in his back. Two thumps propel him to the wall. He smells fresh blood. He smells tire rubber. Another crunch, his thigh exploding. But he keeps to the wall, sweat running down his ruined face, blood drips from his nose, his leg, his back. He feels wet all over. He's a leaking sieve, his life draining away. The pain in his legs screams. The hood fabric sucks into his mouth.

He has to keep going. 'MOVE OR DIE . . . MOVE OR DIE,' a voice bellows in his head. Shrapnel clips his ear. He screeches, feels his guts heave. Another bullet thunders past his head, but he doesn't hear it, just feels the air tremble. Dust and concrete chips hit him in the face. His legs start to buckle, but he refuses to give in.

'MOVE OR DIE. MOVE OR DIE.'

He feels a door, pushes, stumbles through, trips, hits the concrete again. Blood splashes across the floor, up the walls. He pulls up once more.

He's on a roller coaster, at the park with Grandma. He's four years old. Then he's floating in space. No reference points.

He can see nothing.

He can hear nothing.

He senses the air tremble again.

He touches wood. Another door. It moves forward. He's falling . . . and dies before he hits the ground.

Chapter 2

I HEARD THE crash from the other side of the room and for a second I thought one of the hired caterers had screwed up. But then a woman screamed and I was dashing across reception.

I caught a glimpse of my right-hand woman, Mary Clarke, spin on her heel. She's a big, muscly girl but has the reaction time of Usain Bolt off the blocks.

I saw the blood first. A smear, then a dark pool spreading out across the marble. The man lay spread-eagled on the floor, face down, torn apart, gaping holes in his back, his right leg shattered, twisted obscenely under him. A hood over his head.

I crouched down as Justine Smith ran up.

Pulling a tissue from my pocket, I wrapped it around my fingers, turned the body over and tried to remove the hood, but it was tied fast. I glanced up to see Deputy Commissioner Thorogood.

"Jesus!" he said as he lowered beside me.

"Multiple gunshot wounds. Twice in the back, leg," I said and tilted the body so Thorogood could study the ragged circles in the guy's linen jacket.

Darlene, Private's tech guru, squatted down close to the

body. She's usually in a lab coat over jeans, but tonight she was wearing a red cocktail dress that accentuated her incredible curves. She pulled on latex gloves, removed a sharp implement from her clutch purse. Leaning forward, she cut the ties of the hood and eased up the fabric.

"Holy Christ!" Thorogood exclaimed.

Chapter 3

HIS EYES HAD been gouged out. There were two red craters in their place. The skin was jagged, blood oozing. A gray bundle of nerves snaked from the left socket and stuck to the skin of the man's cheek.

It was hard to tell for sure, but he looked like a young kid, maybe late teens, twenty tops. The rest of his face was smeared, his nose smashed to hell.

I heard Johnny Ishmah, the youngest of my team, behind me. I turned to him. "Johnny get everyone out." Then I saw Mary. "Come with me."

The Deputy Commissioner straightened and pulled out his cell as he walked away.

I heard him say "Inspector . . ." His boys would be here in minutes.

"Well, not your average gatecrasher," I heard Darlene mumble as Mary and I headed for the door.

"Blood trail." I flicked a glance at the floor just beyond the door.

"Passage ahead leads to the garage," Mary responded.

There was a slew of blood across the concrete, up the walls.

Picking our way round the puddles I leaned on the second door and we were out onto "Garage Level 1". Plenty of blood still, oval droplets on the rough concrete. The sort of splashes someone makes when they are running and bleeding at the same time.

The poor kid had stopped here, blood had pooled into a patch about two feet wide that was rippling away toward a drain in the floor. The trail led off to the left. Three cars stood there, a Merc, a Prius and my black Spider. Tire marks close to the bend, more blood.

I bent down and picked up a shell casing, holding it in the tissue still in my hand.

".357 Sig," Mary said. She was ex-Military Police, knew a thing or two.

"Pros."

"Must be cameras everywhere." She glanced around.

"Small garage. There's a guard at the gate. He has a security camera system." I turned and led the way back. The road narrowed, a barrier twenty yards ahead. Next to that, a booth.

I could see immediately the place was hit. Glass everywhere, the guard slumped unconscious, a row of monitors an inch from his head. The cable to a hard drive dangling. Standard system . . . record the garage for twelve-hour rotations on a terabyte hard drive. Wipe it, start again.

"Took the hard drive," Mary said nodding at the lead.

I crouched down beside the guard and lifted his head gently. He stirred, pulled back and went for his gun. That had gone too.

"Whoa buddy!" Mary exclaimed, palms up.

The guy recognized me. "Mr. Gisto." He ran a hand over his forehead. "Holy shit . . ."

"Easy, pal." I placed a hand on his shoulder. "Remember anything?"

He sighed. "Couple a guys in hoodies. It all happened so bloody quick . . ."

"Alright," I said, turning to Mary. There was a sudden movement beyond the booth window. A cop in a power stance, finger poised to the trigger.

A second later Deputy Commissioner Thorogood appeared in the doorway, touched the officer's arm. "Put it down, constable."

It was then I saw the third guy, standing next to Thorogood. Middle build, five-ten, hard, lived-in face. I recognized him immediately and felt a jolt of painful memories. Covered it well. I knew he instantly recognized me, but he pretended he hadn't. The devious son of a bitch.

Chapter 4

A COP CAR pulled up to the gate, tires screeching. Close behind, a van, "FORENSICS" on the side.

Outside, Thorogood made the introductions. He seemed oblivious to the animosity in the air. "Craig Gisto and Mary Clarke, Private Sydney – a new investigative agency started by a friend of mine, Jack Morgan in LA. These guys head up the Sydney branch. Craig, Mary . . . this is Inspector Mark Talbot, Sydney Local Area Command."

"And what are they doing here?" Talbot studied my face. I half-smiled back.

"We have an arrangement . . ." Thorogood responded.

"Arrangement, sir?"

"Didn't you get my memo? We help Private, Private helps us . . . Understand? So what do we have here, Craig?" the Deputy Commissioner turned to me.

"Lotta blood. Your forensics guys'll have fun. The hard drive for the security cameras walked." I flicked a glance toward the booth. "And I found this." I pulled the tissue from my jacket pocket and handed the bullet casing to Thorogood.

"That should have been left where you found it . . ." Talbot remarked angrily.

".357 Sig." Thorogood ignored the Inspector. "Okay, so what do you want from us, Craig? Mary?"

"Give Darlene access to the crime scene and ten minutes with the body before it's taken to the morgue."

Thorogood nodded. "Fine."

"What!" Talbot exclaimed and glared at us. Then he saw Thorogood's expression and shut up.

Chapter 5

THE PARTY ROOM was almost empty. Most of the Police Forensics team were still down in the garage, dusting, photographing, videoing, gathering samples. The guard was en route to hospital. A single police scientist in a blue plastic boiler suit crouched beside the corpse. The man looked irritated.

I walked over. Darlene was on her knees, her face close to the dead kid's back. The forensics officer was holding a plastic sample bottle in one gloved hand, a pair of tweezers in the other. Beside him in a metal box lay half a dozen more sample bottles.

"She with you?" the guy asked without moving his head. "She's *really* pissing me off. This is a crime scene."

Darlene treated him as though he wasn't there.

"We have clearance to observe," I told him.

"I'll need that officially verified."

"No you won't," Darlene snapped. "But, if you insist, I'll have my good friend, Deputy Commissioner Thorogood, remind you . . . Oh, and . . ." She nodded toward the box of samples. "I'll need access to those too, please." She gave him a killer smile.

Chapter 6

SUMMER RAIN HIT the windshield as I pulled the Ferrari out of the lot and headed for the North Shore. My mind was churning. Not only because of the dead kid at the drinks reception. My head was buzzing with just three words: "The Bastard's Back". Mark fucking Talbot had returned to Sydney and he was going to get right up my nose, just as Private starts in business. I punched the wheel in frustration, glared at the girders of the Harbour Bridge and the memories started up, couldn't stop 'em.

I'm twelve. My crack-head mom is burned to a crisp in the London project I grew up in. Poor little orphan Craig is shipped out to Sydney and Uncle Ben. Within a week, I go from a mildewed tenement in winter to a four-bedroomed house in Narrabeen and sunshine.

The Talbot family meet me at the airport and there's my cousin, Mark, giving me the sort of hostile look he's never lost. He obviously hates me straight off the bat.

Four years later, I'm alone doing my homework. Mark bursts into my room with a couple of mates. They've been drinking. They stink. I go to get up and Mark slams a fist in my face. One of his friends kicks me in the balls. I spit blood onto the carpet. They hear my uncle turn the key in the front door, run. I spend the next day under the covers pretending I have flu so Ben doesn't see my face until I can come up with an excuse.

Then sweet release. I'm eighteen and go to university to study Law. In my second year I join an exchange program with UCLA, spend a year in the States. It turns out to be the best year of my life. I return home to Oz at Easter – it's the last thing I want.

Ben picks me up at the airport. We jump in the car.

"Mark's engaged," he says.

I look stunned.

"Why so surprised?"

I shake my head. "Nothing . . . just. I didn't know he was even seeing anyone . . ."

"All been a bit quick, I admit. Becky's a babe though. There's a party tonight."

Mark has changed, almost friendly. Amazing what love can do, I think. Then I see Becky and I understand. Love at first sight.

I still don't know how the fight started. I was chatting to Becky in the kitchen and Mark must have thought I was flirting with her – which maybe I was. He was drunk and abusive. He took a swing at me, and that was it. We crashed into the lounge, parting stunned guests like a knife through an engagement party cake. Would have killed each other if it hadn't been for Ben and three other guys pulling Mark and me apart.

When I'd recovered enough to see straight, I realized Becky had slipped away unnoticed.

The next day she called Mark to call off the engagement. It was to be five years before I saw her again.

Chapter 7

DARLENE'S LAB STOOD along the corridor from where Private's launch party had been. It was her fiefdom. In here, she felt relaxed, isolated from the troubles of the outside world. Which was a little ironic, considering what was in the case she dumped on the counter.

She had designed the lab herself and been given carte blanche to install the best equipment available. Better still, through her contacts, she had some technology no one beyond Private would see for years to come. She was very proud of that.

Police forensics had worked through the night and catalogued everything before passing on the samples to Darlene an hour ago. A courier had delivered a case of test tubes and a USB at 6 am. She'd already been at Private for an hour.

She opened the clasps of the sample box and looked inside. Each test tube was labeled and itemized by date, location and type. They contained samples of the corpse's blood, scrapings from under his fingernails, individual hairs from his jacket. She had a collection of her own photographs and a file from the police photographer.

There was no ID on the body. The victim was male, Asian, between eighteen and twenty-one years old. Both eyes removed with a sharp instrument. Wasn't a professional job. By the condition of the wound, it was done at least thirty-six hours before death. Sockets were infected. He was a mess, his clothes badly soiled. They stank of sweat, urine and excrement. He'd probably been in them for days, held captive some place. But the jacket he'd worn was expensive – Emporio Armani – and his hair had been well cut, maybe two weeks ago. He was obviously from a wealthy family.

So it seemed likely they were looking at kidnap, Darlene mused. Maybe the kid had escaped his captors. Maybe he'd stopped being useful. No way of knowing . . . yet.

She removed a selection of test tubes from the case and walked over to a row of machines on an adjacent bench, each device glistening new. She slotted the test tubes into a metal rack, pulled up a stool, switched on the machines and listened to the ascending whir of computers booting up and electron microscopes coming on-line.

The first test tube was labeled: "Nail Scraping. Left *digitus secundus manus*." With the tweezers, she slid out the piece of material. It was a couple of millimeters square, a blob of blue and pink. She placed it on a slide, lowered a second rectangular piece of glass over it and positioned the arrangement in the cross-hairs of the microscope.

The image was a pitted off-white. Set to a magnification of x1000, human flesh looked like a blanched moonscape. She tracked the microscope to the right and refocused. It looked almost the same, only the details were different. She set the tracking going again, back left, past the starting position. Refocused. Paused. Sat back for a second, then peered into the eyepiece once more. "Now that *is* weird," she said.

Chapter 8

I WAS PULLING into the parking lot below Private when my cell rang.

"Hey Darlene. So what'd you find out?" I wiped away a trickle of sweat running down my cheek. My car's thermometer read ninety-two degrees.

"The police have ID'ed the victim. His name's Ho Chang, nineteen, left Shore School last year. His father is Ho Meng, a well-known and very wealthy importer/exporter. The boy was reported missing two days ago."

"Well that's something."

"I found out some other stuff too."

"Great . . . What?"

"I'd rather show you – in the lab."

"See you in a minute."

Mary and Johnny were in reception before me. I was surprised. It was only 8 am. I was even more surprised to see a tall man in a finely tailored suit getting out of one of the chairs across the coffee table. Beside him stood a guy in a gray suit.

A bodyguard, I guessed. He had that boneheaded look about him.

Johnny retreated and Mary led me over. "This is Mr Ho Meng . . . My boss, Craig Gisto."

We shook hands.

"I just heard," I said. "Please accept my . . ."

He raised a hand, shaking his head slowly.

I was lost for words for a moment, then put out a hand to indicate we should walk along to my office.

Mary and Ho sat at opposite ends of my sofa and I pulled round a chair. The bonehead stood by the door, arms folded.

"Mr. Ho and I have met before," Mary began. She was wearing cargo pants and a tight, short-sleeved tee that accentuated the girth of her arms. "Mr. Ho was a Commissioner in the Hong Kong Police Force. I met him when he delivered a special lecture at the Military Police College a few years back."

"I would like you to find my son's killer," Ho responded. His voice was remarkably refined. I guessed Oxford or Cambridge.

"I assume the police are . . ."

"I do not trust the Australian police, Mr. Gisto."

I watched him. He'd drifted off into grief for a second, but then his expression hardened, a carefully constructed shield against the world.

"Well, of course, Mr. Ho. That's what we do."

"My son was reported missing more than two days ago. His death was preventable. The police did nothing."

"I'm sure they tried."

"Don't make excuses for them, Mr. Gisto." He had his imperious hand up again. "They're either incompetent, lazy or lack resources. Whatever it is I won't work with them."

"Mr. Ho, what can you tell us about your son? Any clues how he got into trouble?" Mary asked.

He sighed. "Chang was a wonderful boy. Headstrong, for sure. He was profoundly deaf, but struggled for independence. He was a brilliant lip-reader. Insisted he have his own apartment as soon as he left school."

"He was deaf?" I said, surprised.

Ho nodded. "From the age of four." He glanced at Mary. "I would be the first to admit that this is partly my fault. I've not exactly been a model father. Chang's mother died twelve years ago. I've been obsessed with my business. I could never find the time. I shouldn't have let him leave home so young."

"When did you last see your son?" I asked.

"Thursday night. A family dinner . . . rare." Ho stopped speaking and looked away.

"So that would be three days ago?"

"Yes. I went to his apartment on Friday morning. He wasn't there. I tried to SMS him, emailed him. Nothing. I reported him missing by late afternoon."

"The police called me just after midnight when they'd identified Chang's body. I went to the morgue at six this morning." His voice was brittle. "I saw what they did to him." He looked at Mary and then at me, his face like a mannequin's. "You have to find the killer Mr. Gisto. I am a very wealthy man. I don't care what it costs."

Chapter 9

DEPUTY COMMISSIONER THOROGOOD was coming through the main doors just as Ho Meng was leaving. I met him in reception and we walked along the corridor.

"That was the father of the murdered kid," I said as we sat down. "He's mighty pissed with your people."

Thorogood's face creased into a frown.

"He can't understand why you didn't save his boy."

"So, he's come to you?"

I nodded.

"Well, you know our agreement, Craig. We share Intel."

"He doesn't want to talk to the police."

The Deputy Commissioner blanched, anger building in his eyes. "Well it's not up to him, is it?" he snapped. "If he's with-holding evidence . . ."

I let it go, went to change the subject. There was a knock on the door. Darlene poked her head round. "Bad time? You said you'd . . ."

"Sorry, Darlene," I said quickly. "Come in."

"Deputy Commissioner, you've met Darlene Cooper, haven't you?"

He stood up, extended a hand. "We . . . ah . . . met last night at the . . ."

Darlene gave the man a brief smile. The girl was a cool paradox, beautiful *and* brilliant – the only nerd who could grace the centerfold of *Playboy*. She'd done the whole modeling *shtick* for a year after finishing her degree in Forensics at Monash, became a disciple of Sci, Jack Morgan's resident lab genius at Private LA. Then she'd come back to Oz and our Private.

"You wanted to know the latest," she began before flashing her baby blues at the Deputy Commissioner.

"Absolutely," I said.

She handed me a couple of sheets of paper. They were covered with graphs and numbers. I turned them sideways, then back again.

"Analysis of skin samples, and DNA," she explained.

"Oh, great."

"That was bloody quick!" Thorogood said.

"So what're your conclusions?" I asked.

"I took a range of samples from the body. Unfortunately I haven't been able to get any prints, but I found three distinct DNA profiles. One of these is certainly the victim's."

"Any luck finding a match for the other two?"

Darlene shook her head. "Nothing close on any database."

"Anything else?" I asked.

"Well yeah, actually. I took a sample of material from under Ho Chang's fingernails." She handed me a photograph. I stared at it for several moments, passed it to Thorogood. He sat back, held the photo up to the light.

"It's human skin. I suspect there was a serious struggle. Ho must have taken a chunk out of the other guy."

"But what's the blue?" Thorogood asked, studying the image. It showed a highly magnified ragged rectangle of skin. One corner was dark blue.

"Stumped me," Darlene replied, " . . . for a few seconds. Then I realized it was probably a bit of a tattoo."

Thorogood looked at Darlene, back at the picture.

"Very clever," I said.

"Oh, I'm even cleverer than that."

I flicked a glance at Thorogood who was now giving Darlene a skeptical look.

"I took a sample and ran it through a gas chromatograph that separates out the constituents of a blend. Tattoo ink is a cocktail of many different ingredients. The gas chromatograph pulls these away from each other and gives a readout to show everything that makes up the blend. This is what I got."

I took another sheet of paper from my science whiz. It showed a graph with different colored bars lined up across the paper.

"There were forty-seven different compounds or elements in the ink – vegetable dyes, traces of solvent, zinc, copper. But one thing stood out."

I handed the sheet to Thorogood.

"An unusual level of Antimony."

We both looked at Darlene blankly.

"Only Chinese tattooists use that type of ink. It's most commonly found in the tattoos of Triad gang members."

Chapter 10

Three Years Ago.

IT WAS ONE of those perfect Sydney mornings. Pristine blue sky, not a cloud in sight, a crispness to the air that made you kid yourself everything was right with the world. Even the traffic was light for 7 am and I had the roof down on the old Porsche convertible I'd bought fifth-hand ten years before.

We were en route to the airport. Becky, my wife of nine years, our three-year-old son, Cal, and me. Becky looked amazing. She was wearing a diaphanous dress and a thick rope of fake pearls. She was tanned from the spring sunshine. When she moved her hands, the collection of bangles at her wrists jangled. She'd put on a bit of weight and looked better for it. We'd made love that morning while Cal was asleep and I could still visualize her.

I glanced round and saw her long auburn hair blown back by the warm breeze. She was excited about our trip to Bali. We all were . . . our first holiday in two years. I'd been working hard to build up my PI agency, Solutions Inc., and I was only now able to take a week off, splash some cash on a fancy resort.

I'd woken up that morning feeling more relaxed than I had

for years. I'd had nice dreams too. I was back on our wedding day. Nine years before. It was a bitter-sweet occasion. I'd bumped into Becky by chance one morning at Darling Harbour. The old spark was there, we were both single. It just happened. We were meant for each other. Within a year we were married.

Mark must've heard I was with Becky, but seeing as I hadn't spoken to him since my second year in college, I had no idea what he'd thought about it. He would never forgive me for what happened at his party. I could hardly blame the guy. What did sting for a while was that only a few of my family turned up at the registry office in Darlinghurst. But hell, it was a long time ago and even that wasn't going to ruin my mood.

Cal was strapped in the back, a suitcase next to him. On top of that was the brightly colored Kung Fu Panda carry-on bag he planned to wheel to the plane and put in the overhead locker. He'd not flown before, but I'd told him all about it the previous night in lieu of a bedtime story. Cal had the same auburn hair as his mother, the same eyes. In fact, there wasn't much immediately obvious about his looks that confirmed he was mine. But he definitely had my temperament – patient and calm, but vicious when riled.

"So you looking forward to the trip, little man?" I called to Cal over the noise of the road and the wind and the powerful engine. "I know I am."

He nodded. I saw him in the rear-view mirror, a big smile across his face, baby teeth gleaming.

"What you looking forward to most, Cal?"

He thought for a moment, forehead wrinkled. Then hollered: "Catching fish!"

I glanced over to Becky and we both laughed. I turned back and saw the pickup truck on the wrong side of the road coming straight for us. And I knew immediately that this was the end. I could feel Becky freeze beside me, watched as the ugly great vehicle covered the distance between us. With each vanishing yard, I felt my life . . . our lives together . . . drain away.

Chapter 11

I DON'T REMEMBER the impact . . . no one ever does, do they? The horror began when I started to open my eyes. But at first, everything was blurred and I was stone deaf. I just saw colored shapes. Then my hearing came back . . . but I couldn't make out a single human sound. Instead, a loud, shrill whine, the engine free-wheeling in neutral.

I felt a drip, drip, drip on my face.

My car had rolled and ended up driver's side to the tarmac. I could see a shape close to, almost on top of me. Gradually my vision cleared enough to make it out. Becky's face. Her dead eyes open, staring at me . . . droplets of her blood falling onto my cheek.

I tried to scream, but nothing came out. I couldn't speak, just produced animal noises in my throat. Tried to pull away, horrified, I turned my head slowly. A pain shot down my spine. I could just see Cal in the back. He'd slumped to the side, body contorted.

I managed to twist in the seat and had the presence of mind to feel for Becky's pulse. Then I saw the cut in her neck. She was almost decapitated.

I felt vomit rise up and I spewed down my front. I thought I'd choke and a part of me wished I would. I could visualize the new life if I were to survive. A life alone, my family gone . . . *just like that.*

I turned back to Cal, unbuckled my seat belt, gained enough leverage to slither into the rear of the car.

"Cal? Cal?" My voice broke. "Aggghhh!" I screamed again. Another stream of vomit welled up and out. I started to cry.

"Cal?" I pulled him up. His head lolled, blood trickling from the side of his mouth.

I thought I saw his eyelids flicker. "Cal?" I shouted again. I got his wrist, pulled it up, tried to find a pulse. His arm wet with blood. My fingers wet with blood. No pulse.

"CAL . . . CAL." I shook him.

I reached for my cell, pulled it from my jacket but it fell to pieces in my hand.

There's a gap in my memory after that. Next thing I knew I was clambering through the passenger window. The buckled window frame and remnants of glass were cutting me open, but I didn't care. I landed on the road, guts churning, blood in my eyes diluted by tears flowing down my cheeks. I groaned . . . a primordial sound.

There was a revolting smell . . . petrol, rubber . . . I managed to get to my knees, leaned on the car and pulled myself into a hunched, twisted figure, feeling like an octogenarian suddenly. The front of the pickup truck stood ten feet away, hood crumpled, windshield smashed. I could see the top of the driver's head above the steering wheel.

I shuffled over. From far off came the sound of sirens.

The door of the truck fell away as I yanked on the handle

and I just managed to step back before it landed at my feet. It was an old, screwed-up wagon. The driver hadn't been wearing a belt. His face smashed in, spine snapped. A vertebrae protruded from his shirt back.

I leaned in, caught the smell of alcohol. Then I saw the can of beer on the floor of the passenger side. It lay in a puddle of foaming liquid.

The fury hit me in a way I'd never experienced before or since. It was pure, all-consuming. I grabbed the guy's hair, yanked his head back. His features were just recognizable. He was maybe twenty-five, blond, little goatee.

I felt the vomit rise again, but this time I held it down, lifted my fist, smashed it into the dead driver's face. I hit him again and again. "BASTARD! . . . AAGGGHH!..MOTHER-FUCKER!

I kept hitting and hitting, the dead man's shattered head lolling around.

Then I felt a hand on my shoulder.

Chapter 12

JUSTINE SMITH WALKED into the hotel room on the top floor of The Citadel overlooking Darling Harbour. It was fantastic. Luxurious room, shimmering evening sun. Sliding doors opened onto a walled deck, a jacuzzi sunk into the balcony.

She'd naively hoped the opening of the Sydney branch of Private would offer some welcome relief from the usual death and destruction back home in LA. Fat chance!

She kicked off her shoes and walked into the bedroom. It was cool, the air-con set just right, the bedding turned back, a chocolate placed on the pillow. The room smelled of orange essence.

Unbuttoning her blouse, she turned and caught her reflection in a wall of mirrors. Slipping off her skirt, bra and panties she stood naked considering her body.

"Not bad, baby," she said. Did a half-turn to her left. She had a narrow waist, flat tummy, firm boobs. "Gotta be some benefits from eating nothing and having no bambini, I guess." She did a pirouette and headed for the bathroom.

Then she changed her mind. Pulling on a robe, she went back in to the main room, slid open the doors and felt the crisp heat. A refreshing breeze came in over the harbor. She strode to the chest-high wall, admired the view.

Two minutes later, Justine was naked and immersed in bubbles, a glass of Krug on the side of the jacuzzi. "God! This is the life!" she said aloud and rested her head against the soft cushioning behind her neck. With her eyes closed, she reached for the champagne flute, brought it over and let the bubbles explode inside her mouth.

Her cell rang.

She groaned, and a voice in her head said: "Ignore it". But that wasn't in her nature. She lifted herself from the jacuzzi, padded over to the phone, naked and dripping.

She saw the name on the screen – GRETA. Stabbed the green button.

The first thing she heard were sobs.

"Greta! What is it?"

Something unintelligible.

"Hey, sis . . . slow down."

More sobs. Finally a sentence. "Oh, Justine. One of my friends has been murdered."

Chapter 13

JOHNNY AND I were in my office going over the police report on the Ho kid.

Johnny's only twenty-three, not much older than the victim. Born in Lebanon, he came over here with poor immigrant parents when he was three. Could have ended up a criminal or dead, but he was far too bright for that. He got out of the ghettos of Sydney's Western Suburbs ASAP, found a legit job and took a Psychology degree in his spare time. He was still working on the Psychology degree. I trusted him, and trust is always top of my necessity list when it comes to the job.

"There are two Ho boys, right. Chang's the younger by three years," Johnny said. "Mother died when he was five. Rich businessman father . . . probably never home."

I nodded. "Severely disturbed by his mother's death?"

"Definitely. His deafness made him determined to prove to his father he's every bit as good as his older brother, Dai."

The phone rang.

"Justine . . ." I began and she cut over me. Johnny could see my expression darken and raised a questioning eyebrow.

"What!" I exclaimed. "How long ago? Alright, we'll go to the

Thorogoods' place together. I'll pick you up in five. The Citadel Hotel, right?"

"What's up?" Johnny asked as soon as I clicked off.

I was already out of my chair. "A murder in Bellevue Hill, friend of Justine's sister, Greta."

"Christ!"

"The cops are all over the street. The woman was found in a car just a few yards down from the Thorogoods'."

Chapter 14

I EXITED THE garage and pulled onto George Street. It was almost dark, still hot. Checked my watch . . . 6.57. The city was aglow, shoppers bargain hunting in the January sales.

The traffic wasn't great and it took me more than the promised five minutes to reach the hotel. Justine was waiting in the drive-thru outside the main doors. She looked amazing in white linen pants, a tight top, her hair flowing over her shoulders, slightly damp at the tips.

We merged with the highway traffic. "Did your sister offer any details?" I asked, and tried to put out of my mind the intoxicating smell of perfume wafting from the passenger side.

"She was a mess. The victim is a family friend, apparently. Known her for years."

I drove east down Park Street and onto William Street, and we fell silent. I could hear a siren far off and the rush of air in the sticky night.

Bellevue Hill is mostly old money with a sprinkling of nouveau business gurus and gangsters. From William Street we took New South Head Road, drove about three miles, then hung a right into a wide, leafy street, Stockton Boulevard.

The Thorogoods' house was an ultra-modern place that backed onto the Royal Sydney Golf Club. Its wide, glass-balustraded balconies offered views east toward the ocean.

Justine led the way up the granite path.

Greta, eyes moist, mascara run, opened the door before we reached it, and beckoned us in.

"So what happened?" Justine asked as her sister fell into her arms. We walked into a vast living-room and sat in a horse-shoe of low-slung white leather sofas.

"It was about six o'clock. Brett had just got home. The phone rang. We heard sirens and saw the blue and red police lights, the screech of tires as the squad cars pulled up . . . just over there." Greta pointed through the window. "Brett told me to stay here. But look, the kids are both on sleepovers. So I thought . . . what the hell? I snuck out."

Her face froze for a second. She looked at us, her eyes watering. "I wish I hadn't." She swallowed hard. "Stacy's got three kids . . . There was blood everywhere." She broke down and Justine encircled her in her arms, letting her younger sister sob into her shoulder.

Chapter 15

I FETCHED A glass of cold water from the kitchen and handed it to Greta. She seemed to calm down a little, wiped her eyes, took a deep breath.

"Greta," I said as sympathetically as I could, "is there anything at all unusual about Stacy? Anything that could suggest she would be targeted?"

She looked lost. "No. Stace was just a regular mom. We got to know each other through the school. Her eldest son's the same age as Serge."

"Okay, Greta, I know this might sound insensitive, but were Stacy and her husband happy?"

She shook her head. "Craig, please! I'm upset but I'm not stupid! My husband *is* the Deputy Commissioner!"

"Yeah . . . sorry."

"As far as I know, Stacy and David are, *were* happy. You never can tell, though, right?"

I glanced at Justine. "I'm going to . . ." Flicked my head toward the street. Justine nodded and turned back to her sister.

Outside, the road was dark except for the glow of headlights and crime scene floods spilling around a corner on the far side of the street. I crossed over and ran toward an alleyway, the road brightening as I went.

The end of the lane was cordoned off with crime scene tape. A cop was standing just my side of it. I showed him my ID. He glanced at it, then asked me to wait a moment. Two minutes later, he was back with a young guy I'd seen with Thorogood last night.

"Is the DC . . . ?" I asked.

"Just left for HQ, Mr. Gisto. Inspector Talbot's given you the green light though," and he offered little more than a nod, lifting the tape to indicate I should follow him.

I could see the back of a car in the alley. It was a new Lexus SUV, an LX 570, doors open. The intense white of the floodlights lit up the number plate: STACE. Forensics were already there – blue-suited figures picking and poking around.

I strode toward the driver's side. The dead woman was strapped into the front seat. The seat had been lowered back almost to horizontal.

Mark saw me and came over. "I'm only agreeing to you being here because Thorogood insisted," he said woodenly and lifted his cell to indicate that he'd just spoken to his boss.

I ignored him and walked over to the body. The woman's face was disfigured with what were clearly cigarette burns all over her cheeks and down her neck.

She was, I guessed, early forties, a blondish bob, well-preserved figure, wore an expensive watch. There was a huge diamond next to her wedding ring. She was dressed in a flimsy cotton dress. Someone had placed a green sheet over her from the abdomen down. It was difficult to see how she'd died.

"Tortured and then stabbed repeatedly in the back," Talbot said and pulled the woman forward. A mess of congealed blood, three . . . four long black gashes.

"What's with the sheet?" I asked.

"Look for yourself."

I pulled aside the fabric – and took a step back.

Chapter 16

Three Years Ago.

I WAS TRYING to focus but the florescent strip in the ceiling was too bright. A face swam into view a couple of feet above me. It was probably the last face I wanted to see.

Then it all came flooding back.

Smack.

Filling my world, sending me reeling.

And there was the face.

"You're lucky to be alive, Craig."

I heard the words but they didn't really register. I managed to turn my head a little to the left, then the right. Tubes, machines, a hospital. Yeah – that would figure.

"I do worry about your temper though, mate."

I looked at the face, focused. Mark Fucking Talbot. My cousin Mark.

But I felt nothing, and I didn't care. Mark didn't matter. Nothing mattered. Becky and Cal were dead. I was alive, but I wanted to be dead.

"You smashed that driver's face to a pulp," Talbot went on.

I didn't care what he said. I didn't care.

"You know how I felt about Becky." His face was expressionless, but he knew how to turn the screw. "I never met little Cal . . ." Then his face thawed. For a second, he looked genuinely upset. "They deserved better."

I didn't care what he said. I didn't care.

My cousin had no idea. He must have thought he was really hurting me.

He sighed. "In one way you're lucky, Craig. Sure, you smashed the guy's face up. But . . ." He lifted a thin beige folder into view. "Forensics report. He died on impact."

I didn't care what he said. I was alive but I wanted to be dead.

He started to turn. Stopped. Walked back and leaned in close to my ear. "You got what you deserved, you fuck. And you'll go to hell."

And he was gone.

I didn't care.

Chapter 17

"WELL, YOU ALL know the gist of it," I said, walking into the conference room. "A close friend of Greta Thorogood was tortured and killed a few yards from her front door. Bizarre MO."

I looked around the table. I'd called in everyone . . . the team, plus Justine.

They already knew the basics of the homicide. Bad news travels fast.

I flicked a remote and the blinds closed. A second touch on the rubber pad and a flat screen lit up at the far end of the room. "I shot this on my phone."

It was jumbled up at first but settled down as I'd steadied my hand and set the phone to "Stabilize video".

The inside of the victim's car.

"Stacy Friel," I said flatly, as the horrific image of the dead woman's face appeared. "She was murdered sometime around 5.30 yesterday evening in an alley close to her house in Bellevue Hill. Facially disfigured and stabbed four times in the back as she got out of her vehicle. She was then returned to the car . . . postmortem." The camera moved to show the dead woman straight-on. I had panned down, zoomed in.

There was an intake of breath from the women in the room.

Understandable, I thought, imagining an equivalent for guys.

The victim's lower garments had been removed, her legs spread wide. A bunch of money had been inserted into her vagina. You could see the golden yellow of Australian fifty-dollar bills.

The film stopped. The blinds came up. No one spoke.

I looked round the room. Darlene was staring straight at me. Justine studied the table. Mary was still glaring at where the image had been a few seconds ago. Johnny was counting his shoes.

"Not nice, I know, but there you have it."

"Pretty fucking sick, actually," Mary said with a steely look.

"Yep. Certainly is."

"What've the police found out?" Darlene asked.

"Not a lot. Their forensics people have promised to get a complete set of crime scene samples over to you by mid-morning. Thorogood's being very cooperative. I guess Greta is putting pressure on him to keep us fully involved."

"So am I, Craig," Justine remarked. "Brett's subscribing to the idea that two heads are better than one. He knew Stacy too. He's genuinely upset."

"So what now?" It was Mary.

"Darlene, you work on the samples soon as they arrive," I said.

She nodded.

"Justine, you and me should take a trip to the police morgue. Find out anything we can."

"I've got a very nasty feeling the unfortunate Stacy Friel is only the first victim," Johnny said suddenly.

"Why do you say that?" I asked, swiveling my chair.

"Because, and Justine will verify this," Johnny began, glancing over to where she sat, "the murder was ritualistic."

Justine nodded solemnly.

"So?" I persisted.

"One-off murders are a type – the most common sort," Justine explained. "Someone dies in a violent crime – a bank raid, a gang killing – collateral damage. Or people are murdered in a moment of passion, or slaughtered clinically – revenge, jealousy. A woman who is tortured, killed, dumped in her car and has her vagina stuffed with banknotes is not the victim of a spontaneous act. It was planned and everything about it has meaning. I hope it's not the case, but I think Johnny's right – Stacy Friel is just the first."

Chapter 18

"MARY?" I CALLED her over as the team filed out.

"What's up?"

"The Ho murder. Darlene's found some interesting stuff."

"Yeah, I heard . . . Triads. You're thinking drugs?"

"Possibly, but from what Ho Meng said, his kid was hardly the sort.

Darlene found no evidence he was using."

"May've been dealing."

"Well, yeah. But anyway, it's speculation. It might not be drugs, the Triads are involved in all sorts of shit."

"Maybe it wasn't the kid," Mary replied. "What about the father, Meng? I'd be surprised, but we have to consider it."

"It'd crossed my mind. I don't think he gave us everything he had yesterday."

"I agree."

I looked at Mary. I'd known her for years and I knew she had a soft side, but I think only a handful of people in the world had ever seen it and two of those were her mom and dad.

"You know the guy a little. Reach out to him," I suggested. "Find out if he has connections with the Triads."

"He must have. But he won't like us probing."

"No, he won't," I replied. "But he needs reminding if he wants us to find his son's killer that we have to have everything he can give us – not just about Chang, but about himself too."

She nodded and looked straight into my eyes.

"You okay with that, Mary? The Triads are not nice."

"Oh, please! I'm a big girl and I thrive on 'not nice'."

Chapter 19

THE NEW SOUTH Wales police morgue was part of a modern building in Surry Hills, a couple of miles from the CBD. It was like all morgues everywhere – pristine, clinical, and it stank of chemicals and death.

A tall, well-built man with a graying beard and wearing round tortoiseshell spectacles met us in a small, overlit ante-room. A pass was pinned to his lapel – photo and name, Dr. Hugh Gravely.

He was friendly enough and showed Justine and me into the main part of the morgue. It was low-ceilinged, fluorescent strips. The stink was much worse here.

Stacy Friel lay on the slab. Gray skin, wet hair pulled back, a red, crudely sown up Y-shaped incision dominating her upper half. She would have been a very handsome woman yesterday, I thought. And suddenly a horrible pain hit me in the chest. I almost let it show, but reined it in. I knew what this was. I had been to a very similar morgue . . . after the crash. I had to see Becky and Cal. But later, I wished I hadn't.

"Victim was thirty-nine," Dr. Gravely said, his voice emotionless. "Died from multiple stab wounds. Two distinct thrusts to the thoracic, two more to the lumbar. Each one deep. The knife had a serrated blade approximately eight inches in length. It punctured her liver and right kidney. The lumbar penetrations perforated the large intestine. The victim almost certainly died from heart failure precipitated by shock."

Justine stepped forward and inspected Stacy's lower half. "You've removed the banknotes."

"They've gone to Police Forensics along with the woman's clothes, jewelry – everything on her person."

Justine nodded.

"I did examine them first, of course. But you'll know about them from the police . . . right?"

"No," Justine and I said in unison. "What about them?" I added slowly.

"Well the fact they're fake notes . . . photocopies."

Chapter 20

THE MOMENT THE woman in the $900 Jimmy Choo shoes walked into the offices of Private, I knew something interesting would come of it. I noticed things such as expensive shoes and I knew that women of this type didn't come to places like Private unless there was something serious on their minds.

Before she said a word, I'd profiled her. Lower North Shore Yummy Mummy, maybe Eastern Suburbs, but she looked a little too cool. Professional – once upon a time. Maybe a lawyer back in the day before the kids came along. She'd probably parked a BMW X5 downstairs, almost certainly had a personalized number plate. Kids would be at Shore School or Redlands. Husband . . . let's think, either a stockbroker or a senior exec at one of the big banks.

She exuded confidence as she crossed the floor toward me. "Hi, my name's Pam Hewes," she said, smiled briefly, a New Zealand twang to her voice. "I need advice."

"Well, you've come to precisely the right place. Craig Gisto." I waved her toward the conference room.

I pulled up a chair for her and walked around the table, sat down, my back to the window, waited for her to start.

"Oh God! I don't know where to begin!" She broke eye contact. "My husband . . . his name's Geoff. He didn't return home last night. There's no response to his cell or his office numbers. He didn't show up at home this morning. I went to his office in the CBD. No one's heard from him."

"I imagine this must be unusual or else you wouldn't be here."

"Well, yeah. Geoff works hard, and . . . he plays hard. I knew that about him before we were married. *Quid pro quo* and all that, but he's always kept some sort of balance – even if it was only for the sake of the kids. He has always come home each evening and if there was some emergency and he has to go somewhere suddenly he *always* calls."

"And you haven't heard a word from him?"

"No."

"You haven't contacted the police. Why?"

"Because . . . I'm not one hundred per cent sure that everything my husband does is absolutely legal."

"What does he do, Mrs. Hewes?"

"Please, call me Pam . . . Geoff has fingers in all sorts of pies. Always has some new business scheme. He lends money, he invests in businesses. I find it hard to keep up."

I looked her directly in the eye. "And you, Pam? What do you do?"

"I'm in real estate. I work at H and F Realty on the Lower North Shore."

"Do you have anything to go on? Any leads? Are you familiar with your husband's associates, friends?"

Pam shook her head and looked down at the carpet. "My husband plays his cards close to his chest. He tells me things, but I know it's the tip of the iceberg. But, Mr. Gisto, to answer your previous question, there's one thing you should know about my husband. Geoff does have associates – many of them – but when it comes to friends they're pretty thin on the ground."

Chapter 21

"GOOD MORNING," HO said, standing and extending a hand.

"Thanks for agreeing to meet me," Mary said.

They were in the bar of the Blue Hotel in Woolloomooloo, all oversized concrete buffet counters, post-modern piping and metal grills. She ordered a coffee.

"I wasn't being entirely straight with you and Mr. Gisto yesterday," Ho began. "I don't know Mr. Gisto, but I've done some checking and he seems like a worthy man. And besides," he added with a small smile, "you obviously trust him and that is good enough for me."

Mary kept buttoned up, searched his black eyes.

"The fact is, I believe my son was kidnapped and killed by the Triads."

"I know."

"You do?"

"Our forensics expert found compelling evidence to support the idea."

"I see. Well I have a lot of experience with the gangs, going back years. I know how they operate."

"Your time in the Hong Kong Police Force?"

"I was one of the senior officers involved with breaking up the Huang gang in '94. I then headed up the task force that smashed two other big Triad teams in Kowloon and Macau. I emigrated to Australia with my family, a few years before I met you at the Military Police Training Academy."

"And you think this attack on your family was some sort of revenge?"

"I'm convinced of it."

"Why?"

Ho was silent for a few moments, gazing around the huge, almost empty bar. "I was sent a ransom note."

Mary raised an eyebrow. "Maybe we should start at the beginning, Meng."

"I told you yesterday the last time I saw Chang was on Thursday. I reported him missing the following day. Late that night, Friday, I received a package. A note demanding that I cooperate with a gang who are planning to smuggle heroin from Hong Kong. The note came in a box with one of my son's eyes."

"And you didn't go to the police with this information?"

Ho shook his head. "No, I told you . . ."

"You don't trust the cops . . . Why?"

"I'd rather not say."

Mary rested an elbow on the table and rubbed her forehead. "Okay," she said, a little exasperated. "What happened next?"

"Saturday night I received a call from the gang leader. He said I had twenty-four hours to agree to their 'request', or my son would be killed."

"That would give you until Sunday night. And they *did* murder him." Mary shook her head slowly.

"I've concluded they were going to kill Chang in the car and dump his body in a public car park."

"But why?" Mary said. "Surely they would have been more discreet."

"Quite the opposite, Mary. They would have wanted to advertise it. I'm not the only Asian businessman in this city. If I keep refusing they could go elsewhere. They wanted to broadcast the murder, as a warning to others – that's how they operate – fear and arrogance."

"But you did refuse them," Mary said.

"I could not agree to their demands. They are targeting me because of my past. Helping them smuggle heroin would go against everything I believe in." He stared her out. "You may seem outraged, Mary. But believe me, I will live with that decision for the rest of my life. It was the hardest thing I've ever had to do."

Chapter 22

Thirty-six Hours Ago.

PAM HEWES' HUSBAND, Geoff, was in his favorite chair in his favorite pub, The Cloverleaf in Darlinghurst, and he was feeling pleased with himself.

He'd had a good week so far. That afternoon, he'd won a couple of grand at the races, squeezed over ten thousand more from the small businesses he was lending to in the Western Suburbs and heard that the brothels he managed for Al Loretto, the biggest underworld name in Sydney, had increased their profits.

He was about to take a sip of beer when he felt a tap on his shoulder. He whirled round and was startled to see Al Loretto himself standing way too close. Another man Geoff half-recognized was positioned behind him, arms folded.

"Hey, Al," Geoff said, doing well to disguise his surprise. "How are you?"

Loretto didn't reply for a moment, just stared down at Geoff surveying him with his hard black eyes. He then pulled up a chair, leaned forward. "Geoffrey," he said quietly. "Do I or do I not pay you well?"

"What do you mean, Al?"

"Simple question. Do I recompense you adequately for your services?" Al had made an effort with the Oxford English dictionary. Thought it was impressive.

"Yeah, course you . . ."

He gripped Geoff's lapel and his companion took a step forward. "Then why are you being so disrespectful, Geoffrey?"

Hewes blanched.

"You want to further capitalize on your employment position? Is that it, *amigo*?"

Geoff went to reply, but stopped as Al Loretto tightened his grip, his breath on his cheek. "How did you come to the conclusion that I would be happy for you to install cameras in my brothels? Hmm?"

Geoff tried again to reply, but was cut short.

"Didn't you imagine for a second that it was just a tad disrespectful, Geoffrey? Was there not a skerrick of doubt, not a moment when you thought you might *ask me first*?"

"I didn't think you would have a problem with it," Hewes managed to say.

Loretto stared at him in silence again.

"I thought . . ."

"I don't pay you to think, Geoffrey. Oh no. *I* do the thinking." The gangster tapped his head.

"So, what do you . . . ?"

"What do I want? I want you to cease and desist. Not hard to understand is it, pal? Take the fucking cameras out this afternoon and do what I pay you to do. Any more questions?"

Geoff looked at him blankly.

"Good," Loretto answered, stood, picked up the almost full glass of beer and poured it over Geoff Hewes' head.

Chapter 23

I'D JUST WALKED into the lab at Private. Darlene was at a computer, tapping away. The police had sent over everything from the Stacy Friel murder scene for her to study. "Anything?" I asked.

"Not a lot more than the Police Forensics guys have found, I'm afraid. The banknotes are photocopies . . . high-quality – about the grade of a top-end domestic printer."

"Fingerprints?"

"I wish! No . . . Zip. Actually, to be honest, I didn't expect anything. The killer wore latex gloves. I found traces of the cornstarch powder that coats standard gloves."

"And nothing special about that?"

"Nope. These gloves could have come from any one of a hundred outlets, a thousand – Coles, Woolworths, any drugstore."

"Okay. Anything else?"

"Biological matter from the woman's vagina. I could tell you where she was in her menstrual cycle and whether or not she'd had sex during the past twenty-four hours. But I can't give you anything practical about what was put into her."

"She wasn't raped?"

"Definitely not."

I looked round the lab. Benches on each side. On top of these stood impressive-looking machines with elaborate control panels and flashing lights. I recognized a powerful microscope and a centrifuge, but that was about it. The rest might as well have been Venusian technology.

"The cops gave you all the material you need?"

"Yeah, personal effects plus a file containing several hundred photographs of the crime scene. I've analyzed Stacy Friel's jacket. I can confirm the police pathologist's assessment of the attack – the number of stab wounds, the angle of entry, the type of knife. Although of course, the weapon hasn't been found. I wish I could have been at the crime scene. It's hard working second hand like this. I might have caught something the cops missed."

"I understand," I replied. "And you found nothing unusual with anything Police Forensics handed over?"

"No, Craig. I'm sorry. Hate to admit it – but right now I'm drawing a complete blank."

Chapter 24

I WAS STARVING – it suddenly hit me as I left Darlene's lab and strode into reception. Johnny was there talking to our receptionist, Colette. Justine was coming toward us through the main doors a few feet away. She looked hot and flustered.

"I feel like I'm going to get sunstroke every time I step out-side," she declared.

I laughed. "I thought LA was hot."

"Yeah, but not like this!"

I grinned and glanced at my watch. "I'm going to grab a snack. You hungry?" I asked her. "Or how about a frappaccino?"

She looked surprised for a moment. "Great."

There was a café on the ground floor. We got coffee and muffins and started to head back to the elevator. I checked my watch again, realized I had a spare thirty minutes.

"You got anything to do for half an hour or so, Justine?"

She shook her head as she sipped the frappaccino through a straw.

"Well then, I know just the place for you. I think you'll appreciate it."

"Oh!" she said. "A man of mystery . . ."

Chapter 25

WE WALKED DOWN Macquarie Street close to Circular Quay. Straight ahead of us stood the Opera House, the tiers of wide steps leading to its massive windows just a couple of dozen yards away. People were sitting on the steps drinking Slurpees, coffee, Coke. We turned onto the Quay and I pointed out the sights to Justine. She was quiet, taking it all in, but not "oohing" and "ahhing" as some tourists might. I liked that.

We walked in the shade, an arcade of shops to our left. An aboriginal man was playing a didgeridoo over a hip-hop beat spilling from an iPod plugged into a big speaker.

"Very post-modern!" Justine observed. "So where exactly are you taking me?"

"Don't want to spoil the surprise."

We came to a bar, tables and umbrellas outside, families eating late breakfast. A big flat screen on the wall inside was showing a soccer game from the English Premier League, Chelsea vs. Tottenham. I led the way through the bar and up a flight of stairs. On the wall was a small sign. It said: ICE BAR.

"What's this?" Justine asked and spun round, puzzled.

I stepped up to the counter. A few other customers milled

about. Sixty seconds later, I had two tickets in my hand and guided Justine around a corner. An immaculately tanned blonde was waiting for us by a rack of fur coats.

Justine turned to me again.

"Okay, this is the deal," I said. "You want to cool down? The Ice Bar is set to minus twenty Fahrenheit. Everything is made from ice including the cocktail glasses. We stay in for a drink – twenty minutes. You'll feel a lot cooler by the end of it."

I had to laugh as Justine pulled on a nerdy fur-lined anorak and mittens. It wasn't really her. But she seemed to be loving it all. We went into the antechamber to acclimatize. Here, it was just 18°F. From there we went into the Prep Room, temperature, five degrees. Then the door to the bar swished open and we were inside. The digital thermometer on the wall told us it was minus 20°F . . . and it felt it, even through the thick socks, the boots, the fur-lined anorak and the mittens.

The floor was covered with ice. The chairs around the walls were made of ice, the bar was ice. Everything backlit electric blue.

"This is fantastic, Craig!" Justine beamed, her breath steamy and fragrant. She sipped at the cocktail and I glimpsed the side of her face as the light from the bar caught it. "I could look at that face and never grow weary of it," I thought to myself.

Chapter 26

THE HO MANSION was in Mosman, a few hundred yards from Taronga Zoo. It was new and vulgar and stuck out like a sore thumb among the genteel old-money houses built at the turn of the nineteenth century.

Buzzed in through an electrically operated gate, Mary and I strode up a gravel path that passed over a pond filled with koi. A Malaysian maid met us at the front door and showed us into a grandiose circular hall. A young Chinese guy in a blue tailored suit appeared in an archway to the right of the hall. He had an earpiece in place, a wire disappearing into his shirt collar. I noticed the bulge of a firearm under his jacket.

I showed him my ID.

"You're early," he said and indicated we should follow him along a corridor leading away under the arch. We hung a right, then a left. I glimpsed huge rooms – a gym, a home theater, a couple of living areas, each with the floor space of an average apartment.

We reached a door on the right. Another guard, identical uniform, identical earpiece and jacket bulge, was standing on the nearside of the door. He stiffened as we came round the corner.

The first guy walked off without a word. I flashed my ID again. The second guard opened the door and nodded us in.

It was another impressively proportioned room, high ceiling, sumptuous sofas, a desk, ancient-looking framed Chinese silk prints on dark walls. No sign of Ho.

Halfway into the room, I heard a faint sound from the far corner. There was a door into another room. I noticed a flickering light coming from beyond the doorway but couldn't make out the sound.

I turned to Mary and put a finger to my lips. Stopping a yard from the door, I pulled to the wall, peered in, Mary right next to me.

There was a wide flat screen on the far wall. A sofa.

On the screen a small boy played with a toy train. He lifted his head and beamed a beatific smile. Then the scene changed. The boy was a little older, maybe seven, eight. He was flying a kite on the beach. The camera panned back and I saw Bathers' Pavilion, the landmark café on Balmoral Beach a mile from here.

Ho Meng sat in half-profile staring ahead, transfixed. A line of tears running down his cheek, his body shaking.

I felt a tap on my shoulder and turned to come face-to-face with the dead kid.

Chapter 27

THE YOUNG GUY gripped my shoulders and turned me from the sight of the weeping Ho Meng. I realized it must be Dai, Chang's brother. They were so alike it was spooky. I caught Mary's eye and we crept away across the office, back out into the corridor. Dai led us into one of the living areas I'd seen earlier. He closed the door and indicated we should sit on a sofa, pulled up a chair and leaned forward.

"I'm sorry you had to see that."

I started to reply but he lifted a hand.

"Please. I'm sorry because my father would have been so ashamed if he knew you were there. I'm sorry for him, for me."

I nodded. It wasn't the way I would have thought, but I understood what the guy meant – from his cultural perspective.

"We didn't mean to intrude," Mary said.

"What is it you want?"

"We hoped to talk to your father about your brother's murder."

"He's told me all about the Triads. I grew up with them as a dark presence in our lives."

There was a sound from the doorway. Ho Meng was standing with the light from the hall breaking around him. He strode over as Mary and I got up from the sofa. He gripped my hand and then pecked Mary on the cheek. He had transformed from the grief-stricken father in the home theater, and was once again the upright businessman. But he couldn't completely hide the pain. I saw it in his eyes.

"Please everyone, sit," he said. "I heard what my son told you, and it is absolutely true. The Triads have hung over our lives like a dark shadow, and they still do. In fact their shadow has grown darker."

"Meng, this morning I could tell you were holding back. If you want us to work with you in hunting down your son's killers you have to tell us everything," Mary said.

He held her gaze unblinking. "You are right. The fact is I am convinced my wife, Jiao, was murdered by the Triads twelve years ago, soon after we came to Australia. She was last seen in Chinatown, in the middle of the day. Next morning her headless body was discovered in Roseville. The police were convinced it was the work of a psycho killer, connected it with two similar unsolved murders from three years before. But they never caught the killer."

"And that is why you don't trust the cops," I said.

Ho merely nodded. "They have consistently let me down. First Jiao, then Chang. I reported him missing. They did nothing. Then he died."

I felt like saying that the police could not be everywhere all the time, but thought better of it.

Then Mary said, "But Meng, what I don't understand is this. If you are convinced the Triads killed Jiao, surely when Chang was kidnapped you knew they would be serious about killing him if you didn't agree to work with them?"

Dai went to speak, but his father silenced him with a look. "You're missing the point, Mary. The members of the Triads are not honorable men. They would have killed Chang either way. They would have kept him until I fulfilled my side of the bargain, then they would have slit his throat – he knew too much about them to live. Now, perhaps you begin to understand why I don't trust the police. It was thanks to them I was put in that terrible position."

Chapter 28

I WAS WITH Johnny again in my office at Private, the door open. We heard voices from reception – Colette talking to a man. Without looking up, I heard Johnny shuffle in his chair, then sensed rather than saw him freeze in surprise.

"What is it?" I glanced up from the papers on my desk and saw a man in the corridor staring at us. "Well, well!" I said.

Micky Stevens was quite a bit shorter than I imagined he'd be. Weird how fame and success puts on inches. He was maybe five-eight and looked every bit the globally famous rock star he was. But he seemed jaded. He was wearing a black suit jacket and T-shirt, leather pants and boots. He hadn't shaved for a couple of days and looked like he had used a little too much gel in his spiky jet black hair.

Next to him stood his bodyguard, a massive, bald Maori in a tight-fitting suit. I guessed he weighed over three hundred pounds and had a chest measurement of at least sixty.

"You must be Craig Gisto," Micky Stevens said taking a step into my office. He had a light, jaunty voice, and I could hear one of his songs in my head as he spoke.

"How did you work that out?"

"Got the biggest office," and he glanced around. "You're obviously Top Dog here."

I smiled.

Johnny shook Micky Stevens' hand and was still staring at the pop star with awe. Then he turned to the bodyguard.

"Oh, this is Hemi," Micky Stevens said. "Looks really mean, yeah? But only with the enemy . . . otherwise, he's a pussycat. Aren't you, Hemi?"

"What can we do for you?" I asked.

He spun on his heel, lowered his voice. "Can we go . . . somewhere?"

We walked into reception. The pop star gave Colette a brief, professionally flirtatious smile. She'd been chewing the end of a pen and staring at the young man with a lost expression on her face.

I took Micky and Hemi along the hall and indicated to Johnny he should come with us. "We've a comfortable lounge through here," I said. "Coffee?"

"Got anything stronger? Hemi'll have water . . . sparkling if you have it . . ."

I left the odd couple with Johnny and went back to my office. I had a bottle of Bourbon in a small bar against the wall.

"Great choice, man!" Micky Stevens said as I came back, sat on a sofa opposite and watched him pour a generous measure.

I waited for him to take a sip, but he downed it in one. Meanwhile, Johnny had found a bottle of San Pellegrino and a glass. He handed them to Hemi.

"That's better." Micky Stevens smacked his lips.

I decided to wait for him to start talking, but he seemed a bit confused. "Not used to this sort a thing," he began. "Feels like we're in a Raymond Chandler novel!"

I was a bit surprised by that and must have shown it.

"I'm a big reader. Hated it at school, of course, but on tour there's only so much drinking, snorting and screwing you can take . . . gets boring." He produced a megawatt smile. "Anyway." His face straightened and he looked quickly at Hemi who was pouring water carefully into a glass held in sausage fingers. "I'm here about Graham Parker."

Both Johnny and I looked at him blankly.

"My manager. He's quite well-known, dudes!"

"Sorry," I said. "I'm not really . . ."

"No probs." Micky had his hands up. "You got another?" He flicked a nod at the Bourbon.

"Sure." I refilled his glass. "So what is it about Mr. Parker?"

Micky knocked back his second big Bourbon, wiped his mouth and said, "Well, you see, it's like this. Graham Parker's trying to kill me."

Chapter 29

I HADN'T EXPECTED that. Was the guy high? Was he crazy? Drug damaged maybe? I looked into his face. He seemed stone-cold sober, which was pretty amazing since he'd just drunk about a fifth of Bourbon. Actually he looked pretty cool, reminded me of Robbie Williams. Hemi seemed comfortable, hands in lap staring at the art. I was glad about that at least.

"Okay, Micky. What makes you think that?" I asked.

"I'm worth more dead than alive."

"That doesn't mean . . ."

"The bastard's bent. I've been with him for three years. He picked me up when I was at my lowest point after leaving my old band. He's a ruthless mother. You need that in a manager, but I know he wants me snuffed out." Micky clicked his fingers in front of his face.

"If you really think that, why don't you leave him?" Johnny asked and glanced at me for affirmation.

Micky laughed. "Wish I could! *Really* wish I could. But I'm bound by a watertight contract. Parker has me by the balls."

"There must be . . ." I began.

"Listen, Craig, you've gotta understand. Forget it . . . There's no way out of the contract." He drew a deep breath. "Look, man, it's all about Club 27."

I flicked a glance at Johnny. He stared back, shrugged.

"What is Club 27?" I asked.

"Christ! You don't know?"

"Sorry."

"Almost every dead pop star checked out when they were twenty-seven."

"Really?" I turned to Johnny who seemed suddenly animated.

"Actually, yeah, that's right," he said.

"Kurt, Jimi, Janis, Jim Morrison, Amy Winehouse . . . it's a mighty long list, man," Micky added.

"So?" I said.

"Dude . . . I'm twenty-six."

Chapter 30

"WELL WHAT DO you make of that?" I asked Johnny as the doors of the elevator closed on Micky Stevens and Hemi.

"Seems genuinely scared, boss."

We walked back into reception and saw Colette on the phone. She did well to disguise the fact that she was telling a friend about what had just happened. I frowned and she quickly hung up.

Johnny settled himself back into the chair he'd been in before the rock star visitation. I sat behind my desk, put my feet up on the walnut.

"Refresh my memory," I said. "I was never a big fan. He was in Fun Park, right? Before he went solo and became a massive star."

"Yeah, granddad," Johnny replied with a grin.

"I'm more a Nirvana and Chili Peppers kinda guy."

"Fair enough. Fun Park were big. Three No. 1 singles, a hit album. They've just reformed without Micky."

"But his solo career eclipsed his old band, right?"

"Definitely. He is . . . was, huge."

"Was?"

"Gone off a bit recently. Last hit was well over a year ago."

"Which is an eternity when most of your fans are five- or six-year-olds!"

Johnny laughed. "A bit of an exaggeration!"

"Okay," I said suddenly serious. "Could he just be delusional? He obviously has issues."

"I guess we have to take him seriously," Johnny offered.

"We do? Why?" I paused a beat. "Look, okay. I get it. He's Micky Stevens . . . megastar and, I dunno, he seems like a pretty nice guy. But do we believe him?"

"We obviously need to know a lot more about his manager."

"Alright," I said firmly and lowered my legs from the table. "Let's take Micky seriously – at least until we know otherwise."

Johnny seemed to be lost in thought.

"I reckon this one's for you, Johnny."

"Me? On my own?"

"Most definitely. Right up your alley."

He gulped. "Okay, boss . . . well . . . thanks . . . I guess!"

Chapter 31

Twenty-four Hours Ago.

GEOFF HEWES HAD told himself years ago that he should never show that he was impressed by anything, especially rich men and their big houses. *Most* especially when those rich men in big houses were the ones he did business with. But whenever he went to Al Loretto's palatial home in Point Piper it was a struggle.

A real English butler led him through to a vast conservatory at the back of the house. It overlooked a fifty-yard pool surrounded by palm trees. From each end six-foot-long gold-plated dolphins spewed water, a giant marble mermaid rose up on a plinth in the center of the pool. Loretto was sitting in one of a pair of vast wicker chairs at the far end of the glass-walled chamber. He was wearing a silver colored silk robe and reading the *Sydney Morning Herald*. The butler retreated leaving Geoff standing a couple of yards from Loretto. Aside from the water-vomiting dolphins, the room was silent.

Loretto lowered the paper saying nothing, forcing Geoff to speak first.

"You wanted a chat, Al."

"Not happy, Geoffrey. *Really* not happy."

Geoff flicked a glance at the other wicker chair. Loretto saw the gesture and ignored it.

"May I?" Geoff asked and pointed to the seat.

"No, you may not."

"Okay," Geoff drawled. "What's up, Al?"

"What's up Al?" Loretto mimicked, putting on a silly voice. "I'll tell you what's fucking up, Geoffrey. You are lucky I'm even talking to you. I should have just had you popped in the head." And he made the appropriate gesture with his fingers at his left temple.

Geoff knew what he was talking about. He'd known what this was about when he received the call from Al Loretto's assistant's assistant that afternoon.

Loretto was out of the chair, his nose a foot from Geoff's. "Don't fuck with me." He punctuated each word with a finger poke to Geoff's shoulder. By the third one, it hurt, but Hewes couldn't show it. "You didn't take the cameras out my brothels."

Geoff took a deep breath, feeling sweat bleed from his pores.

"I wanted to talk to you . . ."

"There's nothing . . . got that? Nothing to talk about, Geoffrey. The salient point here is that I asked you very nicely to take the cameras out of the brothels and you did not acquiesce." Another harder finger poke.

Geoff pulled back, eyes blazing, went to grab Al Loretto's hand and missed. The finger stabbed him in the neck.

"Fuck you!" He took a swing and found himself pinned to the ground by two hundred and fifty pounds of security. He hadn't even seen the guy appear.

A fist landed in Geoff's face smashing his nose. A second

blow hit him in the cheek so hard he thought his head was about to split open. Then he was being pulled up to his feet and Al Loretto was smiling at him.

"Geoffrey, Geoffrey . . . why are you doing this to yourself? Just when I thought we were becoming such good friends."

Blood streamed down from Geoff's nostrils, ran over his lips, dripped to the floor.

"Take him to the basement," Loretto hissed.

Chapter 32

STACY FRIEL'S HUSBAND, David, had a very smart office on the forty-fifth floor of Citigroup Tower in the CBD. Greta had eased my path with a call earlier in the day. A secretary showed me in. David Friel got up from his desk and offered a firm handshake. He was tall and athletic, graying at the temples and wearing a conservative tailored suit. I hadn't met him before, but he had the aura of a man who had aged ten years during the past forty-eight hours.

"You haven't taken compassionate leave, Mr. Friel?"

"I was offered it of course," he said, his voice a smooth baritone. "But I didn't see the point. Why would I want to kick around the house? If I'm working I can focus on something other than . . ."

"Makes sense."

Friel was in a daze I realized, no inflection in his voice, face expressionless. It was a state I recognized immediately.

"I've given a full report to the police. Not sure what more I can . . ." He trailed off again.

"Look, Mr. Friel, I know this is tough, but I have to ask some personal questions. I need to get some background. I appreciate it's a raw time. I understand."

"You do?"

I looked around at the white walls, a Balinese wall-hanging softening things a little. "I lost my wife and son three years ago."

He stared into my eyes, his expression still vacant.

"An accident," I added. It felt strange speaking about it with a complete stranger. It was something I never discussed. Perhaps it was simple empathy. I really could feel what the poor guy was going through.

He shrugged. "Ask away."

I paused for a second. "Were you happily married, Mr. Friel?"

"As far as I'm concerned, I was. I think Stace was . . . And, I'll save you asking, Mr. Gisto. I wasn't having an affair, and I'm pretty sure my wife wasn't either. I do realize this is your first port of call. It would make life easier if she had been . . . or if *I* was, I guess."

"Okay, sensitive question No. 2. Money. Everything alright?"

He waved a hand around. "I'm third in line to the throne."

Seeing my puzzled expression, he added, "Sorry, in-joke. There's the boss, Max Llewellyn, then his son, then me. I pull down a seven-figure salary."

I thought how that didn't necessarily mean everything was cool, but moved on. "It may sound ridiculous, but can you think of anyone at all who may have hated your wife?"

"Stace was a normal wife, a normal mom, Mr. Gisto. She cared for the kids, had her book club, her gym class. Who would hate her enough to murder her . . . it's nuts."

"You're absolutely sure? Within your social circle? Any grudges? Any big bust-ups recently, ever?"

He was shaking his head. "No. We are . . . we *were* part

of a big social circle – golf club, yacht club, neighbors, work colleagues." He stared straight at me. "But nothing . . . we were . . . rather boring, actually."

"What about you, Mr. Friel? Do you have any enemies?"

His expression changed for the first time. A bleak smile. "Me? Mr. Gisto, in my business I've acquired so many enemies, if I lined them up, they'd stretch from here to the Harbour Bridge."

Chapter 33

"WELL IT COULD be a lead," Justine said. She'd met me at my apartment in Balmoral. I'd called her while driving home from seeing David Friel and she was now sitting on one of my sofas cradling a cup of coffee and looking, I thought, exquisite.

"I guess these money guys live close to the edge . . . plenty of wars."

"And there's also the symbolism of the money . . . the fake money."

"Of course. All a bit vague though, right?" I said.

"Oh, totally. But we have to start somewhere, don't we?"

"You've talked to Greta. Anything?"

"Just confirmation of what we already know. My sister is part of the same social scene. There're always silly feuds between the moms . . . the usual thing, rich women, bored, overindulged; husbands never there. They crave excitement so they invent problems between themselves. Same in LA, London, anywhere."

"Yeah, but I can't get past the relationship angle. You said it – bored women, husbands never there. Perfect recipe."

"Sure. Look, Craig, Greta told me stuff. Half the women she

knows are having affairs with their personal trainers, tennis coaches, you name it. But she reckons Stacy and David weren't like that."

"She's sure?"

Justine nodded.

"So we check out David Friel's associates. See if any of his enemies hate him enough to kill his wife."

"Find out if he's been a 'naughty boy' you mean?"

"Oh don't even question that!" I said. "The guy lives in a five-million-dollar mansion and earns a seven-figure salary. As he more or less told me himself, he's definitely been a 'naughty boy'."

Justine gazed out at the view across Middle Harbour, checked her watch. "I'd better go."

As I led her to the door she turned suddenly. "Nearly forgot . . . Would you like to come to my sister's fortieth?"

I was startled for a second. "Well . . . er . . . yeah."

"It's at a restaurant called Icebergs at Bondi. Greta raves about it." She took a breath. "She almost called the whole thing off, but Brett and I talked her round. When I pointed out that she couldn't let the bastard who murdered Stacy rule her life, it got her blood up. She can be quite fierce when she's riled!"

"When is it?"

"Tomorrow night."

"Well, I'm honored."

Justine held my eyes and grinned mischievously. "Don't be. You're the only man I know in Sydney!" Then she pecked me on the cheek and left.

Chapter 34

JOHNNY HAD THE smallest office at Private HQ and shared it with the photocopier, which in effect meant he shared the space with the receptionist, Colette. But he didn't seem to mind. Johnny was an expert at filtering out noise and distraction and just getting on with things. It was a skill he'd picked up as a kid. He had to do his homework in a tiny living-room while his father watched the racing, his mother did the ironing and his older brother argued with his younger sister. He still managed to get straight As in his exams.

Now he was staring at the monitor, his coffee ignored on the desk beside the keyboard. He'd been following a paper trail, well a cyber trail, to find anything juicy he could on Graham Parker. But the facts were scant.

He looked away from the screen for a few moments to survey what he had written on a legal notepad next to the coffee cup.

Parker was fifty-six, American, born in Utah. Went to Brigham Young University, studied Economics. He dropped out after two years and became a minor pop star himself. Played on the New York CBGBs scene in the late seventies fronting a band called Venison. Then he became a manager for Toys and, later, Rough Cut, who were pretty successful. He left America in 2010, hooked up with Micky Stevens as the singer was leaving his old boy band Fun Park six months later and turned the guy into a huge solo star.

Johnny returned to the computer and tapped a few keys. The screen showed sales figures for Micky Stevens' three solo albums. He'd peaked with his first, *Love Box*, which had made the US Billboard Top 10. But since then his career had begun to falter. His last CD, *Much 2 Much*, was a flop except in Australia.

"So, there's your motive," Johnny said under his breath. "If Stevens is right and the manager is trying to have him snuffed out, it's because his career is on the ropes. Parker's going for the 'dead pop star revenue'." He spanned back to the screen and began to type.

The next ten minutes were a waste. He went through all the official sites linked to Stevens, Fun Park, old material on the bands Parker had managed in the '80s. Nothing. Well something . . . Parker had been a junkie, had served six months for possession in 1979, spent time in rehab . . . pretty *de rigueur*.

He was about to give up when he found a blog thread about Micky's old band. From there he stumbled upon a chat exchange between half a dozen fans of Fun Park and a couple of people who evidently detested them. Most of it was inane garbage and Johnny began to scroll down faster and faster, until a sentence jumped out . . . *Parker's bankruptcy was the best thing that ever happened to Micky Stevens. What would the useless son of a bitch have done after Fun Park if Parker hadn't left the States to start again?*

Johnny stopped scrolling and reread the two sentences. Then he checked the responses. There were no more comments, they'd just moved on. He threw himself back in his chair, a tingle of excitement passing through him. It was the first chink in the investigation and he was determined to prise it open.

Chapter 35

ELSPETH LAMPARD HAS put the kids to bed and is walking down the stairs when she realizes just how much she needs a glass of Shiraz.

Her husband, Ralph, is away in Europe and won't be back until next week. She feels lonely at this time of the evening – after the kids are in bed and before she falls asleep in front of the TV.

She goes to the wine rack. Nothing. "Damn it," she says aloud. She considers taking something from the wine cellar, but Ralph would hit the roof if he found one of his treasured wines had gone missing. There isn't a bottle in there worth under five hundred bucks.

Dusk is descending over Bellevue Hill as Elspeth walks to the liquor store two streets away. Five minutes later, she is forty yards from her house with a decent thirty-dollar quaffing wine.

It's quiet, sticky hot. Most of Elspeth's neighbors are indoors watching TV or lounging by their blue-lit pools with a cocktail in hand.

She hears a click from behind. Ignores it. Then comes a

shuffling sound. She turns. Nothing. Sidewalk clear. Elspeth spins back again.

The blow comes from behind.

She falls to her knees, confused.

There's a blur of houses, concrete, darkening sky. She hits the sidewalk hard. The wine bottle smashes – red liquid everywhere. Pain shoots up her neck, streaks across the left side of her face. She tries to turn, makes it halfway and sees a figure in an anorak leaning over her. Elspeth can smell her assailant's breath.

She has no time to get up. Her attacker is bigger, stronger. She feels herself being dragged into a narrow alleyway between two gardens. She tries to scream, but as soon as she opens her mouth, a gloved hand comes over it, grips her lips, crushes the flesh about her mouth. Elspeth feels a tooth snap inward. More pain. Terrible pain. It spreads out across her face and around her skull.

She's pushed up against a fence, a cloth comes up against her mouth. The attacker is leaning over her, knotting the material behind her neck. She struggles, but she's drained and the assailant is too strong. Elspeth feels a wire being wrapped about her wrists pinned behind her back.

She can't resist anymore. Her vision is bleary. She sees a head appear in front of her. No detail. The face is in shadow, hooded. She sees a match light, a cigarette lit. The flame illuminates part of the hooded face, but only the mouth . . . pale, thin lips.

Elspeth screams as the cigarette burns her face, but the sound is soaked up in the gag. She can smell her own burned flesh and screeches, helpless, as the cigarette is pushed into her

again, just beneath her left eye. She starts to cry, tears streaming down her face. The pain sears her insides. It feels as though
her head is going to explode. She vomits into the cloth in her
mouth and starts to choke on it.

The attacker grabs her, spins her over onto her front,
Elspeth's disfigured face hits the sandy ground of the lane.

Next comes the knife. Elspeth doesn't know it's a knife. She
just knows something has pierced her back. She feels a strange
dislocation in her spine. In her confused state, submerged in
agony, she imagines she's a puppet and her strings have been
cut.

The knife goes in again and Elspeth convulses and gasps.
But now the pain has gone. She's moved beyond it.

Her assailant turns her over. Peers down into her face, pulls
back the hood. Elspeth is almost totally blind, but she feels
another shock, a new revulsion. Her life is fading away, but she
knows the attacker is pulling up her skirt, spreading her legs.

Chapter 36

TONY MACKENZIE WAS coming to the end of his five-mile run. He always felt a sense of euphoria build at this point in his circuit. He ran the same route at the same time every weekday, and entering Wentworth Avenue marked the final hundred-yard stretch before the wind down.

This morning, he felt energized. The sun was coming up, casting orange light all over the place. He passed the end of an alleyway leading off the sidewalk and kept running. But then something began to play on his mind. Something was wrong. He couldn't figure out what it was, but it nagged him. He tried to push it aside, but it kept niggling him.

Forty yards past the alley, Tony Mackenzie finally stopped. He'd seen something. Something wasn't quite right.

He turned and jogged back toward the entrance to the alley. Looking down the narrow lane, hands on hips, he steadied his breathing. Ten yards ahead, to the side of the alley, lay a dark object, vaguely human in shape. It could have been a bundle of rags. But something in Tony's brain was telling him it wasn't.

He walked toward the object, sweat dripping off him. As he drew closer he realized it was a human being. He thought it might be a homeless person. He stepped forward cautiously, walking past the prone form close to the fence alongside the lane, his eyes fixed on the shape. He half expected it to jump up and attack him at any moment.

Three steps past the strange figure, Tony could finally make sense of it and felt a surge of terror in the pit of his stomach. Then nerves all over his body seemed to fire simultaneously. He jolted, stumbling back against the fence.

Chapter 37

I WAS JUST pulling onto the Harbour Bridge. Glanced at the dash clock. It was 6.59 am. I felt like shit – I'd hardly slept at all last night. In my nightmares and half-sleep I kept going over Stacy Friel's murder. And you know the worst of it? She looked like my dead wife, Becky.

I'd had two strong coffees before leaving the house and had stopped for a Red Bull at my regular gas station in Mosman. The Ferrari is a thirsty bastard, and so was I this morning.

I moved my thumb to switch on the ABC News with the remote control on the steering wheel when my cell rang. I pushed the "Receive" button and heard Justine's voice. "Craig?"

"That's me! Hi, Justine."

"We've got a second murder."

I glanced in the mirror, sped into a gap to my left. "Any details?"

"No. Brett's there now. It's a street away from Greta's."

"No way!" I changed lanes and accelerated along the Cahill Expressway. The traffic was building, but still okay. "Where's the body, exactly?"

"Wentworth Avenue. Runs parallel to Greta's street."

"Know it. How did you learn of the murder?"

"I'm at Greta and Brett's. Stayed over last night. Brett got the call just as he was leaving for HQ."

"Okay. I'll be there in fifteen . . . hopefully."

It was pretty much a straight run and I was there in twelve, stopped ten yards from the police cordon and walked briskly toward the tape. A constable was guarding the sidewalk. I showed him my ID and I was relieved when he let me through without any arguments. Maybe this liaison with the cops could actually work after all, I thought, as I ducked under the yellow tape and paced over to where the forensics team were poking around.

Brett Thorogood spotted me and waved me over. I saw Mark a few yards away, his back to me. He was talking to a man in lycra.

"Runner found the body," Thorogood explained, his expression grim.

I followed the DC over to where the victim lay – another woman, about forty, shoulder-length blonde hair. She was dressed in a blood-soaked Dolce & Gabbana dress. The soil under her and around her was discolored. Her face had been mutilated – cigarette burns.

Her dress had been hitched up over her hips, legs splayed. The end of a roll of fifty-dollar bills could just be seen protruding from between her legs. Blood had dried on the insides of her thighs.

"Same MO," I said unnecessarily. Thorogood just stared at the dead woman.

I turned to see Justine at the tape. The cop who'd let me through was questioning her. I strode over and just as I reached them, he let her under the barrier.

"Same thing as before," I told her as we walked along the alley. Thorogood had moved to one of the police cars on the street. Justine put a hand to her mouth, but as I went to turn her away, she shook me off. "It's okay, Craig!" she said sharply. "Not much shocks me anymore."

I saw Talbot finish up questioning the jogger and decided to leave Justine to it. I walked over to Mark just as another cop escorted the runner toward Wentworth Avenue.

"Oh . . . how nice!" he said.

"History repeating itself."

He nodded toward the dead woman. "Doesn't help that poor thing."

"Might help us though. What do you have?"

He let out a heavy sigh. "Jogger found her about 5.45. The woman had been stabbed repeatedly in the back. We don't know if she was raped before . . ."

"The first victim wasn't."

"No."

"Do we know who she is?"

"Name's Elspeth Lampard. Address: 44 Wentworth Avenue."

"That's just two houses away." I nodded back toward the main road. "Any idea how long she's been here?"

"Ten or eleven hours."

I nodded. "Makes sense. She'd probably have been spotted sooner if she'd been killed earlier. So after . . . what? . . . 8 pm?"

Talbot didn't answer, had started to turn away when he caught sight of Darlene walking toward us with her forensics kit.

"Your turn to poke around," he said sardonically.

Chapter 38

AS DARLENE SET to work, I left Justine behind, plucked out my iPhone and started toward Wentworth Avenue.

I tapped "Elspeth Lampard Australia" into Google and a couple of weblinks came up. She was the daughter of Norman Ruschent, a wealthy mining entrepreneur in Western Australia. And she'd married well too. Her husband was CFO of Buttress Finance Group – a big, global player. Made a name for himself on the Australian stock exchange in the early nineties, served time in London, a big city firm. They'd met over there.

Personal background: the Lampards had two boys, nine and eleven, both at Cranbrook School. I lifted my eyes from the screen of the iPhone as I passed the end of the alley, emerging onto Wentworth Avenue, saw a policewoman a couple of houses down. She was walking toward a squad car with two young boys. The Lampard kids, I realized . . . poor little buggers. I felt for them, I'd lost my own mother when I was around their age.

Leaning against a low wall, I returned my gaze to the screen. So a second victim linked to the financial sector found dead with fake banknotes stuffed inside her body. I wondered if

Elspeth knew the first victim, Stacy Friel . . . or indeed, David Friel? Must have done, I concluded. He was a senior cog at Citigroup. The Friels and the Lampards lived one street apart.

What other links could there be? I started to think laterally. Called Greta.

"Hey," I said gently.

"Is that Craig? Hi."

"Look, I'm calling about the latest . . ."

"Yep," she said. She was clearly trying to keep herself together.

"The dead woman is Elspeth Lampard." I heard a sudden intake of breath. Paused for second. "You know her?"

There was a delay. "Um . . . not that well, Craig. But yeah, I knew her."

"I'm trying to find links, Greta. Links with . . ."

"Okay . . ." Another sharp inhalation. "Er . . . let me . . . let me think. Ralph, her husband . . . he knows David well, David Friel."

"Through work?"

"Yeah, and socially. They're practically neighbors. They play tennis together. Stace . . . she played too. Same club as us . . . down the road. And . . . er . . . the gym. Yeah, Elspeth goes to my gym . . . and Stacy's."

"Okay."

"You think this is some sex thing, don't you?"

"No, Greta. I don't."

Silence.

"I'm sorry," she said after a moment. "I'm just . . ."

I kept quiet for a few beats. Then: "Can you think of anything? Anything unusual? Anything going on? I don't mean tossing the keys into the bowl."

"What *do* you mean then?"

"Elspeth's husband is in finance. So is David Friel. They work for different companies, but could the husbands be working together on something?"

"Craig. I have no idea." She paused for several seconds. "All I know is that Stacy and Elspeth were just nice, normal women . . . until someone killed them."

Chapter 39

THEY'D TAKEN EVERYTHING from Geoff Hewes' pockets – money, cell phone, car keys. Then the man who'd jumped on him had smacked him over the head with something hard and heavy and shoved him into a blacked-out room. When he came to, he could taste blood in his mouth.

Hewes pulled himself up, wincing and cursing, then he felt incredibly sick and vomited copiously, touched his face, it was crusty with blood. His jaw was agonizing.

There was a chink of light from a window high up and he could just hear traffic far off. He recalled Loretto's last words and knew where he was . . . in the basement of the bastard's huge house at Point Piper.

What the hell was Loretto doing? Was he trying to make him cack himself before punching a bullet through his skull? It would be just like him: after all, why just kill someone when you can play with them first?

"Well you're not going to get me you bastard!" Hewes yelled into the empty blackness. Then he slumped to the floor, head in hands.

Chapter 40

"ALRIGHT GUYS, SO, let's take it case by case," I said and surveyed the conference room back at Private. "First, the Ho murder. Darlene has isolated DNA samples but they don't tally with any records. Ho Meng is convinced the police can't help and he's certain the Triads want him to coordinate a smuggling operation."

"There's also the fact," Mary said, "that Ho Meng is sure the Triads are out for revenge. That's why they've targeted him, killed his son. He believes they murdered his wife soon after the family arrived in Australia a dozen years ago."

"So, Mary." I turned in my chair. "You have to dig further. Ho thinks he knows the gang, we have some DNA, but that's it. We need names, we need to know where the gang hangs out. For the moment, Ho refuses to work with the cops, but I don't feel comfortable with that."

"We can't force him to," Johnny commented.

"No, we can't." I scanned the faces around the table. "Okay, Darlene . . . What's your latest?"

She looked down at a short stack of papers. Cleared her throat. "Dead woman: Elspeth Lampard, forty-one. Multiple stab wounds, fatal one to the heart. Tortured, face disfigured. She must have died pretty quick. I've found no sign of sexual assault, no prints, no alien DNA other than background stuff. There are, though, some long hairs that don't match Elspeth's. I found those on her dress. Doesn't mean much. She could've picked them up walking along the road, or at work. The bank-notes are photocopies."

"The victim's husband, Ralph Lampard, is CFO of Buttress Finance Group," I said. "So, I'm wondering if there's a link with big-time corporate money." I looked at Justine and then Johnny before taking in the other two.

"Obviously, our first touchstone has to be money, doesn't it?" Johnny replied. "Both husbands work in the financial sector. Banknotes placed ritualistically."

"But what about the elephant in the room? The fact that the money is fake."

"In *both* murders," Mary added.

"But it seems too much of a coincidence that the husbands are in finance, *and* the two dead women were both abused the same way," Johnny insisted.

"Unless the killer is trying to trick us," Justine commented.

"Yeah, okay, all things are possible." I took a deep breath. "But money *is* the most obvious link we have at the moment, isn't it?"

"No," Justine said emphatically.

"No?" We all looked to her.

"Geography. The two women lived a couple of streets apart in Bellevue Hill. That's as strong a link as the financial one."

"So you really think it's more to do with the fact that the victims lived in the same suburb?" I asked.

"You don't think that's a tangible connection?"

It suddenly seemed obvious. "Well, yeah . . . of course it is."
I shook my head. "We have to think outside the box." The
others were staring at me. "What if," I went on enthusiastically,
"we have some lucky murderer? He's killing women ran-
domly, except for the fact they live within a few streets of each
other . . . Bellevue Hill must be teeming with banker types,
stockbrokers. It's that sort of area."

"I've experienced this sort of thing in LA," Justine inter-
jected and swept her eyes around the table. "The guy could
be going for women with the same hair color . . . Stacy Friel
and Elspeth Lampard were both blonde. He could be targeting women of a particular age. Friel was thirty-nine, Lampard
forty-one. It could be someone at their gym, the tennis club,
the local coffee shop."

"Okay. So basically, what you two are saying is that we've
got nowhere, because the financial link could well be absolutely spurious," Johnny shot back.

"Guess we are," I said, glancing at Justine.

Chapter 41

I GOT THE call from the security firm that supervises our block just as I reached my office – and it was the best news I'd had all day. Mary was passing my door just as I put down the receiver.

"Hey, Mary," I said, coming round the front of my desk. "Got a break in the Ho case."

"What sort of break?"

"The security company for this building, Matrix? They've some images of the guys who killed Chang."

"But the killers snatched the hard drive from the guard booth."

"They have another camera just outside the exit gate of the garage. Separate system. They're sending over the images."

Just as I finished the sentence, my email sounded. I walked to my chair, Mary followed me and leaned in. I tapped open the message, double-clicked the attachment.

"Oh, wonderful!" Mary exclaimed, and I felt my heart sink. The picture showed little more than a pair of blob heads behind the car windshield.

Chapter 42

DARLENE RECOGNIZED THE voice immediately. It came through the speaker in her lab connected to the intercom at the main entrance. Colette had gone out and she was on her own. She stepped out of her lab, strode three paces along the hall, and there he was, one of the world's most recognizable faces – Micky Stevens. Beside him, his legendary bodyguard, Hemi.

"I've come to see Johnny," Micky smiled.

"Ah . . . right . . . Hi . . . I'm, I'm Darlene, Darlene Cooper. Johnny, ah, Johnny isn't here. I'm on my own. He'll be back soon, though."

"That's cool. So, Darlene Cooper . . ." Micky indicated he would like to come in.

"Sorry!" she giggled, and a wisp of blonde hair fell across her face as she held the door open.

"So what do you do here then?" Micky asked as they entered reception.

"Forensics." She was calming down now.

"Wow! Really? That's cool. I love *CSI*. Do you watch that show?"

"Not really," Darlene replied. "I see enough bits and pieces of dead people during the day."

Micky stared at her, then shook his head slowly and grinned. "That is just the most insane job, Darlene!"

"Really? Well, being a rock star's pretty awesome!"

"If you say so."

There was an uncomfortable silence. Hemi stood next to Micky like a lump of rock. He only moved when it was absolutely necessary and his blank expression never changed.

"Er, coffee?" Darlene offered.

"No thanks. Tell you what though. I'd love to see your lab. You do have a lab, right?"

Darlene looked surprised. "Yeah, sure. Along here."

"Oh man! This is really something!" Micky exclaimed as he entered the room behind her. Hemi had stayed back at reception. "You know, my parents always wanted me to become a doctor or a scientist, something like that," he went on. "I got stung by the rock 'n' roll bug, but I always regret not going to college or anything. I love science . . . don't know much . . . but." He laughed.

Darlene was barely able to conceal her surprise. She couldn't take in what a normal guy Micky Stevens was. No, he wasn't just a normal guy, he was humble, in awe of her work of all things!

"It's never too late." She felt stupid as soon as she said it.

"You reckon?" Micky chuckled. "Yeah I can see it now." He put a hand up indicating newspaper headlines. "ROCK STAR BECOMES FORENSICS EXPERT." So, Darlene, what do all these things do, then?"

"God, that would take a while to explain."

"What you working on?"

"Now? Oh, I'm investigating a kidnap and murder."

"Wow!"

"We have some security camera images of the suspects, but they're really not good. I can't make anything out."

"So what can you do about it?"

Darlene led him over to a flat screen. "I'm trying to enhance them with some new software I have."

Micky gazed around the room. "Looks pretty top-end stuff."

"Yeah, it is," she replied proudly. "State-of-the-art. But these stills are just too degraded."

"I can help," Micky said.

Darlene lowered herself into a chair in front of the monitor. "You can?" She couldn't keep the skepticism from her voice.

"Yeah, well not me personally, but I know a really great computer guy. A genius in fact."

Before Darlene could reply, Micky cut across her. "No, listen. The guy's amazing. This stuff –" he swept a hand around the room – "is cool, don't get me wrong, but in the recording studio I use some really hi-tech gear too, and my buddy . . . well, he works for me actually . . . is *the biz*."

Darlene took a deep breath and put up her hands. "Well great, Micky. I'd appreciate any help I can get. What's your colleague's name?"

"Software Sam. I'll send him over."

There was a sound from the doorway. Hemi was filling almost the entire space. Darlene and Micky could just see Johnny trying to get a view of the room over the Maori's shoulder.

Micky came out of the lab and shook hands with Johnny. "Good to see you again, dude. So what's new?"

Johnny nodded to Darlene who smiled back as if to say, "We're done here."

But Micky hadn't finished. He turned back and gave her a peck on the cheek. "Thanks for showing me this," he said and waved at the room. "Fantastic! I'll get in touch with Sam . . ."

And he was gone, Darlene just staring after him.

Chapter 43

"SO HOW CAN I help?" Micky began.

They were in Johnny's small office at the end of the corridor. Johnny had called him the night before. This was the earliest the singer could make it.

"Micky, you claim Graham Parker wants you killed because you're apparently worth more dead than alive."

"Correct."

"But that would imply that he is either very greedy or has money troubles."

"Well, course he's greedy, Johnny. He's a businessman. Only thinks about dollars and cents."

"Yeah, but why didn't you tell us he filed for bankruptcy in the States?"

He shrugged. "Didn't really see why it was important."

Johnny gazed into his eyes and counted to three before responding. "Well of course it is." He glanced over to Hemi who had sunk into a sofa at the back of the room, same fixed expression as always.

"God, this is all so fucked up!" Micky exclaimed and put his head down for a moment. "You got a drink, man?"

Johnny pulled up from behind his desk, left the room for a few seconds and returned with a bottle and a glass. He handed them to Micky, who stared at the label.

"Do you know anything about his finances, Micky?" Johnny asked. "He must know all about yours. Does it only go one way?"

Micky took a swig from the bottle, held it at arm's length. "Good shit."

"I'll take your word for it," Johnny said. "I don't drink."

"Lucky you."

Johnny raised an eyebrow.

"No, I mean it. Wish I didn't have to . . ."

"Parker's finances?"

"I'm not an accountant, man! I don't know much about my own money let alone my manager's!"

Johnny rolled his eyes. Maybe he had overestimated this guy, he thought. Maybe Craig was right, he was drug addled. Perhaps he was just plain dumb . . . or both. "But he must have made a fortune," Johnny tried again. "How could he have ended up bankrupt?"

Micky said nothing, just took another swig.

"Look, Micky!" Johnny snapped. "How do you expect Private to help you if you don't tell us everything you know about the man?"

The rock star looked up and held Johnny's stare. "Yeah," he said finally. "You're right."

Course I'm bloody right, Johnny thought, and waited for the singer to go on.

"Graham had a major problem. Blew fifteen mill . . . apparently."

"How?"

"Compulsive gambler. But look, dude, we all have our demons. I've not seen Graham even dabble since I've known him. Got him drunk a few times and he's told me straight that gambling is a mug's game and he stopped when he came here. Went into therapy, the lot. Gave up his old vices, doesn't even smoke weed now."

"And you believe that?"

Micky considered the bottle again. "Well put it this way, Johnny." He lifted his eyes. "It's up to you to prove it if my manager has been lying, isn't it? And if he has been . . . Bingo! Motive time!"

Chapter 44

MARY HAD TO smile. She saw the car in the lot about twenty yards away. It fit exactly the description the owner gave on the phone the night before. He'd sounded nervous but also full of bravado about his red saloon with the jacked-up rear wheels and the flame spray job along the sides that he would be waiting in on the edge of Prince Alfred Park in Parramatta.

He claimed he had info about the murder of 'that Chinese kid', but refused to come into Private's HQ. He gave a time and place where he would meet someone from the agency, and so here she was.

It was hot as Mary crossed the gravel. She saw the guy in the driver's seat, bleached blond mullet, baseball cap, shades, cigarette. He hadn't mentioned he'd have a very big Rottweiler in the back.

The guy leaned over, pushed open the door. The dog growled.

"Shut up Thor!"

Mary kept her eyes fixed on the dog and slipped into the seat.

"He's cool," the guy said. "Knows who's boss. Don't you, Thor?"

Mary moved to the edge of her seat.

"Buckle up, we ain't staying here," the man said and fired up the engine. It produced a throaty noise, bit like the dog's growl.

"Five nights ago – Friday. I saw a kid that fit the description of that Ho boy in the paper. I found out you guys are investigating. Didn't wanna go to the pigs . . . hate 'em, but I felt I ought to say something. Hate the Chink gangs even more . . . It's them, right?"

Mary kept silent.

"I saw a car pull up about eleven at night. I was with a chick." He gave Mary a wolfish grin and turned back to the road as they took a corner, passed some ravaged tenement blocks.

She gave him a hard look. "You saw this from your window?"

"Yeah, the Chinks were staying in an apartment a few floors beneath mine. I'm on the ninth."

"Can you describe the car?"

He looked affronted. "Course I can, I'm a bloody mechanic, aren't I? '96 Toyota Corolla. Piece a shit. Blue. Faded rear bumper, had an I LOVE MACCAS sticker on it. They dragged the kid from the back. His hands were tied behind him. They were pretty vicious. He was gagged, but protesting, so they kicked him in the balls. I heard him squeal, poor little bastard."

"What did the two Chinese men look like?"

"That's the thing. I only caught a glimpse." He spun the wheel hard left. "It was dark, right? The council haven't fixed the street lights. Besides, those dudes all look the same, don't they? Usual shit . . . short, skinny, long black hair. One was wearing a leather jacket. I thought that was odd as it was about seventy-five degrees outside even that late."

Mary pursed her lips, looked away at the sidewalk flashing by.

"You got the number plate?"

"Oh yeah. I left it for a bit, then I went downstairs."

"You did?"

"Told you. Hate 'em. That's why I'm 'ere."

"Okay."

"It was GHT . . . ah . . . 23R."

"Sure?"

"Absolutely."

"Well, thanks," Mary responded. "Anything else?"

"Yeah. I'm pretty sure they were in apartment 16, third floor."

"Were?"

"They left a couple of nights ago," he said quickly and then pulled the car to the curb, turned in the road and headed back to the park.

"How do you know that?"

"Saw 'em, didn't I?" he glanced over to Mary. She caught a glimpse of the dog, dribble dangling from its chops. The guy accelerated down the street, screeched left and the park lay directly ahead. "I checked with the block manager, Harry Griffin, I know 'im."

"You certain?"

"Of course I'm certain . . . Christ!"

"What's the full address?"

He paused for a beat, reluctant. Pulled back into the lot. "Newbury House, 17, Canal Street. And that's all I got."

Chapter 45

MARY CALLED DARLENE and arranged to meet her an hour later at the address the guy with the dog gave her. Then she rang Parramatta Council. Within two minutes she'd learned that Newbury House was serviced by a private cleaning company called R and M Cleaners.

Their address was only half a mile from where she'd parked and the traffic was light. The office was open, and as she approached the door to the left of a closed shop, a small group of Asian women in overalls came down a flight of stairs. A van was parked at the curb. It had R and M Cleaners written on the side.

Mary paused on the sidewalk to let the women pass and glimpsed the plastic ID each of them wore attached to the straps of their overalls. That's all she needed. Twenty minutes later and a trip to a passport photo booth and a stationery store in the town center and she had a duplicated ID that would pass a cursory inspection. Then she drove on to Newbury House.

The block manager's office stank of cigarette smoke. The manager, Harry Griffin, sat behind a small desk strewn with papers, an overflowing ashtray close to where he had rested his left elbow. He had the racing paper open on top of the mess.

"R and M Cleaners," Mary said confidently. He looked up from the paper, scrutinized her.

"Council sent me. Special clean for apartment 16."

Griffin looked puzzled for a moment. "You got ID?"

Mary pulled the fake from her pocket and held it out.

"Where're your overalls?"

She lifted a small holdall and tapped it.

Griffin shrugged and stood up, plucked the keys for the apartment from a rack on the wall behind him and passed them to her between orange-stained fingers. "When you're done drop 'em in the box outside."

"Will do." Mary walked out, turned left, headed for the elevator. Emerging on the third floor, she saw Darlene waiting by the door to No. 16 already prepped in plastic overalls and holding her metal box.

Mary unlocked the door, eased it inwards. The place was a pigsty.

"Probably best if you leave me here for an hour, Mary," Darlene said as she began to pick through the trash lying everywhere.

"Leave you alone around here? You mad?"

"Alright, but if you're going to nose around, at least put these on." She plucked a pair of latex gloves from her box of tricks.

Mary went into the tiny kitchen as Darlene busied herself with a pile of detritus on a coffee table in front of a ripped gray velour sofa dotted with cigarette burns. The carpet stank of feet and fried food.

The power had been cut off. In the kitchen the only light

came from a tiny window over the sink. She heard a crunching sound underfoot and could make out dried noodles scattered on the cheap tiles.

She walked back into the living-room. Darlene was bagging some cardboard cartons of leftover food, a pair of chopsticks lay against the corner of one. She emptied the ashtray into another bag, sealed it.

"Odd they've been so carefree," Darlene remarked, looking up.

"Show of arrogance," Mary replied. "Think they're above the law."

"In some places they are."

"Not in my city, they aren't!" Mary snapped and turned to search the bedroom.

Moments later she called from the doorway, "Darlene?"

"Yep?" She stopped a foot inside the room. Mary had opened the curtains. The sheets were caked in dried blood. "I think we've found where Ho Chang's eye surgery was carried out."

Chapter 46

GEOFF HEWES PACED around the ten-foot square cellar, swearing to no one, the words echoing back to him.

"That asshole . . . That fucking bastard, Loretto!" he screamed. "You think you can tell me what I can and can't do? Me? Geoff Fitzgerald Hewes? I'm a bona fide genius compared to you! You just got lucky, you wop shit. Then you think you can abuse me?" He looked up to the ceiling, imagined Loretto in his wicker chair.

Then he began to weep, the tears streaming down his face.

Chapter 47

Three Months Ago.

JULIE O'CONNOR AND Bruce Frimmel lived in a fleapit, a project apartment in Sandsville in the Western Suburbs – no-man's land for any respectable Sydneysider. It was a two-room place, cramped living area with a kitchen in the corner, next to that a bedroom, toilet and shower leading off one end. There were bars at the windows, bars at the front door.

Bruce Frimmel was a big guy, six-three, thick arms, hair vibrant red. Julie O'Connor stood five-nine in stockings, big-boned and flabby with straggly bleached blonde hair courtesy of a bottle lifted from the local 7-Eleven. She had bad skin, and six months ago, after seeing a picture of Angie Bowie in the seventies, she'd shaved off her eyebrows. David Bowie had been her idol as a girl.

And Julie loved Bruce. But everything had gone awry.

They wanted a kid, desperately. But nothing was working. So a month ago Julie had gone for an op, an op that had gone spectacularly wrong. She was left infertile, completely and utterly barren. She would never, ever have kids.

Bruce had taken it badly. Very badly.

*

"What'ya doin', babe?" Julie asked. She'd just arrived back from her job at the supermarket across the city. Bruce was in the bedroom bent over a ratty old suitcase on the bed. "We win the lottery?" she chuckled nervously.

Bruce ignored her.

"Babe?"

He turned, face hard.

She sank to the bed. Seemed to age a dozen years.

Bruce tossed a singlet into the case. It landed on top of his footy DVD and *Muscle Car* mag. "I'm movin' out," he announced, hands on hips.

"Moving out . . . why?" Julie's face was twisted. "Someone else?"

Bruce nodded. He made to sit next to Julie on the bed but decided against it.

"Who? That slut from the video store?"

Bruce looked down between his trainers at the worn red carpet. Shook his head.

"Who then?" Julie's voice was far too calm. Then she screamed . . . . "*WHO?*"

Bruce was shocked for a second.

She pulled up from the bed, rushed toward him. He was six inches taller than her, seventy-five pounds heavier, but he stepped back, thought she was about to cry. He'd never seen her cry and an odd thrill rattled through him. A strange moment of pride that even he was a little ashamed of. But she didn't.

"YOU SHIT!" Julie howled and went straight for his throat.

Before the two-hundred-and-fifty-pound hulk of a man could pull her off, she'd drawn blood – deep nail drags across his neck. He caught a glimpse of her expression. She looked like a wild beast.

Then she smacked him across the face. It stung, but it also knocked him into reality. He hit back, made contact with something hard, Julie's jaw. He almost lost his balance, but caught himself, straightened and really went for her.

She stumbled, landing hard on her back. Her head hit the rough carpet. Bruce dived on her, swung his fist round and smacked her in the face.

"Useless bitch!" he screamed. "Can't even do the business . . . Well thank Christ! Who'd wanna have a kid with you?"

He smashed his fist into her face again, pulled himself up. Looked down at the red mess, blood streaming from Julie's nose, her lip split open.

Bruce turned back to his suitcase and finished packing, listening to Julie's rasping breath and the blood gurgling in her throat.

Chapter 48

HE SLAMMED THE front door. Julie lay semiconscious, blood drying on her face.

In her mind she saw her father. He would have sorted Bruce out. She'd always loved her father, Jim. Loved him as much as she'd loathed her mother, Sheila.

Dad had been a cop. Julie's favorite memory of him was the day he took her to work and showed her around the police station in Sandsville. She was ten and very proud of her dad.

They'd gone to the forensics labs in the basement. A man in a white lab coat had shown her the glistening machines and racks of test tubes, told her about fingerprinting and a new thing – DNA profiling. She hadn't really understood much of it. But the next day she took a book from the local library. It was called *Forensic Investigation* and she couldn't put it down.

Julie began to hate her mother when she realized her mother didn't love her dad. There was another man. Julie wasn't sure if Jim knew about him, but she overheard her mother talking to her lover on the phone when her dad was out. And once, she followed her and saw her kissing a heavily set man with a beard.

Then had come the worst day of her life. A policeman came to the door of their house and told them her dad had been killed on duty – knifed trying to stop a burglar. He was only thirty-four.

Chapter 49

JULIE BEGAN TO plot Bruce's murder two days after he walked out on her. She planned everything meticulously. And, as she took one step after the other on the road to killing her ex, she started to enjoy herself.

Bruce was a sex pig. All men thought with their dicks, but Bruce's sex drive was more powerful than most. She knew she could use that.

The first time Julie sent an anonymous email to Bruce's phone she was sure he wouldn't reply. She couldn't afford a computer of her own of course, and besides, emails could be traced. Instead, she'd gone to an internet café in the CBD and written Bruce a flirtatious message under the name Sabrina. Bruce always had a yen for what he referred to as "class ass". And the name "Sabrina" had just the right ring to it.

At first, he was cautious, but after half a dozen messages all sent from different computers, Sabrina ensnared him and the exchanges became more pornographic. He was soon begging to meet her in person.

She coaxed and teased like a pro, made it clear she liked to be screwed rough in filthy places. The more depraved, the more it turned her on. She had him salivating.

She called in at an internet café in Balmain and typed a message: "I want you . . . TONIGHT!"

"When? Where?" he responded almost immediately.

She gave him the place and time, then added, "My panties are getting wet just thinking about it."

Chapter 50

JULIE, OR "SABRINA", arrived at the address she'd given Bruce an hour early. It was a condemned house, fenced off with wire mesh. On the perimeter of the garden stood a large notice-board detailing the new development planned for the site. Other signs told the public to KEEP OUT.

The windows and the front door were boarded up but she made short work of a couple of planks securing the entrance to the decaying old house. Every window was smashed. The hall was strewn with newspapers and pigeon shit.

She'd found everything she needed in the local hardware store, and now it was all neatly arranged in the corner of the dilapidated bathroom – a powerful battery-powered lamp, a hammer and a new knife. She surveyed her purchases, hands on hips. "Not bad," she said to herself.

She waited patiently. The minutes ticked away. She heard someone approach the door, recognized Bruce's sounds as though he had left yesterday. He was a big oaf and moved like one.

"Sabrina?"

She didn't reply.

"Sabrina?" There was a nervous edge to his voice, Julie thought.

"In here," she called from the bathroom down the hall and flicked on the battery-powered lamp. She stood behind the half-opened door.

Julie let him take two steps into the room, crept up behind him, swung her new hammer low and said one word: "Bruce." He made a half-turn and she smashed him behind the right knee with the hammer.

He yelled and stumbled grabbing the edge of the tub. She leapt on him, screaming and bringing the hammer down hard on his head, his neck, his back. She rolled him over, smashing the hammer into his face. His nose shattered, blood plumed into the air, hit the white wall tiles. He put his hands up to protect himself. She raised the weapon again, plowing it into the back of his hands. Bruce tried to scramble away, but she kept hitting him, blow after blow . . . like crushing a roach.

Her face was covered with Bruce's blood. She paused and wiped it away from her eyes. Her ex looked like a sack of potatoes, and he was making a pitiful whining sound. He began to pull himself up. Julie picked up the knife.

Bruce had just managed to shuffle into a seated position, his ginger mullet matted with his blood. He looked up into her eyes as she stood over him.

"Julie!" he gasped.

"Hah!" She leaned forward, grabbed his hair and sliced through his throat with the blade. Blood spewed from the wound hitting her full in the face. She grabbed him, rolled him onto his front and plowed the knife into his back, over and over again.

Julie lowered the knife and crouched down, pulling Bruce over onto his back. His dead eyes open. She brought her face close to his. "Oh, Bruce! You look so pale!" she giggled. "Where's your manly, ruddy face, Bruce?" She pulled his pants down to his knees. "Where's your hard-on, babe?" And she flicked his flaccid, shrunken penis. "What's a girl supposed to do with this?"

Chapter 51

MARY CLARKE SAUNTERED into the bar in Campbelltown as though she owned the place. That was her style and she wouldn't change it for anyone, not even the latest Triad gang to hit Sydney.

She was wearing cargo pants, heavy boots, a black, sleeveless top and a bandana. Heads turned as she pulled up a stool and ordered a drink. For a second, it was like a scene from an old Western, the gunslinger sashaying into the room, the place going deathly quiet.

"Coke, please."

The Chinese bartender looked a little confused. "You sure you in right place, miss?" he asked.

Mary smiled sweetly. "Pretty sure. Now . . . Coke?"

The bartender walked to the fridge. Mary scanned the room. The cops had a pretty thick file on the new Triads, and she recognized some of the patrons from the documents Thorogood had shared with Private. There were two main gangs, one more important than the other. Latest Intel was that they tolerated each other because each was run by siblings who'd once fallen out, but were currently friends.

So apparently, the gangs were working together . . . for the moment.

Mary's concentration was broken by the bartender. "Six dollar."

She put the coins on the counter, lifted her glass and continued surveying the room brazenly. One of the brothers was here, she noted. Lin Sung. An ugly bastard. She had studied his mug shot sent over from Hong Kong that morning. When she'd seen his picture and Craig told her the guy was one of the two brothers leading the Sydney Triads, she'd joked that the poor bugger had obviously gotten the bad genes. Then she saw the image of Sung's brother, Jing, and laughed out loud.

She felt a familiar ripple of power as she looked around. They knew she was either a cop or a PI, none of this lot was dumb. Well maybe some of them were, but they all had street smarts. And at the same time, she was who she was and there was no disguising it. None of them would dare lay a finger on her, at least not yet.

A man got up from a table. It was Lin Sung. He was all smiles, wire thin, snappily dressed, if you happen to go for shiny fabrics and narrow ties, circa 1979.

"Do I know you?" he asked. "What're you drinking?" He flicked a glance at the bartender.

"I don't think you do, Mr. Lin," she said. "And I'm enjoying this Coke . . . don't need another, thanks all the same."

Lin gave a very faint bow. When he looked at her again, some of the pretense had slipped. "Is there anything I can do for you?"

"Nope!" Mary said, smacking her lips, an edge of mockery

in her voice. "Just here to have a Coke. Seemed like a nice place . . . from the outside."

Lin straightened, the fake smile gone. He turned and walked.

But Mary was sure it wasn't the end of it.

Chapter 52

SHE DRAINED HER glass, pulled herself off the stool and paced over to the restroom, fancied a peek around the back of the dive, see what she could find.

It was not the nicest bathroom she'd seen, but she hadn't expected much. There was a square window over the cracked brown-stained washbasin. Stuck fast. She moved a palm over the frame, found just the right spot, hit it with the flat of her hand. It gave and she climbed through.

Outside, behind the bar, it was pretty much as anticipated – stinking, overloaded bins, empty steel beer barrels, a fish skeleton ground into the dirt.

There was a door across the alley. She tried the handle. Locked. A solid kick knocked it in, the bolt snapped, clunked to the ground.

It was a storeroom piled high with large cartons. Chinese writing on the sides. She heaved one down, plucked a Swiss Army Knife from her pants and slit it open. Inside, filled with bags. She moved one aside, sliced along the seam. Rice spilled out over her heavy boots. She closed the knife, pocketed it.

A sound from outside. She ducked down beside a tower of boxes.

The storeroom door began to pivot inwards. Mary charged at it, heard a muffled cry from the other side. Then she was in the open, two men to her left, one on the floor.

She kicked the guy on the floor square in the temple. Severe concussion guaranteed. Spun toward the other two.

One had a knife in his hand, the other, a baseball bat. The one with the knife charged. Mary sidestepped and he stumbled away behind her. She felt a sting of pain in her left hand, ignored it, didn't waste a second on the one with the baseball bat. She was trained in the martial art of Krav Maga, took two graceful paces forward. He ran at her. She lifted her leg and kicked the man in the throat just hard enough to put him in hospital for a couple of days.

Mary heard the guy with the knife pull up and run at her from behind. She was so much faster than him. Did a one-eighty, chopped his legs from under him, leaned forward and with a single blow sent him to La La Land.

Straightening, Mary looked down and saw her flesh ripped open across the back of her hand, a line of blood, white bone. There was a sound from the end of the alley. She looked up, saw Lin Sung standing close to the back door, a faint smile playing across his lips. He'd started to clap.

Mary had her knife out and open in a split second. Lin barely had time to move a muscle before he was pushed up hard against the wall. His smile was still there as he looked down at the point of Mary's blade an inch from his Adam's apple.

"Look at me."

Lin lifted his head a little.

"Who killed the Ho boy?" Mary asked quietly, eyes fixed on Lin.

"Who is Ho?"

Mary stamped on the man's foot, hard.

He did well to cover his pain, kept the smile.

"I would slash your face open," Mary hissed, "but it would do your looks a favor."

Lin chuckled. "What do you people say? Sticks and stones . . ."

Mary kneed him in the testicles, *very* hard.

This time he screeched, gasped for air. The smile gone.

She did it again, even harder. "Who killed the kid?"

Beads of sweat broke out on his forehead, pain clear in his black eyes. "You'll kill me before I speak," he growled.

Mary stared him out for ten, twenty seconds, becoming more and more aware of her own pain, her hand throbbing. She flicked a glance downward and saw a puddle of blood. Pulling away the knife, she turned on her heel and walked away, Lin's laughter echoing in her ears.

Chapter 53

THE $900 SHOES Pam Hewes had worn to the office fit the rest of her lifestyle nicely. The Hewes' home, 20 Simeon Street in Neutral Bay on Sydney's Lower North Shore, was what many people would call a mansion, but it passed for a middle-to-largish house in this neighborhood. Most of the people who lived around here were lawyers, accountants and businessmen.

A path led through a neatly manicured garden to the front door. I spotted a black Porsche Cayenne on the drive. I'd been close when I'd guessed at a BMW X5.

Pam met me at the door. She was in some sort of diaphanous caftan and ethnic sandals. Her longish blonde hair was pulled back and she was only wearing a touch of make-up. "Good to see you, Mr. Gisto," she said. "Come in."

I walked along the wide hall, an impressive staircase swept up to the next floor. Passed a room on my right. Two kids in school uniform sat at a pair of laptops.

"They have to get on with homework as soon as they're home," she said lightly, "or they'll never do it."

She led the way into an expansive living-room – polished

wood floor, massive gray sofas, a couple of huge paintings. I recognized them as Kudditjis, ten to twenty grand a piece.

"So, I'm assuming your husband is still AWOL?" I said sinking into one of the sofas. Pam sat in the other, a bleached oak coffee table strewn with *Italian Vogue* and *Harpers* between us.

She nodded and looked at her clasped hands. "The bugger hasn't so much as called. I'm getting frightened now."

"And you definitely don't want the police involved?"

"No. I'm sure my husband's mostly legit. But I could be doing the worst thing for him if I told the police he was missing."

"Have you remembered anything specific about his businesses?"

"He works a lot with Al Loretto."

"*The* Al Loretto?"

"Yeah, billionaire, investor, gangster, property developer . . . whatever . . ."

"What does he do?"

"For Loretto? Probably wipes his ass," Pam replied, then shook her head. "Sorry. I'm just so bloody angry! I pray Geoff isn't dead in a dumpster somewhere, but when I see him next . . ."

"Okay, Loretto is a start. But I can hardly turn up unannounced at a billionaire's home and start asking questions without a really good reason. If Geoff is acquainted with him, he must know lots of other *interesting* characters."

She nodded. "He does. Keith Newman for one – a retired lawyer – actually, he's a seedy little shyster, but from what I gather, Geoff does a lot of business with him."

"Okay, I'll pay him a visit. See what I can find out." I paused for a second. "I'll be straight with you, Pam. If your husband is mixing in those circles, he's up to his neck in things that are certainly *not* legit. You understand that, right?"

"Of course I understand it!" Pam snapped. "Don't treat me like some ditzy bimbo, Mr. Gisto."

I looked away, staring at one of the paintings. "I'm sorry," I said, placatingly. "I just think we have to be brutally honest with one another. From what you've told me so far, I think your husband is in very deep trouble."

Chapter 54

I LEFT THE house with a list of names. It was like trying to get blood out of a stone, but I knew the poor woman didn't actually know much about her husband's life.

I'd seen relationships like it before. Usual story: a rather average guy who'd never grown up, fancied himself as a player, seen too many episodes of *The Sopranos*. The wife? She was usually the genuinely better half, the one with the straight career, or "home-maker", bringing up the kids, worrying, trying to keep it all together. It transcended class.

Pam had told me I'd find Keith Newman at a pub in Darlinghurst called The Cloverleaf. He held court there.

I Googled him on my iPhone. Over the years, Newman had worked for half a dozen prominent Sydney underworld figures. He was a good lawyer, saved the bacon of some key crime figures in the late seventies. Made a fortune in the eighties . . . sources unknown. He then invested it with some former clients whose business activities were what might be called "nebulous".

Newman's investments had paid off – he'd turned his nest egg into a golden hen and retired to a mansion on Chinamans

Beach on the Lower North Shore, a place known to Sydney-siders as Ka-ching-mans Beach.

The Cloverleaf was exactly the sort of dump a wealthy businessman with a yen for the "dark side" might frequent. It stank of beer, lighting low, lots of slot machines.

I strode in and immediately spotted Keith sitting at the bar. It was still only five o'clock, early for most of the pub's clientele by the look of it. There were half a dozen guys in the room.

"Mr. Newman?" I said, pulling up a stool and glancing at the bartender. "Fosters please."

"And you are?"

"Sorry, Craig Gisto." I extended a hand. Newman ignored it. "I'm actually looking for Geoff Hewes." I withdraw my hand. "Heard he likes this pub."

"Why?"

"Why?"

"Yeah, Craig. Why do you wanna see Mr. Hewes?"

"I'm a journalist. I wanted to get his take on the new lending tax the government's slapping on the industry."

Newman's jaw tightened. "I saw him yesterday. Should be in later."

I nodded.

"So which paper did you say you worked for?" Newman added, studying my face.

"I didn't . . . .But it's the *Sydney Morning Herald*."

A song came on the jukebox. The Moody Blues, *Nights in White Satin*. I've always hated it.

"So you must know Larry pretty well? Larry Pinnard?"

I smiled. "We don't work in the same department. I'm 'Features'."

"Sammy, then? Sammy Taylor? He interviewed me a couple of months back."

I beamed. "Indispensable. Sam the Man!"

Keith lowered himself from the stool. He was much shorter than I'd guessed. He flicked a glance at the bartender who'd been listening as he poured the beer.

A guy appeared at the end of the bar. I couldn't quite work out where he'd sprung from . . . and he wasn't easy to hide. Six-five, six-six, shoulders like a bull, a face like a sow in labor, shock of jet black hair.

"Patrick," Keith said, quietly. "Could you escort this gentleman from the premises please?"

The goon rolled over, grabbed my arm.

"Did I offend you in some way?" I asked.

"Yeah, buddy, you did," Keith Newman snapped. "Sammy Taylor died a year ago, God rest his soul. I hate liars and I hate nosy parkers. So piss off . . ." He nodded to Patrick. I was yanked from my seat and dragged across the stinking, beer-sodden carpet.

"I wouldn't bother putting up a fight," Newman announced. "We call my big friend here 'Borg' . . . 'Resistance is futile'!"

Chapter 55

BUT I DID resist, couldn't help myself. And in return, I got a smack to my right ear that made me feel as though my brain was shaking in my cranium. Maybe it was.

The huge guy they called Borg had literally lifted me off my feet with one hand. Stomping across the room, he smashed open a side door with his free palm. Together, we crashed into the blazing sunlight in the back alley behind The Cloverleaf.

"That was pretty stupid!" Borg growled, then laughed as I tripped over a bin and went sprawling into a pile of rubbish.

I picked myself up, brushed off some wilted lettuce from my shirt and started to walk away.

"What you after with Geoff Hewes then, bud?"

I stopped in my tracks, turned. The bouncer was standing in silhouette a few feet in front of the closed door to the pub, legs slightly parted, hands on hips. Couldn't make out his expression.

"Doesn't matter."

"Might to me, fella," the giant said and took two steps out of the shadow.

I saw a long scar running from the man's brow to his upper

lip. But I also couldn't help noticing his incredible green eyes that weren't totally malevolent. "Why?"

"I'm no friend of Geoff Hewes. In fact I think the guy's an absolute asshole."

"So you know where he is?"

"I didn't say that now, did I? Just said I don't like him. Plenty of others I know don't either."

"Okay."

"Look . . . Couple of my buddies were doing some building work for him – property in Seaforth. They'd agreed cheap rates, right? So what does the shit go and do?"

I stared straight into his eyes.

"He doesn't pay 'em for weeks . . . that's what he does. So, they down tools, right? Next thing we know, one of my pals gets a petrol bomb tossed through his living-room window . . . Coincidence? *Don't think so!*"

"Has he hurt you, personally?"

Patrick blanched.

"He's ruined me. That's why I'm working here." He flicked a thumb toward the pub. "I had a little business – tool-hire shop in Mascot. Borrowed a bit from Hewes to get it started. The business didn't do well. I ended up owing the bastard three times what he'd lent me. Had to sell my house. Wife left . . ."

"I see," I muttered. "So, what does Hewes actually do? I can't get a handle on it. Even his wife's half in the dark."

He laughed. "Course! Wifey's always the last to know. It's simple, our Geoff's a snake-oil dealer . . . a classic . . . Does up houses on the cheap and sells them on to gullible folk for a fortune. He lends money at ridiculous rates. He deals a bit."

"Drugs?"

"Weed, coke."

That surprised me. "Pretty low rent, isn't it?"

"He needs money. Kids in private school, hefty mortgages, car leases. He gets cash from wherever he can."

"Okay."

"He's also right up the asses of some of the richest, nastiest criminals in Sydney."

"Doing what?"

"Works for 'em? Makes himself *indispensable*. It's a trick all these small-time crooks pull. Work your way in with the big boys. Make 'em think you're the hottest thing in town. Gives him access, ready cash, contacts." He counted them off on his fingers. "Plus, no one shits on you . . . Connections, see?"

I saw. I'd witnessed it all before.

"His latest scam is managing Loretto's brothels."

"Go on."

"About a dozen of 'em around Sydney."

"That's interesting, but . . ."

"But, that's not the whole story, buddy." He relaxed a little, took a couple of steps toward me. "Hewes is a cocksucker, oversteppin' the mark, like, big time. He's either stupid or he has balls bigger than a gorilla's."

"Meaning?"

"Loretto's No. 1 whorehouse is in Chester Street, Mosman, okay? Smart place. Gets a better class of customer! But what does the moron go and do? He only double-crosses the Johns!"

"How?"

Patrick took another step forward and leaned against the wall. "He's set up cameras in the bedrooms, right? Records the goings-on. The girls are in on it. He pays them to keep quiet.

Clients include bankers, lawyers, traders, a few judges, politicians . . . usual suspects!"

"So you think Geoff's in serious trouble?"

"You could say that. I actually reckon right now he's the main course for the fishes . . . at the bottom of Sydney Harbour. At least I hope he is!"

Chapter 56

SHE WATCHED THE woman walk across the parking lot behind the supermarket. A warm breeze swept innocently over Bellevue Hill.

The woman's name was Yasmin Trent, five-nine, dressed in designer jeans and a singlet, nice, even tan, jeweled Rolex on her left wrist, bunch of jangling Tiffany on the right.

Julie O'Connor was standing a few yards from the back door of Yasmin's Toyota LandCruiser, merging into the background. She could sense the fear in the neighborhood and reveled in the fact that it was all her doing. In a local shop she overheard women talking about the "serial killer". It was thrilling but dangerous – she knew she would have to tackle this next kill differently.

Yasmin Trent touched the remote, the car bleeped and flashed. She pulled herself into the driver's seat, shut the door. Julie jerked herself into the back.

Yasmin started to turn, screamed.

"Don't move, bitch!" Julie hissed and Yasmin felt something hard and cold at the nape of her neck. She screamed again.

"Once more and I'll slice your pretty head off . . . got it?"

Yasmin shut up.

She could see the figure in the back reflected in the mirror. It was a woman in a hoodie, bleached, crispy blonde hair protruding from under the fabric, no eyebrows.

"Drive," Julie said quietly.

Yasmin had frozen.

"Okay," Julie said a little louder. "I get you're terrified. But you *will* turn the key. You *will* pull out the parking lot. And you *will* drive along the road or I'll not only slice you up, I'll come back for your kids."

Julie felt Yasmin jerk and the engine fired up. The car pulled out of the parking space. Julie kept the eight-inch blade she was holding tight up against Yasmin's slender, tanned nape.

"Good," Julie hissed. "Very good."

Chapter 57

"WHAT IS THIS all about?" Yasmin said. She had calmed down enough to speak coherently, but there was still a tremor to her voice that Julie found gratifying.

She didn't reply. Just looked out the window at the shops lining New South Head Road flash past. They were driving along the main thoroughfare from the Eastern Suburbs toward the business district. Following Julie's instructions, Yasmin pulled the LandCruiser off at the next junction, through a toll booth and onto the freeway, heading west.

"What is this about?" Yasmin repeated.

"About you and me, babe."

"What does that *mean*?"

Julie chuckled. "It's about power, Yasmin, POWER!"

"I don't . . ."

"You don't understand? Doh! Maybe you are as stupid as you look."

She didn't know what to say. Just kept driving. She was trying to rationalize it all.

"So, the Rolex, Yasmin?" Julie said slowly.

Yasmin touched her wrist involuntarily.

"How many blow jobs did that take, eh?"

Julie could see Yasmin's pretty, confused face in the mirror. "Everything costs, Yas, everything costs . . ."

"Is that it? You want my watch? Here, have it . . ." She reached for the clasp.

"No, you stupid, stupid bitch! I do not want your shitty watch . . . although I might keep it as a memento after I've drained you of blood."

The car swerved.

"Careful, honey," Julie mocked. She was pretty sure the woman didn't have the guts to do anything radical.

The car swerved again. This time it was deliberate. Julie pushed the tip of the blade a fraction of an inch into Yasmin's neck making her squeal.

"STOP DOING THAT . . . NOW!"

The car swayed once more. Horns blared. The LandCruiser crossed lanes. Cut in front of another car. More horns, screeching tires.

Julie pulled her mouth up close to the woman's ear. "I will take your twins from preschool, Yasmin. I will take them somewhere very private . . ."

Yasmin abruptly slowed the car, brought it back under control, went to pull over.

"Don't . . ."

She saw Yasmin's face in the rear-view mirror, white as dead flesh. She was staring fixedly at the road ahead.

"You're the killer!" Yasmin murmured, barely able to believe it, even now.

Julie felt a stirring of pride in the pit of her stomach. "Just drive," she said. "Not much further now. It'll soon be over."

Chapter 58

MARY PULLED UP a chair as Darlene turned away from the monitor to face her. They were in the lab.

"I could tell by your tone on the phone you're disappointed," Mary said. Darlene shrugged. "Look, perhaps we were hoping for too much."

"Alright, forewarned."

She noticed Mary's bandaged hand. "What happened?"

Mary glanced down. "Oh, silly accident."

Darlene gave her a skeptical look, stood and beckoned Mary over to a large stainless steel-topped counter, objects spread across it – a pile of blood-stained sheets, take-out cartons, cigarette stubs, pieces of paper, a TV remote – all collected from the deserted Triad apartment in Parramatta.

"The blood on the sheets matches Ho Chang's of course. His prints are all over the bedding, on the food cartons, chairs in the kitchen."

"What about other fingerprints? The guys who abducted him?"

Darlene paced back to her work station, Mary in tow. She tapped at a keyboard. The image on the monitor changed to show several sets of prints.

"I've found four distinct sets in the apartment, excluding Ho's. I've also separated out three samples of DNA."

"That's great . . . yeah?"

"Not really, Mary. One set of prints and one DNA sample belongs to the plumber who'd worked in the apartment a few weeks back. He had a record – petty theft in 1990, meant he was on the database. Another set of prints belongs to the manager's wife, Betty Griffin."

"Could she or her husband be involved?"

"She died last month. Cancer."

Mary snorted. "And the other two?"

"According to my analyzer the DNA comes from two different Asian males."

"And?"

"That's it . . . no matches on any databases. Same for the prints."

"So we've narrowed it down to what?" Mary declared. "About a billion men?"

"Actually, nearer two billion."

Chapter 59

"HERE'S TO GRETA!" Brett Thorogood said lifting his glass of vintage Verve. He clinked it with Greta and their two closest friends, Claudia and Marcus. The doorbell rang.

"I'll get it," Greta's son, Serge, called as he ran from the playroom, his younger sister Nikki close behind.

"That should be Christine, the babysitter," Greta said.

"You're so lucky having a regular girl," Claudia replied.

"Christine's great – works at the local SupaMart during the day."

They looked round as footsteps echoed along the hallway and Greta stood up. A strange woman appeared at the entrance to the lounge. Greta stared at her, confused.

The woman stepped forward a little nervous, a hand extended. "Hi, I'm Julie, Julie O'Connor."

Greta noted the SupaMart uniform and badge.

"Christine went home sick from work. She did call you, yeah?"

"Er, no, Julie, she didn't." Greta forced a weak smile.

"Oh. Well I've a lot of experience. I sometimes babysit with Christine. We're old friends . . ."

"It's not that," Greta said stonily. "It's just, I don't know you . . ."

Julie let out a gentle sigh. "Okay . . . I understand." She turned to leave.

Brett stood up, touched Greta's arm, whispered in her ear. "We're stuck, darling. It's your party, we have to go now, but we can't leave the kids on their own."

"Just a sec Julie," Greta said. "Just let me try Christine." She plucked her cell from the table and hit the speed-dial number. It rang five times then went to voicemail. Irritated, she snapped shut the phone.

"We'll be good," Serge said.

"It's not that, sweetie."

"Too late to get anyone else," Brett muttered.

"Okay! okay!" Greta put her hands up resignedly. "Julie . . . ?"

Julie's face was expressionless.

"I apologize. Would you . . . ?"

Julie smiled sweetly.

Chapter 60

SHE CLOSED THE door. Nikki and Serge were standing together eyeing their babysitter.

"Where have your eyebrows gone?" Nikki asked.

Julie tilted her head to one side, touched her face and feigned surprise. "Aaaggghhh! They've vanished!"

The girl didn't even smile.

"Okay, okay," Julie said frowning. "I woke up this morning and they were gone!"

Nikki was skeptical. "No you didn't!"

"Honest, I did! I think my cat ate 'em!" Julie clapped her hands together. "So what's your favorite game, kids?"

The siblings argued about whether they should play Pocket God on the iPad, Xbox, or the interactive game that came with the latest Harry Potter DVD. In the end, the wizard won out.

Julie indulged them for an hour, then it was bedtime and Julie's turn for some fun.

She'd wanted to see inside a house like this, see how the bitches around here lived. Earlier that day she'd told Christine, the Thorogoods' regular sitter, that Greta had dropped into the store and asked her to pass the message on that she had to cancel tonight. Then she'd slipped Christine's cell from her work overall.

The plan had worked, and now that she was here she was stunned. She'd never been in a house like this and couldn't get her head round the fact that only four people lived in it. It did nothing for her state of mind.

She walked through the main living-room picking up ornaments, settling them back down carefully. The stairs beckoned. She spun round and walked up the wide metal and glass steps to the first floor. The kids were asleep.

She took the second flight of stairs to the top floor, a single expansive area devoted to the parents. A vast bedroom, a wall of windows looking out to the ocean. A bathroom bigger than most people's living-rooms, and a walk-in wardrobe. Julie slipped between the rows of clothes running a hand along the parade of dresses and coats. At the end of each row stood a set of shelves, floor-to-ceiling and filled with expensive shoes.

Beyond the walk-in was a small room, Greta's personal dressing-room. A counter, a chair, necklaces hanging from stands, make-up set out in precise rows.

Julie squatted down and picked a lipstick, applied it carefully and studied the result in the mirror over the counter. She gave herself an approving little nod, found the mascara and put it on, then walked back to the clothes.

She took her time, sifting through the garments carefully. She read the labels, Lanvin, Chanel, chose a bright red dress, slipped into it, managed to zip it up halfway. It was real tight on her, but she didn't care.

She picked a pair of leopard print Christian Louboutin

shoes, crammed her toes into them and strode into the bedroom where a mirror occupied half a wall.

"I was born for this," Julie said to herself and did an ungainly twirl, almost falling off the shoes. That's when she saw Nikki Thorogood staring at her, mouth open.

Julie reacted with incredible speed, whirled on the girl and grabbed her before she could take a single step back, brought a rough hand to the girl's mouth and pulled her backwards against her body. Nikki's petrified squeals muffled by Julie's large fingers.

"Shut up," Julie hissed in Nikki's ear. Twisted her to face the mirror. She slipped the stiletto off her right foot and lifted the blade-like heel to the kid's throat. "Tell anyone about this, Nikki . . . and I will come for you in the night and I will kill you very, very slowly. Do you understand me?"

The kid was too terrified to move. Julie tightened her grip. "DO YOU UNDERSTAND ME, NIKKI?"

The girl nodded and slowly Julie loosened her grip.

Chapter 61

THE THOROGOODS HAD booked out the entire restaurant for Greta's birthday party. A hundred guests. I had to admit the place was a great choice. Icebergs is ultra-chic, sits on the side of a cliff, has an amazing, panoramic view back across a stretch of ocean to Bondi Beach.

Justine looked stunning in a tight-fitting white cocktail dress. She'd put her hair up and wore a delicate, jeweled head-band, Audrey Hepburn circa *Breakfast at Tiffany's*.

I felt her tug my arm and she led me toward a balcony across the room, plucking two champagne flutes from a surf dude who'd brushed his hair and put on a uniform for the night.

"Greta seems to be having a fun time," I said. She was dancing with Brett and did look happy, a champagne glass in one hand, laughing at something her husband was saying close up to her ear.

"It's good to see. Hasn't had the best time recently."

We stared out at the darkness broken by the lights of Bondi, a half-moon revealing the silver shimmers of a calm ocean.

"Ice," Justine said suddenly.

"What?"

"We seem to have a thing for ice, you and me. You took me to the Ice Bar and now I get you here, Icebergs." She produced a gorgeous smile.

I looked into her eyes. "Where next?" I said. "Would you like dinner somewhere with Ice in the name?"

"Ah," Justine said. "I'm flattered but . . ."

"Sorry."

"No, don't be. But . . ."

"You're taken . . . lucky man."

"It's Jack, Craig. Jack Morgan. We've been . . ."

I raised a hand. "No need. I didn't realize, Justine."

There was an awkward silence, then she said, "So, Craig . . . How did you end up here, doing what we do. This crazy job?"

"Nice diversion, Justine!" I laughed. "Long story."

"Got time." She took a sip. I turned, leaned on the balcony. "I was born in England. Mom died when I was twelve. I never knew my father. I was sent to Australia to live with my uncle and his family."

"And why PI work?"

"Ah, well that was thanks to the love of a good woman."

She raised an eyebrow.

"I studied Law, but when I actually got round to practising it I found it bone dry. At the same time, I met my future wife and fell in love. Becky was a free spirit and pushed me into trying something I really wanted to do. So, I set up my own company: Solutions Inc."

It was clear Justine knew something of what happened to my family and trod carefully around the subject . . . "Another?" She held up her champagne flute.

My cell trilled. I recognized the Private Sydney number. "Darlene . . . you're working late."

"Sorry to ring you at the party. Just had a call from Police HQ. There's been another murder."

Chapter 62

THE BRUNETTE LAY on her back, face horribly disfigured, legs akimbo, a roll of fifty-dollar bills in place.

"This is becoming bloody repetitive," Darlene snapped as she knelt beside the body. "This bastard's getting me down."

I stood beside her staring down at the corpse. The woman's blood had pooled on the concrete beneath her, clothes drenched red. I'd already learned her name was Yasmin Trent, forty-one, mother of three young boys, lived in Gervaine Road, Bellevue Hill, fifty yards from Stacy Friel and Elspeth Lampard. Yasmin had been a home-maker, and her husband, Simon Trent, a dentist. So that pretty much wiped out the finance motive theory.

There were two Police Forensics officers working on the body. They'd mellowed toward us recently. Realizing we weren't going away, I guessed. Plus they'd benefited from Private's resources. I caught a glimpse of Mark at the wheel of his car, the door open. He was talking to a sergeant.

I left Darlene to it and nosed around. It was a patch of waste ground behind a gas station in Sandsville in the Western Suburbs. The late evening traffic was light up on the freeway beyond the forecourt. The place was scrappy and grimy. A rusting car stood to one side. A few weeds poked through the concrete nearby. A dead palm stood close to the rear wall of the gas station building.

The MO had altered. It was another new disconcerting aspect to this case. Killers rarely changed their MO, even subtly. The dead woman was from the Eastern Suburbs. She'd probably never even been to Sandsville before. Maybe just seen it on TV when Channel 9 News carried an item about a knifing or a house blaze in the West. It was only, what? Thirty miles from here to Bellevue Hill? But the two places may as well have been in different solar systems.

So what was Yasmin Trent doing here? Killed here or in Bellevue Hill? Much of the MO was the same – facial disfigurement, multiple stab wounds to her back, vaginal ATM in reverse. We were looking for one sick mother-fucker.

I felt a tap on my shoulder, turned to see Darlene. She had her box of forensics equipment in her left hand.

"That was pretty quick."

"I've learned what to look for. That part of it's predictable. The hard work comes later. But you know what, Craig? There's something not quite right about this."

"You mean the body being here?"

"No, it's not that. I can sense something isn't right. I can't put my finger on it. But I will."

Chapter 63

HO DAI WAS thinking about hitting the sack. He'd just got back to his apartment after leaving his father's house, walked into his tiny kitchen, got a glass of chilled water, turned and heard a sound.

He held his breath. The noise came again. He saw two shadows pass by a glass wall close to the front door, then watched as the handle turned and released.

He padded across the floor and into the bedroom, reached the built-in wardrobe, pulled inside and eased the door shut. It was dark but he knew where he kept the gun his father insisted he have. He felt the handle just as the intruders made it through the front door and into the hall.

Dai pulled the weapon down from a shelf and pointed it directly ahead. He heard someone enter the room.

"Mr. Ho," a voice said. "We know you're in here."

"I have a gun," Dai panted. "Open the door and I'll shoot."

A bullet thudded through the door and smacked into the wall a foot to Dai's left. He felt his bowels loosen, just managed to control himself. A second bullet sent shards of wood flying in the dark and crunched into the wall at the back of the wardrobe. It was so close splinters flew into Dai's arm making him cry out.

"Open the door a crack and drop the gun outside, or we'll shoot again," said the same man.

Dai stood rigid trying to think, trying to rationalize.

"I'm counting to three. One . . ."

Dai was wreathed in sweat, breathing hard. He couldn't win, he was dead meat whatever he did.

"Two . . ."

The kid could barely move. Had to force his arm forward. The door opened an inch, two inches. He tossed the gun onto the carpet and slammed the doors outward, propelling himself into the bedroom. He tripped, crashed to the floor and felt the cold barrel of a gun on the back of his neck.

Chapter 64

ANTHONY HILARY WAS feeling really horny. Everything had been arranged with Karen. He would surf at 6 am with his buddies, Trent and Frankie, and then he would meet her at the empty old house he'd found the day before. When he'd first suggested it, Karen was reluctant, but he'd eventually persuaded her.

"I can promise you the most comfortable and cleanest sleeping bag in Sydney," he'd told her with a grin.

"Oh! I'm touched!" she'd responded. "I must remember to mention that to my parents when they quiz me over why I'm leaving the house an hour early for school." But then she had shaken her head and smiled. "Okay, Ant. 7 am."

The surf was good this morning, but Anthony's mind wasn't on it. Frankie and Trent noticed. "Dude, what's with you? You totally wasted that wave."

"Yeah, sorry, man," Ant responded. "Look, I'm gonna bail."
"What?"

"Can't focus. I'll put the board in your car, right, Frankie?"
His friend waved and slipped back into the surf.

Half an hour later, Anthony was standing outside the house on Ernest Street, Bondi, watching the shifting morning light on the roofs across the road. He didn't normally do this sort of thing. He and Karen were good kids from the same co-ed school. But he loved her and he believed she loved him. They were seventeen, Year 12. Some kids their age were parents already, but he and Karen could never be alone together, watched over 24/7. It pissed him off no end.

Karen was fifteen minutes late and Ant was growing increasingly frustrated as the seconds passed. When she arrived, he just managed to stay cool.

"Okay, lover boy," she said sexily, sidling up to him and reaching on tiptoes to kiss him full on the mouth. He looked down at her gorgeous tanned face ringed with dark curls, feeling himself harden almost instantly.

"Come on," he said, and took her hand.

The front door was broken and hung half off its hinges. Ant escorted her along a narrow passage to the second room on the left. She could hear music drifting along the hall and glanced at her boyfriend as she recognized the tune, Angus and Julia Stone's *Big Jet Plane*.

Karen stood at the entrance to the room, holding Ant's hand, entranced. He had cleaned it up, swept the floor, made a bed of sleeping bags. The curtains were drawn, two dozen candles glowed. An iPod played softly through a portable speaker system. The song ended and was followed by Karen's favorite, *No One* by Alicia Keys.

"Oh! Ant. This is . . . just lovely." She turned and kissed him again, sliding her tongue between his teeth and producing a low moan in the back of her throat. Ant felt he would burst there and then. He swept her up, lowered her gently to the soft layers of the sleeping bags.

The music flowed over them, and when it was over, they lay together, looking up at the shabby, pitted ceiling.

"Back in a sec," Karen said softly, pecked Anthony on the cheek, and pulled herself up. "Bathroom!"

"Hey, take this." Ant reached into his bag for a large bottle of water. "No mains supply!"

Karen looked pained and then crouched down to kiss Anthony again. "That's very thoughtful," she purred.

He watched the girl's naked form in the candlelight and threw his head back onto the makeshift pillow. He thought that this was the high point of his life. That things could never be better than this.

Then he heard Karen scream.

Chapter 65

INSPECTOR MARK TALBOT felt unwell, and days like today, the ones that started out really crappy, were almost impossible to bear.

He'd woken up at 6 am with a sore head from a big night out with his buddies and had dragged himself into the station by seven-thirty. Forty minutes later the call had come in – another grisly find. It was all getting a bit ridiculous.

The traffic was terrible all the way to Bondi, and about eight o'clock it turned stormy – black clouds rolling in over the ocean. He switched on the radio, pushed the button for Classic Rock FM and felt better as Steely Dan's *Reeling in the Years* filled the car.

"Alright, what's the story?" Talbot said as he got out of his car and a sergeant led him to the empty house, the rain crashing down around them.

"Best see for yourself, sir."

Talbot dashed into the hall, his jacket soaked. Forensics were everywhere. Huge spots blazed, powered by a portable generator. None of it did his head much good. At the end of a corridor there was a bathroom, two officers in plastic suits crouching down. The tub, toilet, floor and white walls were splashed with pints of dried blood. A lab guy was photographing the scene. Talbot saw a line of dry red-black dots leading from the room out toward the kitchen and the rear of the property.

The stench hit him as he entered the yard. The smell of death. He knew it well.

The blood trail stopped one side of the back garden. There was a large stain on the patio close to the fence. His team had already lifted the pavers and dug away some soil. Talbot, hand over his mouth, could see part of a corpse, a woman, face-up in the dirt.

He waved over one of his sergeants standing the other side of the shallow grave. "The basics," the Inspector insisted, his voice phlegmy.

"Young guy called us about seven-thirty. By the time we got here, the place was deserted."

"What was he doing here?"

"Looks like the kid was a vagrant . . . evidence someone had slept in the front room last night."

"Obviously wasn't here long. Probably nothing to do with the crime. Needs checking out though."

The body lay no more than a couple of feet beneath the surface. Three men in blue forensics suits lifted the dead woman out of the opening and laid her on plastic sheeting.

Talbot and his sergeant took two paces toward the body.

One of the forensics officers leaned in and brushed away some soil.

Most of the woman's clothes had rotted away. Her flesh barely clung to her bones.

"Dead for weeks," the forensics guy muttered, his voice muffled by his mask.

"Clear the soil from her pubic region," Talbot said.

The officer moved the brush down the dead body, swept away the sand and grains of soil. Some skin and flesh came away with it. A roll of fifty-dollar bills had been wedged into her vagina.

"You want me to call Private?" the sergeant asked.

"No, I don't think so," Talbot responded without looking round. "Not this time."

Chapter 66

COLETTE POKED HER head around the door into the Private lab.

"What's up?" Darlene asked. She saw a tall, skinny guy with hair like a giant bird's nest standing just outside the room trying to peek inside.

"Er . . . this is . . . What did you say your name was again?" Colette asked, turning and deliberately obstructing the doorway.

"I-I-I'm, S-S-Sam," the man stammered.

Darlene looked at him blankly for a second and then the name registered. "Software Sam? Micky's friend?"

"The very s-s-same."

Colette glanced at Darlene, then at the tall guy and stepped aside.

"Micky reckons you're a whiz with computers," Darlene said leading Sam into the room.

He was gazing around, taking it all in approvingly. "Yeah . . . I-I-I am. So, w-w-what's your problem?"

"Look, I don't mean to be rude, but this equipment . . . Well, it's all pretty new. Most of it's one-off stuff, custom-made. I wouldn't expect you to be able to help with it."

"I could g-g-give it a go."

Darlene studied him. "You look ridiculous," she thought. "But then so did Einstein!"

"Okay. I'm having a problem with my image-enhancing software." She led him across the room. "I'm working on some blurred images from a security camera." She pointed to a large Mac screen, sat and tapped at the keyboard. Sam stood beside her chair.

A pair of indistinct faces came up.

"Th-th-they're the o-o-originals, r-r-right?"

Darlene looked up. "No, Sam. They are the best I can get."

He whistled. "Wh-wh-what software package you using?"

"It's a custom-made one from a friend of mine in LA. He calls it FOCUS."

"Yeah, well it's c-c-crap, isn't it?"

Darlene produced a pained laugh.

"C-c-can you open up the p-p-program for me?"

Darlene shrugged. "Okay." She brought up the appropriate screen, then offered her chair to Sam.

The screen filled with symbols and lines of computer code.

"I'll c-c-clone this first," Sam said. "As a b-b-backup." He tapped at the keyboard with lightning speed. Darlene watched as the algorithms and rows of letters and numbers shifted subtly. Sam paused for a second, peered at the screen, then his staccato key-stabbing started up again.

Two minutes of concentrated effort and the visitor pushed back Darlene's chair. "Th-th-that sh-sh-should do it," he declared.

"What've you done?"

"B-b-boosted the r-r-response parameters, r-r-realigned the

enhancement s-s-software to concentrate on th-th-the contrast and the w-w-warmth c-c-components."

Darlene returned to her chair and clicked the mouse a couple of times to bring back the main screen. She opened the FOCUS software package, clicked on the image from the security camera and pressed "import". A new screen opened showing a crisp, sharp image of two Asian men, the picture so clear you could almost make out individual pores.

"That's incredible!"

"I-i-it is pretty c-c-cool, i-i-isn't it?"

Darlene stood up. "I'm so sorry I ever doubted you."

"No probs." Software Sam looked a little embarrassed. "Oh! Almost forgot. M-M-Micky gave me these." He held out a bunch of invitations. "H-h-half a dozen p-p-passes to his b-b-birthday bash tomorrow night at The V-V-Venue."

Darlene was stunned. "Fantastic!" she said.

Chapter 67

I WAS STARING at the monitor on the desk in front of Darlene.

"That's just amazing!" I exclaimed as the image of the two men who'd killed Ho Chang came up.

"I'd like to take credit for it," Darlene said, "but it was Micky Stevens' buddy, the guy they call Software Sam."

"Yeah, Colette told me he'd been here – some sort of weirdo."

"A genius more like. So what do we do now? We going to share this with the cops?"

I contemplated the image. "Oh, I don't think so . . . not yet, anyway."

Darlene gave me a quizzical look.

"If we do that," I went on, "someone will blab, and these bastards . . ." I waved a hand at the monitor, "will vanish into thin air. No, this is ours, Darlene. At least for the moment. You been able to do anything with it?"

"I've tried. Spent all afternoon attempting to match up facial characteristics with databases all over the world. Not getting very far. Same old problem. The Triads bribe the authorities in Hong Kong so nothing's on record. If there's nothing on the two men, then the CIA, MI6, the Australian

Intelligence Agency can't get a handle on them. These guys have no DNA records, no fingerprint or photo presence at all. As far as the investigative agencies are concerned, they don't exist."

Chapter 68

I DIDN'T HAVE a problem with brothels, per se, but this one bothered me. They all stank of deceit and hypocrisy, but this one was smack bang in the middle of a wealthy suburb bordering Neutral Bay, where the Hewes lived. It seemed to me the locals at Loretto's brothel might actually get off on the idea they were shitting on their own doorstep.

I'd made a booking through a website called "Kinkies" and chosen a girl, Ruthie.

The house stood in Chester Street off Military Road, the main highway running through the Lower North Shore. It was a totally nondescript building. I rang the bell and a woman in a business suit opened the door. I gave her the password I'd been sent online.

"Okay, sweetheart," she said and I followed her up a narrow staircase.

Ruthie was a petite girl with long black hair and a plain face, wearing a see-through camisole and a lot of make-up. I guessed she was no more than twenty.

I was experienced with surveillance, so I knew right off where to look, spotted the camera in five seconds.

Ruthie got up from the end of the bed. "Pop your clothes off, honey," she said, her voice bored, flat. "Back in a sec."

She stepped behind a curtain and I saw a red light come on over the lens of the camcorder, pulled up a chair with my back to the machine and when Ruthie returned she looked a bit surprised to see me still fully dressed. Her expression changed. "Oh, a talker, are we?"

"Sorry?"

"Just wanna cosy chat . . . Bitch about the wife, the job, life in general? Still costs the same."

"S'pose I am. Just feel lonely. I'm a bus driver. Need some company."

She gave me a blank look, stood up again and tottered back to the curtained area. The red light went off.

Ruthie sat on the bed again, cross-legged.

I glanced over toward a small stereo on a low table. "Can you put on some music?"

The girl obliged, bending over provocatively as she pushed "Play". When she turned back, she saw I had a roll of fifty-dollar bills clenched in my right hand. I peeled two from the top of the wad. "Need some info," I said very quietly.

Ruthie looked confused for a moment, then frightened. "What . . . sort of . . . information?"

"About the set-up here."

Blood drained from her face. "I don't know . . ."

"Of course you do." I separated a third fifty and held out the notes.

Ruthie eyed them. "You're not a cop, are you?"

"No. I'm a private investigator."

She snatched at the bills but I pulled them back. Her

fingers grasped air.

"Ah, ah," I tutted. "What're the cameras for?"

She looked at her feet, black high heels with fluffy balls over her toes. "We record everything important. We're told to turn on the machine before the client . . . you know . . ."

"Who've you filmed?"

Ruthie stared at the money. I handed her two of the fifties, peeled off a fourth and held out the two notes.

"Shit! I dunno. Dozens of blokes."

"Anyone you recognized? Anyone you've seen on TV, for example?"

I handed her a fifty. Kept the other. "Okay, so what happens to the tapes?"

"How should I know?"

I nodded and stood up pocketing the rest of the money. "Alright, Ruthie. If you do manage to recall anything useful, ring this number." I handed her a slip of paper. "It's a secure line."

Chapter 69

WHEN THE DOOR opened, Geoff Hewes had no idea how long he'd been in Al Loretto's basement.

They'd given him water and some bread. They left a bucket in the corner for him. It stank. He'd slept, on and off.

The big guy who'd smashed in his face came for him. Hewes heard a series of strange sounds, then suddenly felt water blasting his face and chest. He panicked for a second then realized the big guy was hosing him down, like a dog.

The force of the water pinned him to the wall. He struggled to get away but he couldn't.

"Strip off you idiot!" the big guy bellowed and Hewes felt something hit him in the guts. He looked down and saw a bar of soap on the concrete floor.

He took off his filthy clothes, used the soap, and a couple of minutes later the water stopped. He was flung a towel and some old clothes, jeans and a tee.

"Get those on and get out of my house, Hewes."

Geoff followed the sound and saw Loretto at the top of the stairs into the basement. "I'm only having you washed because I don't want you messing up my carpets. Show your face again and I'll have it blown off."

Chapter 70

I WAS IN the NSW Police Path Lab with Darlene. She was leaning over the dreadful remains of the dead woman discovered in the old house in Bondi. I watched her work methodically, felt a growing anger we hadn't learned about the corpse for at least five hours after it was found. Even then it was only because Darlene heard about it third-hand from a friendly cop at Police HQ. In the time since then she'd caught up pretty fast.

The victim was Jennifer Granger, thirty-eight, of Newmore Avenue, a street perpendicular to Wentworth Avenue in Bellevue Hill where Elspeth Lampard had been found. It was within spitting distance of the other victims' homes.

"I spoke to one of the sergeants at the station in the CBD," I said. "Jennifer Granger was reported missing three weeks ago, December 15."

Darlene didn't look up. "Who reported it?"

"Her husband. She was supposed to be on a girls' weekend in Melbourne, but didn't show. Her girlfriends didn't tell her husband, a gynecologist called Dr. Cameron Granger, until the Sunday morning."

Darlene lifted her head at that.

"Two of them knew Jennifer was having an affair. They

concluded she had used the weekend as a cover without telling them. The same two women tried to SMS her. When they got no reply, they phoned her cell. No response. Straight to voicemail. We've followed up on the calls, their story holds up."

"Probably dead at least twenty-four hours by then."

I stared at the mess of rancid flesh that stank of newly applied chemicals. I tried and failed to imagine her as a beautiful wealthy woman engaged in an affair.

"What's the husband been doing all this time?" Darlene asked.

"The sergeant at the station told me that Dr. Granger called them at least once a day," I said. "Went to the station half a dozen times, offered a reward of ten grand for any info. That was all in the first week after she vanished. One of Jennifer Granger's friends finally enlightened her husband about the affair. But he still kept up the pressure on the cops. In fact, he doubled the reward."

Darlene raised an eyebrow. "I reckon this poor woman is the first victim."

"Is that based on anything empirical? Apart from the fact that she died three weeks ago?"

"No, just a hunch. The murder is a bit different to the others . . . done with less confidence."

I tilted my head.

"The murderer got the woman to come to him . . . in a derelict house, away from Bellevue Hill. Now though, he's literally on the victims' doorstep."

"He was you mean . . . What about Yasmin Trent?"

"I'm convinced she was snatched. Probably close to where she lived. The cops found her car fifty yards from her body."

It was my turn to look surprised. "I didn't know that."

"They checked the odometer. The last journey in the car was thirty-one miles. Precisely the distance from Bellevue Hill to where Yasmin Trent's corpse was discovered in Sandsville. I reckon our killer is beginning to feel the heat in Bellevue Hill and mixing it up to keep us off his scent."

I was about to reply when the door opened and Mark Talbot walked in.

"Just passing," my cousin smirked.

"We need to talk," I said through gritted teeth.

Chapter 71

"WHY THE HELL didn't you tell us about this woman?" We were in a deserted storage area at the back of the building.

"One of my officers caught a pickpocket in Darling Harbour this morning, Craig," Talbot said. "Should I have told you about that?" He took a step toward me, intruding into my personal space. "Oh, and that pesky graffiti artist who keeps daubing a wall just off George Street in the CBD? Got him too. Sorry . . . forgot to mention . . ."

"You may think you're being very clever, Mark," I said with robotic calm, "but we have a deal with the police, don't we?"

"*You* have a 'deal' with the Deputy Commissioner."

"And you have to abide by it."

Talbot came even closer. He was about my height. We were eye-to-eye.

"This morning I used my professional discretion."

"No you didn't. You did this deliberately to screw me over. And you just showed up here to gloat."

He shrugged. "Well, yeah, maybe I did."

"Thanks to you, we lost five hours of precious investigation time."

He laughed in my face. I could feel his breath. "Just listen to you . . . You fucking smart-ass . . . 'Precious investigation time!' Who the hell do you think you are? You're a PI, dear cousin! You can fool the Deputy Commissioner, but you don't pull the wool over my eyes."

"I'm very disappointed."

"You what?"

"I'm disappointed."

He leaned in, his eyes narrow. "Disappointed! You cocksucker! Who do you think you're talking to?"

I went to gently push him back. And that's when he took a swing at me.

I blocked his fist and he stumbled back a step, went for me again, his right arm swinging round.

But he wasn't in the best of shape. I dodged his fist so easily it was embarrassing . . . which enraged him more. His left fist came up, slower, but at an oblique angle. It grazed my shoulder. I grabbed his wrist and bent his hand back.

"Don't, Mark!" I said in his ear.

His breath was on me again, hot, his mouth close to my left cheek. I bent his hand a little more and sensed him shift position, his right knee moving up toward my groin. I turned my body away and his knee hit me in the hip. It stung. Still gripping my cousin with my left hand, I swung round, sending a right hook to his face.

He fell back and landed heavily on the floor, blood streaming from a cut just below his left eye. He made to get up.

"Stop!" I hollered, but he wouldn't listen.

"Asshole! You always have been . . . !" He growled, got to his feet with surprising speed and rushed me. I whirled round, elbow out, and he ran straight into it, nose first. I heard the cartilage crunch. He spun, hit the floor again, lay still for a few moments, face down. I heard him groan, crouched beside him, keeping my guard up. He glared at me with a look of pure hatred, blood streaming from his nostrils. His left eye was already puffed up.

I offered him a hand but he spat at it. His saliva landing on the floor between us.

"Suit yourself," I said and walked away.

Chapter 72

I TRIED MY best to look composed as I returned to the morgue.

"You alright?" Darlene asked, concerned.

"Yeah, fine."

"You don't look fine." She dusted my shoulder.

"You found anything?"

She pointed to Jennifer Granger's corpse. "It's very similar to all the others," Darlene said gravely. "Face burned and cut, stabbed in the back repeatedly. The same money dump . . . *fake* money dump. No sign of sexual assault. No DNA."

"But?"

"But what?"

"You've found something, haven't you?"

She smiled. "You should be a detective! I've found a partial print on one of the photocopies."

"Oh."

"Which convinces me even more that Jennifer Granger was the first victim. The killer was less practiced. He made a mistake."

Chapter 73

DR. CAMERON GRANGER was wearing an open-neck shirt, loafers and an expensive suit. I knew because I'd seen it up-close in Armani the week before.

He was tall, broad shouldered, strong jawed. He had a big house in the Eastern Suburbs, probably a million-dollar yacht moored somewhere exclusive and used maybe twice a year.

He indicated a plush suede sofa, sat one end, me the other. He looked suitably morose.

"I've been to the morgue. Been briefed. Given my report to the cops."

"You seem very calm and collected."

"What can you do? I've had some time to absorb it all. After Jennifer failed to show up with her friends, I assumed she'd either run off with her lover or she was dead."

I appraised the man again. Was he using bravado to overcome his grief?

"You had no idea your wife was having an affair?"

"Oh, right . . . What more traditional motive for murder is there than being cuckolded?"

I held his eyes and he looked away.

"Strikes me as odd," I said provocatively. "Why would a wife risk losing such a lavish lifestyle by messing around?"

Granger surprised me by simply shrugging. "You tell me, Mr. Gisto. Maybe she thought she'd never be caught."

"When did you see your wife last?"

"I went through this with the police." He sighed. "I kissed her goodbye in the hallway of our home. Waved as she got into her car. She was leaving for the airport – apparently – to see her girlfriends in Melbourne."

"Then, later, you got a call from one of them."

"Yes, Helene Fromes, over thirty-six hours later actually. She'd tried and failed to reach Jen by phone . . . got worried . . . Stupid bitch."

"You sound pretty angry. Wasn't this Helene Fromes doing you a favor?"

"Oh yeah! The sisterhood keeping my wife's infidelity a secret . . . Great. I'm touched!"

"Right," I said evenly, thinking about all the times men had closed ranks and kept their buddies' secrets to themselves. "Well, you obviously would like the killer brought to justice . . . you've doubled the reward."

"I doubled it again earlier this afternoon."

"Is there anything you can think of that might help us . . . and the police?"

"Look, Mr. Gisto, I've told the police everything I know. I saw Jennifer leave the house. I assumed she was doing what she said she was going to do and meet her mates in Melbourne. I didn't hear a thing until Helene called. That was three weeks ago. Maybe you should speak to the guy Jennifer was seeing."

"We've only just tracked him down. My colleague is with him as we speak."

"Oh, do wish the man well, won't you . . ."

Chapter 74

JUSTINE STUDIED THE man sitting in front of her and wondered how any woman could find him attractive. Nick Grant was Jennifer Granger's lover. He was tall, thin, in a vest and shorts, his left arm a full-sleeve tattoo. He'd agreed to meet on neutral ground – a pub on Napoleon Street, Bondi.

"Look," he said, fixing Justine with a confident gaze. "Me and Jen . . . it was a casual thing, right? She was getting quotes for an extension on her house in Bellevue Hill. Took a shine to me right off." He gulped his beer, gave Justine a faintly flirtatious smile. Then his expression turned serious. "I was sorry to hear what happened . . ."

"She was with you the weekend she was murdered?"

"No! That's just it. I hadn't seen her for weeks. As I said, it was casual. I think we only did it three, four times. She'd arrange everything – swanky hotels in the city, call me up with half-an-hour notice. Tell me to put on something clean . . . that she was in Room 131 at the Four Seasons, or Room 42 at the Hyatt, wearing nothing but high heels." He grinned stupidly. "Well, what do you do?"

"And the weekend of December 14th/15th? You were in Sydney?"

"No." Nick Grant shrugged. "I wasn't."

"So where were you?"

"In Melbourne."

"Melbourne?"

"Yeah . . . you look surprised."

"No, no go on."

"Rugby piss-up. Me and the lads. We went to see the Waratahs at the AAMI Park. Fantastic game . . . and afterwards! Sunday . . . whoa! . . . a complete blur. Took Monday off. Went back to work Tuesday. We're on a big job in Mona Vale." He nodded toward the Northern Beaches.

"So when did you hear that Jennifer Granger had gone missing?"

"One of her friends called me out of the blue. I didn't know what the woman was talking about at first. She was another stuck-up bitch . . . Sorry. I mean she was . . . Oh fuck! You know what I mean!"

Justine simply stared at the man.

"This woman," he went on. "Helene? She said Jennifer hadn't shown up for a girls' weekend. Why you telling me? I said. Apparently, Jen had mentioned my name and the company I worked for and this Helene tracked me down. Cheeky bitch. I got a bit pissed off with her. Told her she'd better not tell anyone where to find me, especially Jen's bloody husband."

"And nothing else happened?"

"No. Not another word 'til this morning."

"So when was the last time you saw Jennifer Granger?"

Nick Grant took another gulp of beer and pondered the

table top. "Well, let me think . . . Must have been two weeks before the Melbourne weekend. Yeah . . . early December . . . at the Sheraton."

Justine shivered. "What a terrible mess some people create for themselves," she thought, recalling the gruesome photographs of the woman's shallow grave.

Chapter 75

THE PARTIAL PRINT from Jennifer Granger's body appeared two feet wide on the flat screen. Darlene studied the lines, what analysts called "whorls" and "loops". Darlene remembered a stat from college – a one in sixty-four billion chance of any two people sharing fingerprints.

The partial on the screen looked completely unremarkable. It was perhaps two-thirds of a full print, limited in value, but better than nothing.

Darlene double-clicked the mouse and highlighted the image, then moved the picture to an icon on the screen. The file disappeared and a box came up with the words: "Global Database Analysis in Progress." Beneath this, a line, a tiny red dot to the left and the words: "Estimated time remaining: 42 minutes" – the time it would take for the powerful computer system at Private to compare the partial print with every database it was linked to throughout the world, some two billion records.

She pushed her chair back, ran her fingers through her hair. She felt incredibly frustrated. Here she was with some of the best forensics equipment in the world and she'd spent three days drawing a blank on four connected murders. At the back of her mind something was nagging her. It'd been needling her for at least twenty-four hours, but she couldn't pinpoint it.

She got up and walked across the lab to a bench. She'd filed away every piece of data she had on the four murders. Most of the info was on the computer and there were a few written reports kept in a filing cabinet. Here on the bench stood ninety-six test tubes in a dozen racks. Each one was carefully labeled. Each contained something from the murder scenes.

She scanned along the racks. There were slithers of cloth, particles of soil, fragments of body tissue, blood-soaked fabrics, hairs. Hairs! She moved the racks forward, one after the other, taking care to keep everything in the correct order. Then she saw what she was looking for . . . a test tube containing a single whitish-blonde human hair.

Darlene felt her heart pounding. She strode over to a powerful drive that stored all crime scene photos. Tapped the mouse. Brought up the photo collections from the past three days. Clicked a folder entitled: "Yasmin Trent." Scrolling down, she stopped over Image No. 233. A smile spread across her face.

Chapter 76

DARLENE WENT STRAIGHT from her lab to the house in Bondi where Jennifer Granger had been found. She knew the Police Forensics team would still be there and she wanted one more search around the place herself.

A cop Darlene recognized met her at the front door, gave her a warm smile. "Darlene," he said. "Back again?"

"Can't keep me away from a good murder scene, Sergeant Tindle," she quipped, reading his ID badge. He was young and good-looking, she'd spotted him at the earlier murder sites and knew that he'd definitely noticed her too.

"It's Howard," he said leading her through the hall. They stopped at the door to the bathroom splattered with blood.

"The murder was committed here," the sergeant said.

"You don't say!" she laughed. "So, I heard you got tipped off by a vagrant who slept in the front room last night."

"That's what we thought at first. A young guy called us early this morning. We followed up. He'd dropped his driver's license would you believe! Turns out he's an eighteen-year-old schoolboy. He and his girlfriend snuck in here for a quick one. They're both respectable kids from good families. But they picked the wrong spot. They're in a lot of trouble with their parents now!"

"Poor things."

They emerged from the dark interior into the blazing afternoon sun. Darlene saw four men in boiler suits digging up the lawn and the overgrown flowerbeds to the rear of the house. Two CSOs were sifting through the soil searching for further clues.

Darlene heard a cry from one of the diggers and ran across the yard.

Two of the men were bending over an opening in the ground. Darlene skirted the edge and crouched down. Decayed human bones. Patches of white caught the light of the sun – a forearm protruding from the dirt.

The forensics guys ran over, saw the bones and settled down beside Darlene. "Keep digging, but gently," one of them said to the men with shovels and started to clear the soil near the arm with smaller spades.

The grave was shallow, barely two feet deep and soon the outline of a large man could be seen. A few patches of gray-brown flesh remained on his dead bones, strands of red hair clung to his skull.

Chapter 77

IT HAD PASSED 6 pm and Johnny was leaving the office when the phone rang. A young female voice told him she was calling from Bonza Records and inviting him to a "VIP concert" starring Micky Stevens starting at 8.30 that night.

He just had time to get home, get changed and get a cab to the venue – a rather macabre place called the Old Quarantine Station near Manly.

The cab pulled into the lot, Johnny paid and walked toward the noise. He knew this place from when he was a kid. For over a century since it was built in the 1820s, it was the place where visitors to Australia were quarantined before being allowed into the country. Thousands had suffered terribly in this place. Decades ago it'd been turned into a national park novelty: "The Most Haunted Place in Australia."

Close to the old shower block and the mortuary, the original boiler house had been converted into a swish restaurant and conference center. Johnny emerged onto a cobbled courtyard lit up by massive lights on rigs. Directly ahead stood a stage strewn with musical equipment, men in black jeans and T-shirts testing mics. There were perhaps a hundred people milling around in front of the stage. Most were wearing suits, drinking champagne, chatting animatedly.

Johnny strode over to a waiter carrying a tray, took a glass of orange juice. A leggy blonde approached with a clipboard. Johnny gave her his name.

"Ah yeah!" she said. "I was the one who called you earlier. Mel . . ." She extended a hand.

"So what's this all about?"

"Promo for the suits. Even stars as big as Micky need to lay on a show for the execs and the sales guys."

I nodded. "Weird choice of venue."

"Oh, we like to be a bit different!"

There was a sudden hush as the strains of a famous classical piece Johnny couldn't put a name to flowed from the speakers either side of the stage. A man wearing a cream linen suit and a Micky Stevens T-shirt walked out stage right, radio mic in hand. It was Graham Parker.

"Ladies and gentlemen . . . welcome." His voice was deeper and softer than Johnny had imagined. He smiled at the crowd, pointed at someone at the front, laughed good-naturedly. "Thanks for coming along. It's a sort of celebration of Micky's birthday tomorrow, but the real party's at The Venue – and, of course, you're all invited. Now . . . Micky's well and truly wired and he is RARING TO GO! So, please, give it up for my boy . . . Micky Stevens."

The lights died, the entire stage turned black. A drum rhythm started and a bass guitar came in. Then the lights burst on, thousands of watts of color. And there was Micky Stevens dressed entirely in white, crouched, microphone in hand. He screamed and the music came crashing in.

The crowd, lubed on expensive champagne and free cocaine, went wild. The song rocketed along, growing more and more powerful as it went.

Johnny had seen videos of Micky Stevens of course. His latest song already had a million hits on YouTube, but seeing him live and only fifty yards away was something else. He looked round and saw Mel nodding appreciatively. Then he turned back to the stage, hardly able to believe how the demure shy character he'd met at Private could transform himself into this massive personality, this rock god parading in front of them.

Chapter 78

I'D NEVER SEEN Darlene so excited. "What's happened? The latest copy of *Forensics Now* arrive early?"

She gave me a phony smile and tilted her head to one side. "Just got back from the house in Bondi. There's a second body in the garden."

I stood up. "Really?"

"A man. From the level of decomposition I'd say he's been dead two maybe three months. Severe facial disfigurement, multiple stab wounds. Sound familiar?"

"But it's a totally different MO . . . a male victim. It doesn't make sense."

"I've taken samples. Police Forensics are all over it. There must be some link. Has to be the same killer."

I must've looked shocked, or at least deeply concerned because Darlene said, "There's some other news."

"That's good."

"I think I have something on this killer."

I came round my desk and we sat on the sofa. Darlene had a file in her hand. "Something was niggling me about these crimes."

"Yeah, you said something in Sandsville . . . Yasmin Trent's murder."

"It came to me a couple of hours ago." She pulled a test tube from the pocket of her lab coat and held it out.

I took it and lifted it to the light.

"A strand of hair?"

"Specifically, bleached blonde hair. Found on Elspeth Lampard's blouse."

"Not one of hers? She was blonde."

"I don't think so. I've just had it under the scope. A particular bleach was used. Every brand is very slightly different. This is a cheapie, slightly higher peroxide level than the more up-market dyes. Doesn't sound like the sort of stuff a woman like the victim would use. Also, see how a good third of the hair is dark? The woman this hair came from doesn't keep up with her color. She let it grow out. Again, doesn't fit Elspeth's profile."

"I don't see . . ."

"Okay . . . the thing bothering me was that when I first arrived at the scene of Yasmin Trent's murder I ran off a couple of hundred shots on my camera and must have subconsciously noted a strand of blonde hair lying across the dead woman's arm. I was distracted by something and had to talk to one of the cops for a couple of minutes. By the time I got back, the Police Forensics guys were packing up, and I set to work."

"You'd forgotten about the hair?"

"I don't think I really registered it consciously."

"But the camera did."

Darlene pulled a photo from the folder. It showed a magnified white-blonde hair lying on a piece of dark fabric.

"And Yasmin was a brunette," I said.

"She was." Darlene took back the photo. "I called forensics straightaway. One of the guys there, Martyn Gofner. He's okay, seems to like me. He checked their files. Sure enough, they have a blonde hair from the Yasmin Trent murder scene."

"Wow!" I exclaimed.

"Yep . . . They profiled a DNA sample from the hair. Couldn't match it with any database. They sent the profile over." She pulled a piece of paper from the folder and held it out. It was a chart showing the analysis of the sample. "And this," she said proudly, "is the profile I have from the hair I had, taken from Elspeth Lampard's body." She handed me a second sheet. The two charts were identical.

"Hair from the same person."

"Absolutely no doubt . . . and the DNA does not match either blonde victim, Stacy Friel or Elspeth Lampard." She flicked a glance at the sheets of data I held in each hand. "There's one more thing . . . the DNA, and therefore the hair, is definitely from a female – no Y chromosome in the profile. Our killer is a woman."

Chapter 79

DARLENE HAD GONE back to her lab and out of the corner of my eye I noticed Mary walking along the corridor from reception to her office. I hadn't seen her or heard from her all day. But Johnny had told me what'd happened to her at the Triad place. I pulled up from my desk and tapped on her open door. She looked up and knew I wasn't happy, followed me over to my office.

"I'm really pissed with you, Mary. What the hell were you thinking?"

She sat down, kept her bandaged hand just out of sight deliberately. "Information gathering, Craig. I went into places worse than that friggin' Triad dump all the time in the force."

"You could have gotten yourself killed. Besides, you might as well have put up a billboard on George Street . . . 'Triads . . . We're after you'!"

"They knew already. Word travels fast in this city. Besides, that's exactly the desired effect, Craig. I wanted to give them the shits!"

I let out a deep sigh. "Okay." I put my hands palms down flat on the table. "It's done. How is it?" I nodded toward her hand.

"Just a scratch."

"Yeah right! A sixteen-stitch scratch!"

"God!" Mary exclaimed. "Can't a girl keep anything secret around here?"

The phone rang.

"Mr. Gisto," Ho Meng said down the line. "I need you to come here to my home immediately. There has been . . . a development."

Chapter 80

JOHNNY WAS WALKING toward the exit gate at the Old Quarantine Station where the cabs were lining up when he heard someone call his name.

He turned just as a black limo pulled up. Micky Stevens had his head out the window, a big grin on his face.

"Jump in."

Johnny strolled over and peered inside. There was a stunning girl on the back seat next to Micky. She had mile-long legs and a perfect model pout. Hemi was in the front passenger seat next to the driver.

"I'm good, Micky."

"Dude! You're coming to the after-gig party, right?"

"Party?"

"My place. Come on, hop in." He spread his arms. "Plenty of room."

"Okay."

The car pulled away as the door closed and Johnny landed on a seat facing Micky and the girl. There was an ice bucket in the middle of the floor, two uncorked bottles of champagne inside. Next to that, a mirror with half a dozen lines of coke. Johnny noticed white powder on Micky's upper lip.

"Johnny . . . meet Katia, my girlfriend. Katia, this is Johnny, a good friend of mine."

The girl looked at him seriously, didn't move a muscle. She had jet black hair cut in a severe bob with a high, straight fringe, huge dark eyes and amazing cheekbones. She was dressed entirely in black except for what looked like a miniature sword about an inch long on a pink ribbon at her incredibly pale throat.

"I know you don't drink, Johnny, but do you . . . ?" He nodded toward the cocaine.

"Er . . . no, thanks, Micky."

"How dull," Katia said. Her English was almost perfect with only the merest hint of an accent Johnny couldn't quite place.

"Each to his own," Micky said matter-of-factly. "Katia is a brilliant guitarist, Johnny. She's Russian and was in a band in Moscow. They were called Khuy."

"Which translates as penis," the girl said blankly.

"Isn't that fuckin' great, man? I fell in love with her when I learned that. Six months ago . . . Longest relationship I've ever had!" He turned to the girl. "And I love her."

Katia smiled for the first time and leaned in to kiss Micky. They stayed glued together for five minutes while Johnny looked out the window at the buildings flashing past.

Finally Micky pulled away, wiped his mouth and refilled his and Katia's glasses.

"So man, you like the show?"

"I was knocked out," Johnny replied earnestly.

"Excellent. Excellent." Micky downed the champagne. "Well, I think you'll enjoy the party even more." And he gave one of his huge smiles.

Chapter 81

MICKY'S SYDNEY PAD was a penthouse in Woolloomooloo. Spartan, clean lines, massive windows looking out toward the harbor, a ten-mill price tag.

By the time the limo got there the place was packed. Micky and Katia vanished and Johnny was left to wander around clutching another glass of orange juice. The place was filled with the sound of ridiculously loud rock music.

Part of him was still in a state of shock just knowing Micky. He was, after all, just a poor boy from the Western Suburbs. At least that's what so many people wanted him to believe. He never had accepted the label and that was partly how he'd clawed his way up the food chain. Now he had real friends, people who appreciated him, a great job, prospects. But meeting Micky and finding him so easy to be with . . . that had been totally unexpected.

He felt a tap on his shoulder and turned to see Katia.

"Can I speak with you?" she said seriously.

"Sure."

She led the way across the main room, a vast space filled with men in suits, a couple of recognizable faces from TV and YouTube, a lot of beautiful young women. Johnny noticed Graham Parker talking to Micky on the far side of the room. Katia motioned toward the balcony just as Johnny saw Parker hand Micky a small package.

Outside, a mellow breeze ruffled the water.

"I'm sorry I was so rude earlier."

Johnny shrugged and thought how refined her voice was. She was clearly educated. "You weren't . . ."

"I didn't realize you were the guy from Private. Micky's been singing your praises."

Johnny looked stunned.

"I'm very concerned for him," Katia went on.

"Because of this Club 27 business?"

"Of course."

"He's convinced that Graham Parker . . ."

"I'm very aware of that . . . But," Katia said, her voice thick with . . . what? Concern? Irritation? "But . . . oh, I just don't know . . . I'm worried Micky's losing it . . ."

"Drugs?"

"Everything, Johnny. Everything. It's almost as though he has some weird death wish."

"So you think Graham Parker has nothing to do with it?"

"You're the PI."

He fell silent, looked back to the room filled with people. There was a sudden commotion. A woman ran over from a doorway in the far wall. She was shouting something, but Johnny couldn't make it out over the thumping music.

Katia was at the door to the main room. Barged her way through the packed room sending drinks flying. Johnny followed in her wake.

The music stopped abruptly and a hundred threads of conversation died with it.

They had reached the far side of the room and Johnny followed the girl through a door. The woman who'd rushed into the main room a few seconds before was now back, standing in the doorway. Katia ignored her and plunged into a cavernous bathroom, Johnny a second behind. Three men stood around a prone form on the floor. A fourth was leaning over the figure, an opened case beside him.

"Fuck . . . Yob . . . Govno," Katia screamed, mixing her languages. She fell to the floor.

Micky was semiconscious, drenched in sweat, foam at his lips. His arms and legs twitched.

Katia suddenly seemed to recognize the man with the case. "Dr. James . . . " she said.

The man ignored her.

She went to grab Micky.

"Please!" the doctor snapped.

Dr. James pulled a syringe from the case, squeezed the plunger a fraction of an inch letting liquid dribble from the tip. Then he leaned forward, and with one shockingly violent movement he thrust the syringe into the middle of Micky's chest, right through to his heart.

Micky jolted upright. Then, as the doctor withdrew the needle, the rock star slumped back, his eyes snapping wide open. He rolled to one side and vomited.

Johnny noticed the package he'd seen Parker hand to Micky ten minutes earlier. It was opened on the floor, a used syringe and an empty vial lying on a rectangle of cloth.

Chapter 82

HO WAS SITTING on his living-room couch, dressed in cream chinos and a polo shirt. As he rose to shake my hand, I could see that he'd shaved badly, a line of bristles missed close to his chin.

"What's happened?" I asked heavily.

"Dai has disappeared. I called his cell and home number half a dozen times. Went to his apartment. No response. I let myself in. There were signs of a struggle. A gun had been fired into the wardrobe."

"Any blood?"

Meng shook his head, gazed at the plush cream living-room carpet.

"And you haven't contacted . . . ?"

Ho looked up. "No, Mr. Gisto, I haven't called the police."

I sighed. "There's more, isn't there?"

"A ransom note. Same as before. Either I do as they say or my son dies."

The man looked drained, his skin almost translucent in the light from ceiling halogens.

"An ultimatum?"

"Midnight tonight. I say 'yes' or Dai . . ."

I nodded.

"And there was this. He leaned over to a side table, picked up a small cardboard box, removed the lid and handed it to me. I peered inside and saw an ear nestled in a bed of bloodied cotton wool.

"This changes everything," I declared. "Forget about us trying to catch the two goons who kidnapped and killed Chang. We have to get the police involved and go much higher up the gang hierarchy."

Ho closed his eyes for a second.

"This has gone too far for Private to deal with alone," I insisted. "And actually, by not going to the police you're in danger of breaking the law yourself."

Meng sniffed at that but slowly nodded. "I know."

Chapter 83

PAM HEWES HAD just checked on the kids. They were both sound asleep. She went back downstairs and found a half-empty bottle of white wine in the refrigerator, plucked a glass from the cupboard over the sink and was walking through to the living-room when she heard a sound from outside the front door.

She froze and listened. Nothing but the regular domestic sounds, the washing machine in the laundry going through the end of its cycle, the distant hum of traffic on Military Road, fifty yards away. Then it came again, a scratching, shuffling sound from just the other side of the front door. She tiptoed across the hall and put her eye to the spy-hole.

There was nothing unusual there, the garden path, the gate to the street. A face reared into view making Pam scream and stumble back in shock. The glass and bottle slipped from her hand and shattered on the wooden floor sending wine and shards of glass across the hall.

"Pam? It's me," came a fractured voice.

It took her several seconds to recognize it. She yanked on the bolt and pulled the front door inwards.

Geoff stumbled into his house, unshaven and disheveled. "My God, Geoff!" she exclaimed. "What the hell happened?"

Chapter 84

GEOFF PULLED HIMSELF upright, winced, but lifted a hand. "I'm okay."

"You don't look okay, darling. You're cut." She went to touch Geoff's face.

"It's alright, Pam . . . really."

"What can I get you?"

"Look, I need to make a call."

"What?"

"It's super urgent. Then I'll have a shower and eat something." He pecked her on the cheek, turned toward his study and shut the door behind him.

Pam couldn't resist listening at the door. She heard Geoff walk round his desk, tap at the phone, then start to talk.

"Brian."

Pam could just make out the words. Her husband was speaking deliberately softly.

"Listen, buddy, I'll tell you about it when I see you," he said. "What's happened at my Mosman place? . . . Yeah, Chester Street . . . Yeah . . . yeah. Damn, I knew it!"

Quiet for a moment.

"So, Loretto's guys just turned up and ripped out the cameras? When? Bastard! Right, Brian . . . listen. I want you to go back to Chester Street tonight . . . Yes, tonight . . . I'll pay you extra . . . yeah . . . come on! . . . Don't worry about that . . . I want those cameras reinstalled."

Quiet again.

"It's got nothing to do with you, Brian. Don't worry about Loretto . . . he won't touch you . . . Yeah . . . I'll take the responsibility . . . Of course I will . . . Good. Right, you got it then? Tonight . . . Right away. I'll show that fucker . . ."

Chapter 85

THERE WAS A bad atmosphere in the briefing room at Police HQ.

Five of us in the room, Mark Talbot, Brett Thorogood, a senior detective called Matt Yender who was in command of the police assault force, Ho and me. The Deputy Commissioner was commanding proceedings from the head of a large table.

"Mr. Ho," Thorogood said, looking directly at the man. "You know these people better than any of us. Do you have any idea of the identity of the men behind these crimes?"

Ho sat still as a statue. In one sense he seemed to have diminished but in another way, he'd grown. He now possessed some sort of Zen-like calm that to my eyes covered a seething anger and horrible pain.

"As you are aware, the lead operatives in Sydney are the Lin brothers, Sung and Jing," Ho said stiffly. "They are 426s."

"Which means?"

"The Triads have clear distinctions between ranks and positions in the gang. They are each given numbers based upon the *I Ching* numerological system. The leader of the Triad is 489. His name would be 'The Mountain' or 'The Dragon'. I believe the gang in Sydney is a fragment of the Noonan, perhaps the most powerful of the Triads. The Dragon, the 489, is a man named Fong Sum. I met him once in Hong Kong. He's there now."

"So he'd be like a Don in the Mafia?" Talbot asked.

Ho nodded slowly. "There are many differences, but very broadly speaking, yes, he would. He controls a global network. The Sydney gangs are just a small part of it."

"And the Lin brothers . . . how many people work for them?" Yender asked.

"That I do not know for certain."

"Ballpark?"

"I would estimate perhaps forty to fifty foot soldiers in the city," he responded.

"Foot soldiers are the rank and file, right?" Thorogood queried.

Ho nodded again. "They are known as 49s. I would suggest the men who abducted Chang and later Dai would have been their best 49s, men who are working their way up the pecking order. This would have been a big job for them."

"As this whole heroin project is for the Lin brothers too," I remarked.

"Indeed."

"Okay," the Deputy Commissioner said. "So do we have a consensus as to what to do next?"

I watched Ho, waiting for him to respond.

"I have come to the conclusion that the only chance we have of saving my son is to convince the gang that I will do what they want."

"And that will provide us with a platform for a sting operation," I added.

Mark looked at me with contempt. "Us?"

"We are happy to provide any assistance you wish," I said directly to Thorogood, giving my cousin nothing. "But we're not going to be part of this unless we're armed – like the rest of you. My assistant, Mary Clarke and I are licensed to carry firearms."

"I appreciate your contribution," the Deputy Commissioner responded, looking directly at me. "I think we can work together on this."

Chapter 86

HO MADE FIRST contact from his home phone about 11 pm.

The cops were at the house with tracking equipment. Talbot, Yender and Thorogood were there to babysit. I had Mary and Darlene with me this time.

Ho tried to keep the call going, but the foot soldier at the other end wasn't dumb. The call ended before the police expert could locate the caller to less than a square mile. Ho gave the anonymous Triad member a cell number. The guy clicked off before saying when he would respond. We just had to wait.

"We brought along some technology that might help," I said. Mark gave me his usual contemptuous look, but Yender and Thorogood were all ears.

Darlene paced across the room carrying a couple of small boxes, put them on a low table and opened the lid of the top one. Then she plucked out a cell and removed the back cover. "Put your SIM in here," she said to Ho Meng. "When they call you we can get a better trace on them than with the conventional gear." And she flicked a glance at the police operator with his suitcase-sized tracking unit resting on the couch close to the home phone.

Darlene then picked up the second box, prised open the lid.

We could all see inside. A white pad with a black dot the size of an aspirin on top. "A micro transmitter," she said. "We can place this anywhere on your body and it'll pick up conversations and relay them to a receiver. You'll be close by in a van, right?" Darlene asked the cops.

"I'll be with the assault unit," Yender replied. "Inspector Talbot will be in the van."

I glanced at him. He ignored me.

"Okay." Ho nodded. "So what happens now?"

Thorogood looked up. "We're ready when they are. Just need the word."

Chapter 87

JULIE O'CONNOR HAD fallen asleep in front of *Australian Idol* and was dreaming about her father again. In her dream, none of the bad things had happened. He was still alive. She'd finished school, gone to college, become a Police Forensics officer.

She was woken by the crowd on TV roaring and shrieking as the winner was announced. And it all came rushing back – the reality of her life. She closed her eyes again and there was her mother screaming at her. When she hadn't reacted, Sheila had begun to torture her. She had kept her locked in her bedroom for days, forced her to shit in a bowl left stinking in the corner, gave her only beetroot to eat.

Later, the torment got worse. Sheila would tie her to a chair in the kitchen, gag her and burn her arms with cigarettes.

On her eleventh birthday, the first since her father's death, she received nothing. Then, just before bedtime, Sheila tied her to the chair again and told her that if she made a sound she would have her feet put in the fire in the lounge. Her mother had then pulled out an incisor with a pair of pliers.

This treatment continued for four years. She could never say a word for fear of worse torture. She hid the scars and the marks, made excuses for every lost tooth, every bruise. Then, one day something snapped inside her.

On the evening of her fifteenth birthday, Julie knew she would be in for a traditional 'gift'. As Sheila busied herself getting ready to go out, Julie slipped a kitchen knife into the back pocket of her jeans.

Her mother appeared in the doorway to the kitchen. She was wearing far too much make-up. There were two lengths of cord in her left hand.

"In the chair."

When she didn't move, her mother began to smile. Took a step toward her. "At last . . ."

Julie pulled the knife from her pocket and swung it round, stopping two inches from her mother's face.

The woman screeched, the smile vanishing instantly.

"You! In the chair," Julie hissed. And when her mother didn't react, she'd moved the knife an inch closer.

She tied Sheila with the cords meant for herself, gagged her with a tea towel and then brought the knife to the center of her forehead.

Sheila was shaking, her eyes filled with terror and hatred.

Julie had moved the knife a fraction of an inch, scoring her mother's flesh. The woman screamed under the cloth but it came out as nothing more than a muffled hum. Julie heard a rush of liquid and saw her mother's urine flow over the front of the chair and onto the floor.

"You didn't once make me do that, you useless bitch!" the girl announced proudly. She pulled the knife away and pocketed it again, turned and walked out.

Chapter 88

THE CALL FROM Lin Sung came ninety minutes later, close to twelve-thirty. Listening to Ho manage the call, I could see how he'd been such a successful cop in Hong Kong and then made a lot of money with his businesses in Australia.

Darlene had an iPad on her lap and with a new App sent over from Sci's lab in LA she could pinpoint the caller in under ten seconds. It was impressive, but actually not much help. Lin was calling from a payphone outside Luna Park in North Sydney.

"We would like to meet you," Lin said, his voice coming softly through a small speaker away from where Ho stood. The words went straight to a digital recorder.

"You will have my son?"

"Not this first time."

"Then there will be no meeting."

Silence from the other end. I held my breath.

"You are hardly in a position to negotiate, Mr. Ho."

Ho paused for a moment. "I entirely disagree."

Lin gave a small laugh. "Ah! A little game of bluff."

"I'm not bluffing." Ho's voice was stony.

Another, longer pause.

"Very well. We'll bring the boy. But we will only consider an exchange if all our conditions are met. Do you understand?"

Ho said nothing.

"I'll assume that is a 'yes', Mr. Ho. And if you invite a third party to our meeting, your son will be killed before your eyes."

When Ho still did not speak, Lin said. "Blackball Reserve, forty-five minutes," and hung up.

Chapter 89

WE WERE ON the freeway ten minutes short of Blackball Reserve near Manly when the agreed rendezvous was changed. I was in my car, Mary in the police surveillance vehicle with Mark, and next to him, a plainclothes officer driving. A hundred yards ahead of them was Ho's Bentley which he was driving alone. The news came from Mary calling my cell. "New destination," she intoned wearily. "A warehouse near the airport."

We all turned off at the next junction and headed south. I couldn't see the Bentley, but kept a steady distance back from the cops. My car was fitted with a police tracker set to a broad range of frequencies. I could hear their comms and knew Central Control had quickly redirected the assault team in a chopper to the new location. They'd be much faster than us and in position before we got there.

We reached the place in thirty minutes, pulling up fifty yards short of the warehouse. I parked behind the surveillance vehicle and ran over silently, watching Ho's car vanish into the shadows. Mary opened the sliding door and I climbed in. Mark and an operative were at the controls. We could hear every sound Ho made through the tiny transmitter.

"Assault Officer 1," the operative in the van said. "This is Control, come in." AO1, I knew, was Matt Yender.

"Control. We're in position. AO4, 5, 6 and 7 are in a small room across from the main warehouse building. I'm with AO2 and 3 the opposite side. I have visual contact with Mr. Ho's vehicle."

A screen on the wall of the control-room of the van lit up with a night vision video feed from AO1's helmet. It showed a fuzzy image of Ho's Bentley entering the derelict warehouse, lights ablaze. It stopped, Ho dimmed the lights and the image improved dramatically.

As we watched, a black Mercedes with tinted windows, registration LS1 entered through the north end of the dilapidated building. It crunched over the pitted floor strewn with pieces of metal and crushed concrete, stopping twenty feet short of the Bentley.

Ho stepped out of his car, took a couple of paces toward the Merc. The car's engine was still running, rear doors opened each side. Two men slipped out. They were slender, black-haired figures. The slightly taller one of the pair was Lin Sung. He was dressed in his usual vintage narrow-lapelled jacket and skinny tie. His brother, Jing, was in a blue tracksuit, white trainers. They walked slowly toward Ho as the driver clambered from the front of the Merc to stand by the hood.

"It's a pleasure," Lin Sung began, and put out a hand which Ho studiously ignored.

"Where is my son?"

Lin Sung chuckled and flicked a glance at his brother. "There is great value in patience, my friend."

"I'm not your friend." Ho looked from one brother to the

other. "I'm here to make a deal with you as we provisionally agreed."

"Yes, and . . ."

"I want my son released, *then* I will cooperate."

Sung sighed, cackled.

"You find it funny?" Ho asked coldly.

"You don't?" the younger brother butted in. His voice was oddly effeminate, completely at odds with his macho stance.

"Ho's hanging tough," I whispered to Mary who was standing beside me in the police van.

"Hope he doesn't overdo it."

I turned back to the screen and saw Lin Sung take a step closer to Ho. "We have the boy," he said slowly, "but we need assurances. Surely you understand that? If we return him to you, what is to say you will cooperate?"

"You have my word."

It was the younger brother, Lin Jing's turn to produce a half-assed laugh. "Ah! Your word!" he said, nodding his head. In an instant his mirth had vanished and he pulled a gun, a Type 64, from his waistband. His brother, Lin Sung, saw it and glared at him, but he didn't flinch.

Ho looked from one man to the other.

"This isn't going well," Mary hissed in my ear.

Yender's voice came through the comms. "Hold positions. No one move 'til I say."

Sung deliberately moved closer to his brother and slightly in front of him. "We are all reasonable men," he said and tilted his head slightly as he appraised Ho Meng. "I understand you want your boy back, but you have to put yourself into our position, Mr. Ho." Then he turned and snapped his fingers at the man standing by the hood of the Merc. He walked to the back door and opened it.

"You may see your son."

The driver leaned in and helped Ho Dai climb out. The young man's hands were tied behind his back and he looked petrified. He had a bloody wound where his left ear had been. He caught sight of his father and went to speak. "Say nothing!" Lin Jing barked, then whirled round to Ho again, his gun raised.

"There. Your brat's safe. Now we talk."

"What is it you want from me?"

"At last . . . !" the younger gangster exclaimed, but his brother cut over him.

"Your business provides a perfect cover for one of our . . . trade plans."

"Drugs . . . You want me to get heroin in."

Sung smiled, nodded.

"And in return?" Ho flicked a look at his son who was still standing by the car, the driver gripping his right arm.

"When you have proven your worth, he will be released."

Ho gave Sung a venomous look. "No deal," he said and started to turn.

"You mother-fuc . . ." the younger brother bellowed and began to squeeze the trigger of his Type 64.

"GO!" yelled Yender through the comms.

Chapter 90

FOR A COUPLE of seconds it was sensory overload. Shouts from the assault team, yells and thuds from the warehouse floor. On the screen, a smudge of movement through the night vision lens. Ho fell to the floor. I couldn't tell if he'd been shot or dived to avoid a bullet. Then Sung spun on his brother. Ho rolled to one side as the younger brother fired a second bullet. Sung was just yanking Lin Jing's arm down when the assault team in full body armor burst through into the warehouse from two different directions, screaming as they went, Enfield SA-80s leveled.

The younger Lin reacted instinctively. Pumped up, he dived for cover, headed for a pile of metal drums to his left and fired at the approaching cops. Before he could reach the barrels he was ripped open by at least three different weapons and crumpled in a heap.

Sung whirled round, reached the Mercedes. Dai and the driver were crouching behind the car. The driver had pulled a gun, the kid looked like a puppet, cartoon eyes, limbs limp. Sung reached cover, pulled out his own weapon, a semi-automatic, Bulgarian-made Arcus 94.

Lin grabbed Dai and we all heard the gangster yell out.

"Hold your fire," Yender's voice boomed through the speakers.

On the screen, I could see the fragmented image of Lin Sung rising slowly from a crouching position. He had the semi-automatic at Dai's temple. The driver shuffled away, slipping behind a hulking lump of rusting plant machinery. Then Ho Meng stood up slowly, apparently unharmed. He started to walk toward his son.

"Let the boy go," he yelled.

Lin Sung ignored him, took a step forward, opened the driver's door with one hand and simultaneously shoved Dai inside the Merc as he slid in beside him. They disappeared from view behind the tinted windows.

Ho reached the car but was forced back as it roared away. The cops had their machine guns raised, jumping aside as Lin accelerated toward them. The car skidded on the uneven floor, drifted for a second, tires screaming. Lin got it under control and slammed his foot to the floor.

I didn't wait another second, slid open the door of the surveillance vehicle and ran across the gravel to my Ferrari, hitting the remote as I went.

Chapter 91

I SPUN THE car backwards on the gravel, turned into a pitted lane beside the warehouse and shot away.

I couldn't see the Merc, but I knew Lin had gone this way, it was the only route to the perimeter fence. Careering round a bend-topping sixty, I hit a yard-wide hole in the tarmac, bounced out, the suspension stretched to breaking point. I almost lost grip on the road as the rear end came out, just pulled it back.

The entrance to the freeway lay fifty yards ahead and I caught a glimpse of Lin's car as it shot through the gates and accelerated up a slip road. I dodged another pothole, swung left, then a hard right, opened up the engine and tore onto the M5, headed west.

The Merc was quick but my Spider was quicker, and driven by someone in my state of mind it was *fantastically* fast. If Lin wasn't aware of the stats, they were impressed upon him when I started to gain on his car, halving the distance between us in less than thirty seconds. The M5 freeway was almost deserted and I had the Merc in my sights only twenty-five yards ahead. The speedometer read a hundred and twenty.

Lin took the next junction, screaming onto Rocky Point Road toward Rockdale. It was a smart move, a slower road, more chance of urban traffic, plenty of turn-offs. It leveled the playing field . . . some.

At 1.15 am the street was pretty much empty of traffic. Lin pulled the Merc off the dual carriageway into a side street, took it wide and almost hit an oncoming car. I screeched after him, missing the other car by an inch.

It was a narrow suburban street, rows of modest houses, parked cars to the left. Lin jumped the lights. I slowed and checked, followed him over the junction. He took a right, a left. More residential roads, a church, a grocery store. I caught a sign for a sports field and glimpsed a line of trees.

Lin left it to the last second, roared into a narrow lane just before the park. I braked and flew round the corner.

The Mercedes had disappeared from view. Then I realized I'd shot straight past it. Lin had taken a hard right off the road and pulled up onto a rutted track at the edge of the field.

I reversed and caught movement in the rear-view mirror. The gangster was out of his car, gun in hand and rushing round to the passenger door. He yanked it open, dragging Dai to the ground.

I stopped, slipped out, kept low. The Merc was ten yards away. Lin was pulling Dai up, the barrel of his gun at the kid's temple.

I was in the shadows, but Lin knew exactly where. He could have taken a pop at me, but then he risked losing Dai. "Stop," he shouted into the night, "or I'll kill him."

I pulled back and crept behind a line of bushes. I knew he wasn't sure where I was now. I moved fast. Lin and the boy dropped out of view for a few seconds, then I found an opening in the bushes and saw they hadn't moved.

I picked up a stone, tossed it to my left. Lin whirled round. He had his free arm around Dai's throat.

"Stop the stupid games," Lin said, an edge to his voice now. I was getting to him.

I moved hard round to his right and could see the back of his neck wet with perspiration. Leveled my gun to his head.

"Let him go."

Lin spun round.

"Let. Him. Go."

"No!"

Some instinct told me I'd pushed him too far. I fired and his gun went off simultaneously. Lin flew backwards, the hood of his car breaking his fall, a cloud of red exploding from his head. Dai jolted, screamed and collapsed to the ground.

I rushed over expecting the worst. Blood was running down Dai's cheek, dripping from his jaw. But he must have had the same awareness Lin was going to shoot as I had. He'd moved just in time. The Chinaman's bullet had just grazed the boy's temple.

I pulled Dai to his feet. He was shaking uncontrollably. I untied the cord around his wrists and he started to cry, tears streaming down his cheeks. He put a hand to his face and came up with bloodied fingers.

We could hear sirens. "It's okay," I said, realizing I was pretty shaken up too. "Just a scratch. You're going to be fine, Dai. It's all over, buddy."

Chapter 92

I GOT EVERYONE into the conference room real early. I hadn't slept and had gone straight to Private from Police HQ. They'd questioned me for nearly three hours before they were satisfied I couldn't have done anything different with Lin. Mark had gloated his way through the grilling of course and had taken pleasure in my discomfort. Nothing new there.

I surveyed the others. Everyone was exhausted. I had that morning's paper in front of me. The headlined screamed: "Sydney Slasher Claims Another Victim."

I exhaled loudly and felt a stab of frustration. "We're getting nowhere fast with this," I lifted the *Sydney Morning Herald*. "Darlene, anything?"

"Only what I said yesterday afternoon. I'm sure the killer is a woman."

The others had been told about Darlene's DNA findings.

"Not conclusive though," Mary said. "We know the victims were all acquainted. The blonde hairs could have come from a mutual friend."

Darlene looked at the table, nodded.

"But what if they *were* the killer's? Let's run with that for a sec," I said.

"There's no match on the database." Johnny commented.

"Means nothing. Maybe the murderer had never committed a crime until . . ."

"Alright," Justine said suddenly. "What if she happens to be a 'respectable' bleached blonde friend of the dead women and part of the same social circle? Maybe the motive was some relationship mess or simple jealousy."

"The wife of a banker or a corporate suit gone gaga?" Darlene looked up. "Maybe it *is* a sex thing. An Eastern Suburbs mom taking revenge on women her husband's slept with?"

I raised my hands. "Hang on, let's calm down!"

"Actually, I don't believe that," Darlene backtracked.

"Why?"

"For a start, the hair was not recently bleached. There was significant regrowth. That in itself suggested the woman didn't pamper herself. How many wealthy women walk around with weeks of roots growing out?"

"Search me!" Johnny said, rolling his eyes at me.

"And my sister insists that Elspeth and Stacy weren't messing around," Justine commented.

"Besides," I added, "the banknotes don't fit the theory, do they? The very fact that the notes are fake suggests the killer isn't a rich woman living in the same area as the victims . . . unless that's a trick."

"Oh for God's sake!" Mary exclaimed. "We're going round in bloody circles!"

"No, no . . . rewind," I said suddenly excited. I stood up and started pacing close to my chair. "Let's say it's *not* a trick and that the killer *is* poor . . . a woman from outside the area. She can't afford real fifty-dollar bills. She photocopies them. Yes!" I gazed around the room at the faces of the team. For a moment they all looked a little perplexed.

Then I remembered something. "Darlene you told me the other day, the fakes are high-quality photocopies. What if our killer photocopies the notes at a shop instead of at home? And what if . . . What if the murderer, this woman who's left hair strands, doesn't live in the Eastern suburbs, but works there?"

"I'll get onto it – visit all the copy shops in the area," Johnny said as excited as me. "I think you're onto something, boss."

Chapter 93

"SO, WHAT D'YOU have?" I asked Johnny as he came into my office two hours later looking jaded.

"There're five copy shops within a two-mile radius of Bellevue Hill. First three drew a complete blank. Guys there had no idea what I was talking about when I asked them if any suspicious-looking women had been in. Made me feel bloody stupid, actually!" He grinned endearingly.

"What about the others?"

"Fourth shop was on New South Head Road, about a mile from Bellevue Hill. The manager was a nice guy. Said he'd seen one particular woman come in a few times during the past three weeks. She didn't look 'suspicious' exactly, just miserable, rundown. But get this. He described her. Above average height, well-built, bleached blonde."

I rubbed my hand over my chin and stared at Johnny silently. "And the fifth shop?"

"Jackpot! A very sweet girl running the place."

"Yeah, yeah . . ."

"She'd seen the same woman at least twice during the past month."

"There's more. I can tell by your tone."

"The last shop keeps surveillance records for a month at a time. I gave the girl a hundred bucks and she ran off a copy of the disc for me."

Chapter 94

IT WAS A poor-quality recording, but good enough. It showed a woman coming into the copy shop, moving from the counter to a self-service machine. She placed something indistinct on the machine's tray and watched as half a dozen copies emerged. She then paid for them and left.

"Quite a powerful-looking woman," I said.

"And piss ugly!" Johnny remarked.

I exhaled.

"Sorry!"

"Can't see much of her. But she definitely has bleached her hair."

"First thing I noticed," Johnny replied.

"Take it through to Darlene. See if she can do anything with her souped-up imaging equipment."

Chapter 95

DARLENE WATCHED THE short clip taken at the copy shop. Johnny was leaning on the back of her chair peering at the screen over her shoulder.

"It's pretty crappy," she mumbled.

Johnny said nothing.

"But, thanks to my new buddy, Software Sam, I might get something out of this. It works just as well for video as it does for still images."

She ran her hands over the control panel of the image enhancer. Then she turned back to the computer keyboard and slithered her fingers over the keys.

The screen went blank for a second and then the film spooled back to the start. Darlene tapped another couple of keys. The clip was 500 per cent clearer.

The woman came into the shop. She was wearing a shapeless blue sweat top, handbag on her right shoulder. They could see her straight-on. She had a wide face, flat nose, small eyes. Her shoulder-length hair looked greasy. It was bleached blonde. Not dyed well – a bottle from a pharmacy. She wasn't wearing make-up and she'd shaved her eyebrows.

"Not the prettiest specimen," Johnny remarked, a little more diplomatically this time. "What would you say? Five-seven, five-eight? Hundred and seventy pounds?"

"Five-nine, one seventy-five."

"I bow to your superior skills," Johnny retorted.

They continued watching as the woman walked over to the photocopier.

"Can you close in on her there?" Johnny asked.

Darlene played her fingers over the keyboard, slowed the film, zoomed in and adjusted the enhancer to sharpen the picture. She was straining the software to its limits.

Tugging the mouse gently, she moved the center of the image to see what it was the woman was placing on the copier. They both noticed she was wearing latex gloves. She plucked a sheet of paper from her bag. It was impossible to see what was on it.

Darlene let the film creep forward a few frames a second. The first copy began to emerge. She shifted perspective, closing in on the paper spewing from the copier. It appeared slowly. She moved in closer still. Darlene toggled the controls on the enhancer, prayed the software would hold up.

And there, in the plastic collection tray of the photocopy machine, lay a sheet of paper containing the image of four fifty-dollar bills.

"Wow!" Johnny exclaimed.

"We still don't know who she is," Darlene commented. "I'll get this over to the police. They may know something we don't."

Chapter 96

JUSTINE WAS WITH me in the office when Pam Hewes called to suggest we meet.

"You look exhausted, Craig," Justine said as I put the phone down.

I gave her a wan smile. "Felt fresher."

"Can I help?"

I was about to say, "No, everything's cool," then changed my mind. I told her all the details of the Hewes' case. She looked intrigued.

"Would Pam mind if I helped out? Would you mind?"

I cocked my head. "It's my call . . . I run my own show. And, well, I've persuaded myself it would be good to have you along!"

Pam Hewes arranged to meet me at a small café close to the Opera House. Justine and I arrived early and sat admiring the view.

We didn't notice her come in. She lowered herself into a chair beside me and gave Justine a quizzical look.

"Hi, Pam, this is my colleague from the LA office . . . Justine Smith."

The women shook hands.

"What you drinking?" I asked.

"Double espresso, please."

I leaned back and called over the waitress.

"So Craig's filled you in on my husband's antics, I imagine," I heard Pam say to Justine.

"What's been happening?" I asked.

"Geoff's returned."

"You don't seem that relieved."

She exhaled. "No, I *am* relieved, but I'm also suspicious."

"Did he explain where he'd been?" Justine asked.

"Oh, in that way he has," Pam sighed. "Claims a couple of his drinking buddies played a prank on him. I don't believe that for a second."

I raised an eyebrow. "Does sound a bit . . ."

"Far-fetched?"

"I was going to say ridiculous, actually."

"I agree. He's up to something," Pam said. "What've you found out?"

I told her straight, all about the brothels. Pam was my client and a big girl.

"Well, that makes sense. Is one of them in Chester Street, Mosman?"

I gave her a surprised look.

"The first thing Geoff did when he got home was to call one of his pals . . . I 'overheard'!" Pam added, seeing my puzzled expression. "He was talking to some guy called Brian about cameras installed in Chester Street. Apparently Loretto had them removed. Geoff was telling his friend to reinstall them . . . right away."

"That's bad. Very bad," Justine said. "From what Craig has told me, Loretto's not the sort to mess with. If your husband has put cameras in the guy's brothels . . ."

Pam looked pale. "You spoken to Loretto, Craig?"

"He's out of town. But as soon . . . Look, it sounds like he held Geoff somewhere – maybe a final warning to back off?"

"So, what now?" There was a tremor to her voice.

"Well, Pam," I said, "I reckon that's up to Geoff. If Al Loretto was giving him one more chance and he takes notice, that's one thing. If he chooses to ignore it . . ."

Chapter 97

"YOU'RE NOT GOING to believe this!" Darlene gushed as she came round the open doorway into my office. She had a paper file in her hand.

I got up from the desk.

"Just off the phone. Sergeant Tindle called. They've ID'd the remains of the man at the Bondi house." She sat at the other end of the sofa from me, opened the file. "Name's Bruce Frimmel."

She handed me a photograph of the man from police records.

"He'd served time. Assault charge five years ago. His DNA was on file. He vanished two months ago."

"And you reckoned the guy in the garden had been dead for two to three months."

"Police Forensics have also identified two distinct sets of blood splatter in the bathroom at the house. One is Frimmel's, the other Granger's blood. They were both killed in the same room."

"Interesting."

"It gets much more interesting. Bruce's girlfriend, Lucy . . ." Darlene glanced at the file again. " . . . Lucy Inglewood . . . was questioned when Frimmel vanished. She told the police he had crossed a few people. There was a biker gang in Blacktown he'd upset and a few months earlier he'd broken up acrimoniously with his last girlfriend who he'd lived with for a few years."

"The police looked into these I take it?"

"They interviewed everyone who'd known Bruce Frimmel. Sergeant Tindle worked with Inspector Talbot on it. They talked to twenty-odd of Frimmel's associates and those close to him, including his ex, Julie O'Connor. The sergeant called me, Craig, because he had just seen the security camera stills of the woman in the copy shop I sent over this morning."

She plucked two sheets of photographic paper from the file and handed one to me. "This," she said, "is the best image from the security camera."

I stared at the woman approaching the copier.

"And this is the woman Sergeant Tindle interviewed two months ago, Julie O'Connor."

I glanced at the second photo, held the two images side by side. "We have our killer," I said.

"And you know the best bit? According to police records, as of two months ago, she was working at SupaMart in Bellevue Hill."

Chapter 98

"JESUS! MAGGIE . . . MY favorite madam!" Geoff Hewes exclaimed as the woman in the red silk dress walked in. They were in Geoff's office in the CBD.

She rolled her eyes and helped herself to a chair directly opposite Hewes. In her late fifties, she was heavily made-up, saggy cheeks. She'd clearly lived, and then some.

"Must be important," Hewes added and looked past Maggie through a pair of glass doors toward the reception area. "So how is my Mosman House of Sin? All the pervs having fun?"

"I try to make sure of that," Maggie retorted. "And Geoff, baby, I try to please you too."

He raised an eyebrow, giving her a skeptical look.

"Can't say I'm happy about these bloody cameras going in and out of the place."

"Ah yes, well, we have Mr. Loretto to thank for that. But it won't happen again, Maggie. They're there to stay."

She let out a heavy sigh and held up a DVD.

"What's that?"

"I was unsure what to do with it. It's a film from one of our rooms, recorded just before Mr. Loretto took the cameras out.

I was thinking of chucking it. I didn't want to get into any trouble. But then . . . the man on this –" She waved the DVD in front of her face, "– came back in last night and acted like a right pig."

Geoff was surprised. "Isn't that what the punters pay for?"

"We have a strict house rule," Maggie replied. "No fists. If a John wants that he can find some backstreet slut who's willing . . . not my girls."

"And this guy was violent?'

"He booked one of the prettiest girls, Jill. The bastard fractured her nose, broke two of her teeth, cut her face up. The poor kid won't work for weeks."

"I see. So, you thought . . ."

Maggie handed him the DVD. "Do what you want with it," she said.

Hewes slipped the disc into his computer and tapped a couple of keys. The inside of a room in Maggie's brothel appeared. A bed, a low ceiling. A woman in a corset, high-heels and stockings came into shot and lay on the bed. A man appeared. Geoff couldn't see his face. He flicked forward. The office filled with the sounds of copulation, the man grunting loudly. The prostitute was straddling him now. She moved to one side, and there, lying on his back, was the prominent Liberal MP, Ken Boston.

Chapter 99

GEOFF WAS STARING into space, still a little shocked. Maggie had just left and the DVD case lay open on his desk, the disc still in the machine. Then he reached for the phone.

"Ken Boston's office, please."

A female voice picked up. "Mr. Boston's rooms."

"Good morning," Hewes began. "Could I speak to Mr. Boston, please?"

"Who's calling?"

"Mr. Geoff Hewes."

"From?"

"I'm a Sydney businessman and a constituent."

"Does Mr. Boston know you, Mr. Hewes?"

"Not yet."

"I see. I'm afraid I cannot put you through, but I can convey a message."

Geoff smiled. He hadn't expected anything more. "Okay. Could you please tell Mr. Boston I've called about Chester Street. He'll know what I mean."

A pause. "And what was your name again, Mr . . . ?"

"Hewes. Geoff Hewes. My number is . . ."

Chapter 100

I CHECKED MY watch as we drew up outside the branch of SupaMart in Bellevue Hill. It was just past noon. Mary stood on the sidewalk, pulled on her shades and waited a moment for me to get out of the car and lock it. I led the way to the store, keeping the keys in my hand.

The manager's office was at the back. A girl standing on some steps filling shelves pointed the way.

"Take a seat, take a seat," the manager, Matt Jones, said enthusiastically.

"Obviously bored," I concluded. "Slow day in Bellevue Hill."

"We're looking for Julie O'Connor. Understand she works here."

"Julie? Yeah, she does. Should be here now, but isn't."

"What do you mean?"

"Didn't turn up for her shift this morning." He frowned. "So what's this all about? You cops?"

"No," Mary said. "We're from an investigative agency. We've had a call from one of Julie's relatives," she lied. "An old aunt has died and the family wants to reach Julie."

"Really? So she might be in for an inheritance!"

"Maybe."

"Well of course . . . I understand . . . Mustn't assume anything."

"No," I responded. "You couldn't give us Julie's address, could you? And maybe a phone number?"

Jones looked doubtful for a few moments. "That might not be possible. There's a certain confidentiality . . ."

"Sure," Mary said in her sweetest voice. "It's just the family is *desperate* to get in touch with Julie. She apparently left her relatives in Queensland under a cloud, years back."

"I didn't know that," Jones responded. "Might explain a thing or two."

I gave the guy a questioning look.

"I like Julie, but she's never been the most . . . communicative of my staff. Never made friends with the others. She's a bloody good worker though – that's why I kept her on." He paused. "Okay, I can't give you her number – she doesn't have a phone. But the address . . ." He turned toward a mini filing cabinet on top of his desk. Flicked through the cards. "Yeah, here it is: 6 Neptune Court, Impala Road, Sandsville. Let me know what the outcome is, will you? It would be good to know if Julie will ever be coming back!"

Chapter 101

JULIE WAS SITTING on her threadbare sofa. The TV on, sound off. Beside her lay her scrapbook and a notebook. She picked up the notebook first. She kept this in her overall pocket at work. In many ways, she had the perfect job for her purposes. Working at the checkout of SupaMart in Bellevue Hill each day she would see potential victims. Each day, a parade of spoiled wives of successful Eastern Suburbs bankers, brokers and doctors passed by. These women came into SupaMart Gucci-clad and dripping Tiffany to buy zero-fat milk and goat's cheese with their private-school-uniformed brats. To them, she was either invisible or an object of contempt. She loathed them.

But she had access to their personal details. She had their credit card data, she caught their names when they bumped into their snooty friends and had a little "chat" at the checkout. She noted down everything she heard. The same women, perhaps fifty of them, came in each week, often several times a week. A month of listening and note-taking and she knew a great deal about Samantha, Sarah, Donna, and dozens of others including Yasmin Trent, Stacy Friel, Elspeth Lampard and, of course, Jennifer Granger, the wife of the bastard who'd started it all.

Returning the notebook to the top pocket of the lumber-jack shirt she was wearing, she picked up her scrapbook. She'd devoted a double page to each of the murders, numbered them. 1. JENNIFER GRANGER. 2. STACY FRIEL. 3. ELSPETH LAMPARD. 4. YASMIN TRENT. Beneath these, descriptions of each murder recounted in her scratchy handwriting, every other word misspelled. Interspersed with the words, Julie had pasted in pictures of babies taken from magazines.

In the middle pages, she'd itemized everything she'd learned at SupaMart . . . credit card numbers, addresses, friends' names, husbands' details, where they worked, kids' schools. All of it had been routinely transferred from the notebook, keeping the original as a backup.

She flicked through the pages of the scrapbook, studying all the information she'd transferred over the months. "Tabatha," Julie said aloud. "Married to Simon, a 'very handsome' broker at Stanton Winslow. Address: 8 Frink Parade. Four kids . . . Shit! Busy girl!" Turning the page . . . "Mary, ah, nice Catholic girl, Mary. Irish ancestry, no less. Works for a local charity – 'Homes for Rejected Pets'. How lovely! Two kids, Fran and Marcus. Husband, a spinal surgeon at Royal North Shore Hospital . . . tempting, very tempting."

She flicked to the last page. A newspaper article about the murder of Jennifer Granger. Skipped forward. Stopped, read a name at the top of a double-page profile. Let her eyes drift down to the material she had collected on this woman.

"Well, hey . . . looky here," she said in a whisper. "Just

looky here. I'd almost forgotten . . . Oh, that would be perfect!"

She leaned forward, the scrapbook on her lap, turned back to her pages listing the murdered women, flicked to a fresh page and wrote: "NUMBER FIVE." Then a name.

Chapter 102

JULIE SMILED. "SOMETIMES," she thought, "I can't believe how easy all this has been." She switched on a lamp with a pink shade she'd bought for two dollars from a charity shop, swung back round and saw Bruce on the TV screen.

She felt a shiver pass through her and quickly ramped up the sound.

". . . the body has been identified as Bruce Frimmel," the newsreader said, and the camera held the image of the dead man. "He is thought to have disappeared in November and was probably killed soon after . . ."

Julie jumped up at the sound of tires screeching outside. She dashed to the small window of her first-floor apartment and saw a white car pull up hard on the other side of a small scruffy courtyard.

She snatched up the scrapbook, ran into the bedroom, tossed it on the bed, scrambled in the bottom of her wardrobe for her backpack already prepared with the things she knew she would need sometime soon. In the kitchen she found a box of matches, darted back to the bedroom, struck a match and flicked the flame over the end of the scrapbook.

The paper resisted. It felt to Julie that seconds were passing as minutes. She had to quell the rising panic. The match expired without the flame catching properly. She'd just singed the edge of the flimsy cardboard cover. She struck another match and steadied her fingers by gripping her wrist with the other hand, blowing gently on the flame.

It caught. She couldn't wait a second longer, dashed out of the room and into the hallway, leaving the door ajar. She could hear footsteps on the stairs, a woman's voice. She sped up to the second level, round the bend and onto the next flight taking her to the top floor.

She leaned over the railings and saw two people, a man and a woman, approach the door to her apartment. As they slid along the wall and disappeared inside, Julie turned on her heel, pushed the exit door onto the roof.

She'd moved here after splitting with Bruce, it was cheaper. Within a week she'd explored every nook and cranny of the block and had quickly found the caretaker's shed on the roof. He was always careful enough to keep it locked, but she knew where he hid a spare key.

The roof was eerily quiet, just the hum of traffic on the main road, the occasional squawk of a lorikeet. Julie crouched beside a utility pipe running along the edge of the roof, felt around for the brick she knew was there, found it, shifted it, plucked up the key.

She ran back to the shed, slotted the key into the lock, pulled open the door. After the glare of the midday sun the inside of the shed seemed almost black, but her eyes adjusted quickly. She scanned the shelves of jam jars filled with nails and screws, tins of paint, rolls of wire, bits of plastic tubing and a bench scattered with tools. On the floor stood a five-gallon plastic drum, "FLAMMABLE" written in large black letters around the middle. She locked the door from the inside and crouched down, keeping her breathing shallow and listening for approaching feet.

Chapter 103

SANDSVILLE IS PROBABLY the worst part of Sydney. Happen to be there at the wrong time, in the wrong gang in the wrong street and your life expectancy would make a mayfly proud.

Realizing that driving my Ferrari into Sandsville would be about as clever as vomiting over the Queen, Mary and I had taken a detour back to Private and switched to her sensible and unassuming white Toyota.

The apartment blocks of Neptune Court looked as though they would collapse any moment. I guessed they were mid-'80s vintage. There were three buildings clustered around a scrap of land, the grass worn to nothing.

The three buildings had six-foot-high digits written on their south-facing walls. Nos. 1-20, 21-40 and 41-60. We headed for the first.

We could hear a horrible clash of sounds. Kids screaming, a baby's cry, several different TV shows, a rap track. From my right came a bass drum throb and the growl of some God-awful death metal band.

The door into Julie O'Connor's block was closed, but the

steel-reinforced glass had been smashed in. I climbed through the hole, Mary half a second behind me.

Number 6 was on the first floor, but I smelled the smoke before I'd reached halfway up the flight of stairs. Mary went ahead, leaned on the wall next to the door, then swung inside. I was right behind her. She turned into the living space, swept the room, proceeded to the only other part of the apartment, a tiny bedroom.

Yellow flames swirled up from blackened sheets. The fire was small – a pile of papers, but smoke had filled the room. We grabbed a pillow each and smacked at the fire, then I found a quilt on the floor, threw it over the small blaze and snuffed it out.

"This was just started," Mary said.

"Must've missed her by seconds. You search the place. I'll be back in a minute."

I ran onto the landing. No one around. I noticed half the doors were boarded up. There were two more floors above this one. I ran up, saw no one, reached the top floor. There was a ROOF EXIT sticker on a door. The door had been pushed outward.

I approached it cautiously, eased out onto the roof. It was deserted. I spotted a workman's shed in one corner, paced over to it slowly, carefully. I tried the handle. It was locked.

I did a three-sixty, saw the black metal railings of a ladder descending from one corner. Walking across the roof, I peered over the edge. The ladder dropped three floors to the ground. No one in sight.

Chapter 104

I FOUND MARY sitting at a kitchen table that was shoved up against the wall between the stove and an ancient fridge. She'd pulled on latex gloves and was leafing through a clutch of charred papers.

"Something I picked up from Darlene. Always handy . . . if you'll pardon the pun," she wiggled her fingers at me. "Here." She fished out a second pair from her cargo pants. Tossed them over. The place still stank really bad.

"Tried to open a window," Mary said. "Sealed tight." She flicked a glance toward a small window along the wall near the bedroom. "Checked every cupboard. No one in any hidey-holes. Looks like Julie O'Connor left in a hurry, but there's no sign of a handbag or purse. Found this on the floor over there," Mary added, picking up a five-dollar bill.

"Probably dropped it after snatching notes from this," I replied, indicating a jar lying on its side on top of the fridge. A few coins had been left inside.

"So what'd she set alight?"

"It's hard to tell." Mary nodded at the crispy papers. "Some of it's just burned to nothing." She pointed to a pile of black, fire-ravaged paper, then carefully shifted through a few pages of what looked like some sort of a scrapbook. "Don't want to damage it more, Darlene'll kill me!" she commented. Prising it open about halfway through, she glanced at the pages.

I walked round and peered over her shoulder. There was a scorch mark running across the paper. "Personal info, descriptions," I said. "That set of numbers halfway down the left side." I hovered a finger over the damaged papers. "List of credit card numbers . . . always sixteen digits, batches of four."

Mary nodded, turned a page carefully. "She's headed each double page with a woman's name."

I felt a tingle pass up my spine as I saw the name at the top of the first pair of pages. Elspeth Lampard. "Alright," I said. "Let's bag this stuff. Get it to Darlene." I glanced round to search for a plastic container. That's when we both heard, from the hallway, the sound of smashing glass.

Then a loud "whoosh".

Chapter 105

THE FIRE SHOT along the short, narrow hallway like the jet from a flame-thrower. "A Molotov!" I yelled above the roar of the blaze.

Mary was up in a flash, her chair flying across the kitchen floor as she ran for the bedroom. I scanned the room desperately and spotted a plastic trash bag scrunched up beside a garbage bin. I plucked it up. Moving as fast as I could, I scooped the material on the table into the bag, then tucked it inside my jacket.

Before I'd finished, Mary was back in the living-room clutching a pair of blankets. The flames from the hall had spread, tendrils reaching toward the ceiling of the main room. A tatty sofa close to the hall end had caught fire, the cheap foam adding to the stench as it melted.

Mary ran over to the sink, pulled on both taps, twisting them to "max". "Got to wet the blankets!" she hollered and threw them under the running water. I caught a sodden blanket. Following Mary's lead, I ducked my head under the stream of tap water. Then I wrapped the wet blanket about my shoulders, across my front, letting the bottom edge knock against my shins.

"Go!" I bellowed, and without wasting another second, I ran straight for the flames and the hallway.

The fire had engulfed half the living-room. I could sense Mary a foot behind me as we stumbled into the hallway.

The heat from the fire hit me like flames from hell. I knew I had to keep running. The floor was alight, scorching my shoes.

Gripping the blanket, I reached for the latch and twisted. It was locked.

I felt panic rise up in my chest. It was getting hard to breathe. I turned to Mary. I'd never seen her scared before. Then we both reached the same decision at the same moment and charged forward, slamming into the door together.

I heard the wood splinter and managed to stagger back. My chest was screaming at me. My feet felt like I was walking barefoot on hot coals, but I knew that if I didn't keep going we would both die.

Mary obviously thought the same thing. We ran for the door again. A pain shot across my shoulders and up my neck. The door gave, but only opened a fraction. We charged a third time, the sense of desperation growing. The door fell outwards, and I collided with Mary as we crashed onto the concrete landing.

We pulled ourselves up but I tripped on the blanket, falling heavily against a door on the other side of the landing. Shrugging off the pain, I tossed the blanket aside and felt something hit me hard across the face and chest. I looked up and saw Mary leaning over me beating out a line of fire with her blanket, yellow flames searing across the front of my shirt.

Chapter 106

WE STAGGERED OUT onto the smudge of ground between the buildings. I was leaning forward, hands on my knees, gasping for air. A couple of teenagers saw us and ran over. Mary was coughing from her gut and then she spun round and vomited. I saw the first guy approach as I straightened and felt a terrible pain in my jaw. I stumbled back and caught a glimpse of the other kid as he jumped on Mary's back.

Before I could take in that the bastard had hit me, he swung his fist again. I dodged it, lashed out and caught him on the side of his face.

I heard a crash from behind and saw the kitchen window of Julie O'Connor's apartment shatter outwards, a great sheet of flame spewing out. The teenagers were distracted and Mary had recovered amazingly quickly. She whirled round, a string of vomit running down her vest top, threw the teenager clinging to her back straight over her head. He crashed to the ground, face first. I landed a second punch to the side of the other kid's face and Mary connected her right boot with his balls. He doubled up, moaning.

I noticed the bandage around Mary's hand was bloodied.

"You alright?" I gasped almost inaudibly.

"Felt better, Craig. You?"

I started coughing and couldn't stop for at least ten seconds, then groaned. Fire alarms in the apartments began to wail.

Mary had plucked her cell from her pocket. She nodded toward the car as she called 000. We ran over, leaving the two thugs groaning in the dirt.

From the corner of my eye I saw a group of people run out of the building.

Mary was giving instructions into the receiver as we crossed the patch of ground. I was limping like an injured footballer leaving the field and totally in awe of how incredibly fit and powerful Mary was. She was recovering so fast.

It was only as we got fifteen feet from the Toyota we realized all four tires had been slashed.

Chapter 107

JULIE O'CONNOR CAUGHT the train from Sandsville, headed for the CBD. She had close to two hundred bucks in her pocket and a stolen credit card. She had formulated a plan.

She thought about the apartment she'd destroyed. There was nothing there of value. She had nothing, nothing but her notebook, the bag she had with her, the two hundred bucks and a credit card. She still felt the buzz, the thrill she had experienced – making the petrol bomb from the materials in the shed, tossing it into the apartment, descending from the roof of her block using the metal ladder and slipping away in the commotion.

Ten minutes into the journey she left her seat, walked calmly past a family in the next aisle and into a corridor. Pulled open the door to the washroom.

Yanking her backpack from her right shoulder, she let it drop to the floor. Leaning down, steadying herself as the train swayed, she found the plastic bag she'd put in the bag earlier. She placed it on the small sink.

Pulling out a dark wig, a fake moustache and a baseball cap, she arranged them on the side. Tugging on the wig, she tucked a few loose strands of bleached blonde hair beneath the edge, found the tube of glue she'd purchased, ran a line of it along the back of the moustache and put it in place. Then she tugged on the cap. Looking at her reflection in the mirror, she had to smile.

She was wearing jeans, boots and her lumberjack shirt. She turned to her handbag, pulled out the roll of banknotes – real ones – three fifties plus a twenty, a ten and a few coins. There was a second roll wrapped in an elastic band – ten fifties, photocopied money . . . ready for later.

She then removed the stolen credit card, a packet of mints and her favorite baby picture, one she had salvaged from her scrapbook. It showed a real cute kid – about nine months old – a girl wearing a nappy. She had an adorable fat tummy and was crawling toward the camera, a big smile on her face.

Julie stuffed all these items into the pockets of her jeans, opened the window of the washroom and tossed out her hand-bag. Then she checked herself in the mirror again and brushed a stray bit of wig under the cap. Taking a deep breath, she leaned into the mirror, real close, her face filling her view. She bared her teeth. "You can do this, Julie O'Connor," she hissed. "You can do this . . . *baby*!"

Chapter 108

"JUST IN FROM one of our cars out in the Western suburbs, sir," said Sergeant Tim Frost. He handed a sheet of paper to Inspector Mark Talbot. "Thought you might find it interesting."

Talbot scanned the report and grinned, touched the Steri-strip across his nose. Craig Gisto had almost been barbecued, then beaten up by a couple of teenagers in Sandsville.

"He's not in the Serious Burns Unit of the Royal North Shore by any chance?"

"Not this time, sir," the sergeant replied.

"Shame," Talbot remarked under his breath. Glanced at his watch. "Hell. I'm late." Turning, he strode down the hallway.

He crept into the conference room just as Brett Thorogood was about to start talking, found a seat and manned out Thorogood's glare.

There was a buzz of excitement in the room. Even Talbot could sense it. This is why he'd joined the force – a man-hunt, well, a woman-hunt in this case. He felt his heart beat faster.

"This is the suspect," Thorogood announced pointing to a large photo of Julie on the smart-board. "A snap taken when she started work at SupaMart."

"Hideous bitch," Talbot thought.

"Don't have much on her," The Deputy Commissioner went on. "Name: Julie Ann O'Connor. Age: 26. Current address: 6 Neptune Court, Impala Road, Sandsville. No record. So far, so ordinary. Her father was a cop, Jim O'Connor . . . killed in the line of duty in 1996. She disappeared in 2000, off the radar until 2004. Cropped up in State records as a cleaner for a small engineering firm, Maxim Products, Campbelltown. Our friends at Private have come up with some useful stuff."

Talbot felt a knot in his gut. He couldn't bear even hearing the word "Private".

The DC clicked a remote and footage from the copy shop came on screen.

"Appears the woman is underprivileged, lives in a slum, works in one of Sydney's most affluent areas. Some sort of motive for her killings we suppose. She copies the banknotes using a couple of different copy shops near Bellevue Hill."

"Underprivileged?" Talbot said and looked around at the five other officers in the room.

"Yes," Thorogood replied. "Your point?"

He had none, just hated the term. The stupid bitch was a complete klutz. Didn't she know you could photocopy at home on a printer? But she probably didn't have a computer, big satellite TV dish, for sure, but no computer. She'd probably never touched one, had no clue. Douche bag.

Thorogood was talking again. "Private have confirmed a positive DNA match to place this woman at two of the murder scenes for sure. She was also in a long-term relationship with the male victim, Bruce Frimmel, whose DNA was found at the same murder scene as Jennifer Granger. Both bodies were found in the yard of the house on Ernest Street, Bondi."

Talbot wanted to retch. That word again. Private. Thank God it had been one of his boys who'd put the pieces of the puzzle together, matching the photos of the O'Connor bitch.

"Where is this Julie O'Connor now, sir?" It was Chief Inspector Mulligan, Talbot's immediate superior. He was leaning back in his chair, arms folded across his chest.

"Good question. We don't know. But we will. I've just heard that about an hour ago Craig Gisto and Mary Clarke from Private almost caught O'Connor at her apartment in Sandsville. They were lucky to escape with their lives though, the bloody woman fire-bombed the place with them inside."

Mark exhaled loudly. Thorogood gave him an odd look.

"I'm pulling out all the stops," the Deputy Commissioner went on. "Closing the airports, putting up roadblocks ringing the city, every spare man out on the streets. We'll get her, and when we do, she'll live out her days in a ten-foot square cell."

"Not if I get her first!" Talbot thought.

Chapter 109

IT WAS BUSY in the CBD. Julie glanced at her cheap digital watch: 5.03 pm. She'd left the apartment hours earlier, thrown in the Molotov, slashed the car tires. Now she was walking around town dressed as a man, feeling increasingly confident. No one seemed to bat an eyelid. She just merged . . . merged into the pool of humanity. She knew she was not like *them*, not like *them* at all. She was a different breed to the people she brushed shoulders with, different to the ones she stared at, the ones who merely glanced at her.

They all had homes to go to, people who loved them, people they loved. They had lives, careers. Julie had nothing . . . and for the first time ever she actually felt liberated. Free. Totally, totally free. She was her own powerhouse. She could do anything. She could even be a he!

Chapter 110

GEOFF WAS PULLING his Audi A6 onto King Street in the CBD when his cell rang. He pushed the button of the Bluetooth and a voice familiar from TV and radio came into his car.

"May I speak to Mr. Hewes, please?"

"Mr. Boston. Nice of you to call back."

A silence. Hewes kept quiet.

"What is all this about?"

"Well you see, it's like this, Mr. Boston. I have a rather entertaining video clip of you and a young lady who, I'm pretty sure, is not your wife."

Another long silence.

"And?"

Geoff grinned and looked out the window at the pedestrians streaming past. "Fucker thinks he's so cool," he thought.

"Well," Hewes said slowly, deliberating on each word. "I think that perhaps this clip is worth rather a lot of money. After all, we wouldn't want it to fall into the wrong hands now, would we?"

"Mr. Hewes, I feel it's my duty to warn you. You don't know what the hell you're getting yourself into."

Geoff snorted. "Thank you for your concern, Mr. Boston. I'm touched. But I think I do know what I'm doing. Now, listen to me."

Boston tried to cut over him, but Hewes simply raised his voice. "I think this DVD is worth at least five million dollars. But I am a fair man. I will accept four million delivered to me *in cash* by this time tomorrow." And he pushed the red button on the dash, cutting the call.

Chapter 111

THERE WAS A tap at the door. Johnny looked up from his desk and saw Micky Stevens' girlfriend, Katia, standing at the entrance. She looked even more stunning than the night before. Today she was dressed entirely in white – a long flowing dress that reached the floor, the miniature sword on the pink silk ribbon still about her neck.

Johnny came round the desk. "Katia."

She gave him a faint smile.

"How's Micky?"

"Oh, he's absolutely fine."

"Fine?"

"Up by two this afternoon and off to a rehearsal at three."

"But . . . ?"

Katia gave him a broader smile. "You're pretty naive, aren't you, Johnny Ishmah? That's sweet."

He blushed. "I don't know much about the rock world, but I'm not exactly naive."

"Micky has an incredible constitution, but he keeps Dr. James close by. Graham insists upon it. Micky can't stand the guy. Thinks he's a grossly overpaid . . ."

Johnny perched himself on the edge of the desk. "Last night, you were starting to tell me what you thought about this Club 27 thing."

"Yes. I really don't know what to think anymore. I've been with Micky for six months. He was a user when I met him. He drinks heavily. But . . . you know . . . he's a rock star . . . That's what rock stars do, isn't it? But he's become a lot worse in the last two months."

"And you think that's because he's approaching his twenty-seventh birthday? Or do you think Parker is pushing him into killing himself?"

Katia folded her arms and looked as though she was about to burst into tears. Johnny was shocked for a moment.

"Look, Katia," he said, "last night I saw something."

She fixed him with her huge dark eyes.

"The smack. I saw Parker give it to Johnny just before he went into the bathroom."

Katia exhaled through her nose. "Of course he did," she said, her expression cynical. "Micky was a prize racehorse. He used to be Graham's most valuable asset. Now though, even with his career on the slide, the guy's still Micky's filter for everything . . . even his Class A drugs."

Chapter 112

JOHNNY HAD BEEN tailing Graham Parker for over two hours and he'd ended up here – Kings Cross, the stretch of strip clubs, discos and gambling haunts called The Strip.

Parker had ducked into a joint called The Roxy. Johnny stopped outside, stepped past the bouncer at the door and pulled out his wallet as he approached a woman in a short black dress with a plunging neckline that revealed acres of cleavage. She was sitting on a stool, legs crossed, a cash register on a shelf next to her. A sign on the wall behind her shoulder read: ENTRANCE $50.

Inside, the thump of some nameless dance track, all bass drum and bubbling synthesizer. There was a circular stage, spotlights moving in a crazy random pattern sending splashes of color across a couple of girls wearing G-strings and nothing else. Several punters stood near the edge of the stage looking up at the girls and the glare. A bar in one corner was surrounded by UV lights.

Johnny scanned the room, but it was hard to make anything out. He moved slowly around the edge of the space trying not to make himself obvious to the half dozen men sitting at tables.

He couldn't see Parker. Then he caught movement in the corner of his vision, a man slipping under an arch. A notice to the side said "Private Rooms".

Johnny made his way over, slowed as he reached the arch and took a couple of paces into a narrow corridor lined with closed doors. At the end stood an emergency exit left ajar and opening onto an alley. The music was quieter here, just the thud of the bass drum. He paced along the corridor and heard voices coming from beyond the exit, recognized Parker's voice. He pulled in close to the wall and held his breath, straining to hear what was being said.

Then came a thumping sound, a groan and suddenly Graham Parker was flying toward the emergency exit, grasping the doorframe to break his fall. Johnny couldn't help himself, he reacted instinctively, jumping aside and into full view of the men in the alley.

Chapter 113

JOHNNY TORE THROUGH the doorway and right, into the lane, gaining a few seconds lead before the men realized what was happening.

The alley was dimly lit, the surface cratered with potholes and strewn with garbage. He tripped, almost went down but managed to keep going. He flicked a glance over his shoulder and saw two thugs running toward him through the shadows. Beyond them, the rear lights of a car.

He reached a turning to his left, dived in, sped through the darkness. He could hear the two men had reached the opening and were coming after him, gaining on him.

Johnny's heart was thumping, sweat ran down his cheeks, but somehow he found some new energy. He ripped along the narrow laneway emerging from the end onto a brightly lit road. People were out with their friends, in restaurants and bars. He could merge in maybe. But these guys would get him somehow. It was their turf.

Directly across the street, a dark entrance to another alley. He darted across the road, barely looking where he was going. A driver blasted his horn, Johnny swerved, gained speed and flew into the passageway. But the men were faster, they crashed into the lane a few yards behind him. Johnny put on a final burst of speed, reached the end, a T-junction. He swung left and tripped, hitting the ground with a spine-jarring crunch.

Chapter 114

THEY WERE ON his back in an instant, pulling him to his feet. One of them stepped away, the other rammed Johnny against the wall, hand at his throat.

"A bit nosy, aren't we, kid?"

Johnny stared into the man's face. He had a shaved head, big brown, malevolent eyes that searched his questioningly.

"I was just leaving the place."

"Yeah, sure."

"Look, I'm not interested in what you were saying."

The other guy laughed, took a step forward. The first man loosened his grip on Johnny's neck, grabbed his left arm, pulled it up hard behind his back making him cry out in pain.

"A little word with the boss, I think," he said and pushed him forward, back to the lane, and then the street beyond.

Thirty seconds later the two men had marched Johnny to the rear entrance to The Roxy, a big car stood in the lane.

Johnny struggled to get away but it was hopeless, the two men had an arm each, gripping him like a vice. They came round the side of the vehicle and the one on Johnny's right opened the door with his spare hand, pushed down on his head shoving him into the car before sliding in beside him. The other guy ran round and jumped into the driver's seat.

"You a little out of breath?" the boss asked, turning to the henchman in the back. "Gave you a run for your . . . Johnny? *Johnny Ishmah?*"

Johnny stared at the boss. He had a flabby face, small black eyes and was wearing a big grin.

"Jerry Loretto!" Johnny said, amazed. "It's been a long time . . ."

Chapter 115

"ALRIGHT YOU TWO . . . piss off," Loretto snapped at his men, and without a word, they stepped out into the alley slamming the doors.

"Well, well!" the boss exclaimed. "Never thought I'd see you again, Johnny. What the hell you doin' here?"

Johnny had regained some composure, took a deep breath. "Could ask the same of you, Jerry. You watching one of your dad's places?"

Jerry snorted. "My own, you cheeky bastard. I'm a big boy now!"

Johnny knew Jerry Loretto was only twenty-four, although he looked at least ten years older. He'd known Jerry at school. Not that Loretto had been at school much. Even then he'd been a petty criminal, a kid gangster, following in the footsteps of his father.

Johnny had studiously avoided Jerry. He was bullied at school because he wanted to get on, do well, get out of the Western Suburbs. Jerry Loretto was one of the school thugs, a thoroughly nasty piece of work even at the age of eleven. But then one day Loretto crossed the path of another tough kid from a neighboring school who had intruded into Jerry's "patch" selling cannabis and ecstasy. Loretto had been jumped, knifed and dumped by the roadside. Johnny had found him and Jerry had begged him not to call an ambulance because he didn't want anyone to know what he'd been up to.

Johnny had helped Jerry get home, and after that, Loretto was his guardian angel. He was never bullied again.

"I'm here on an investigation," Johnny said, a little embarrassed. "I'm a PI."

"What!" Loretto's eyes widened and then he burst out laughing. "Well, I guess that figures, Johnny, you always were a goody-two-shoes," and he slapped him on the back. "You're not investigating me, are you?" he added, eyes narrowing.

It was Johnny's turn to laugh, a nervous edge to it. "Nah, your buddy, Graham Parker."

"That shyster?"

"He manages one of our clients."

"Micky Friggin' Stevens?"

Johnny nodded.

"So what do you want to know about Parker then, Johnny Boy?"

"Well, he's obviously up to his neck in it."

"Up to his eyeballs more like . . . Up to here." And Jerry indicated a level six inches above his head.

"Gambling?"

Loretto nodded. "Stupid bastard must be the worst punter in history, but he don't give up."

"How much does he owe you?"

Jerry frowned, then tapped his nose. "Client confidentiality," and laughed loudly. "Let's just say *a lot*."

"And you've given him an ultimatum?"

"One he probably can't meet."

Johnny nodded. "He really is up to here . . ." He imitated Loretto's earlier gesture.

"Oh yes, Johnny Boy. I wouldn't want to be in his shoes in three days' time."

Chapter 116

I GOT THE call from the hooker Ruthie just as I was dropping Justine off at her hotel. The girl sounded nervous as hell and at one point I thought she'd change her mind and hang up.

"Can we meet?" I said.

"Where?"

"There's a bar in Crows Nest, The Corporal Jones."

"I know it."

"I could be there in half an hour."

I lowered the phone and turned to Justine. "That was the prostitute I met at the place in Chester Street. Wants to talk."

"Let's go then."

We got there on time and sat nursing glasses of insipid pub wine for almost twenty minutes before Ruthie showed. She saw us at a table by a window and walked over.

I did the introductions and fetched the girl a double vodka and tonic, then waited for her to start talking.

"This business with the cameras," she began, looking from

me to Justine and back. "Can't handle it no more. Something's going on at work. It smells rotten. I want out."

"I can understand that," Justine commented.

"Can you?" Ruthie replied sarcastically.

Justine took a sip of wine.

"Is that why you called me?" I asked.

The girl gave me a hard look. "I want five hundred bucks."

"Do you now!"

"I think when you've heard what I've got to say you'll think it's cheap."

"Go on."

She had a hand out on the table, palm up.

I took out my wallet as surreptitiously as I could. I'd suspected something like this would happen and stopped at an ATM on the way over. I pulled out a handful of fifties. "Two hundred now," I said. "Two hundred more if I consider your information important enough."

She snatched the notes and gulped her vodka and tonic, looking around as she swallowed. "A few nights ago, I had a client I recognized from TV. He's a politician, seen him on the news. He was in several nights in a row just before the cameras were taken out. I recorded one of the sessions."

"Do you know his name?" Justine asked.

She shook her head. "Called himself Pete, but I know that's crap."

"Describe him," I said.

"He's a big, rough bastard. I was lucky. The night after he was with me he beat up one of the girls. He's banned now. He's old . . . about forty. A big fat thing, spiky silver hair. I noticed he had a bit of a limp."

I stared at the girl, shaking my head slowly.

"What?"

"You've just described the government minister, Ken Boston."

Chapter 117

WE SAW RUTHIE to a cab and walked quickly back to my car. Closing the door, I pulled out my cell and punched in Pam's number. No response. I went to put in her home number, saw Justine staring at me and put the phone down.

"I was calling Pam," I said, "but maybe it's not the smartest . . ." Then I came to a snap decision. Turning the key in the ignition, the car sprang to life. I hung a right onto the main road in the direction of the freeway.

"Where are we going?" Justine asked.

"The Hewes' house is only ten minutes from here."

Chapter 118

GEOFF WAS SO drunk it was a minor miracle he made it home without totaling his car or failing a breath test. He'd started drinking that afternoon after speaking to Ken Boston.

Pam had also gotten through half a bottle of red. She saw him walk a little unsteadily into the lounge and just knew there would be trouble. She took it carefully. "Hi, darling." She pecked him on the cheek. "You eaten?"

Geoff shook his head. "Not hungry, babe." He sounded excited.

"You look pleased, honey. What's happened?"

"Oh, just the biggest break I've ever had, Pam."

She stared warily at his back as he walked over to the drinks cabinet, poured himself a generous whiskey and meandered back to the sofa, swirling the drink in the glass.

"So, you going to tell me?" she asked enthusiastically, and sat in the opposite sofa, leaning forward, arms folded on her knees. She realized Geoff was actually more drunk than she had at first thought.

"You know Al Loretto? Big businessman?" he began.

Pam nodded. "Heard of him."

"Yeah . . . I should think you have. He's a huge name. I do

some work for him from time to time. Anyway, he knows lots of influential people."

Pam nodded and kept looking keen.

"Some of the guys he knows have been . . . well, indiscreet."

"How?"

Geoff waved his free hand in front of him. "Oh, don't worry about that, babe. Let's just say, Al has evidence, which I helped him get."

Pam said nothing.

"Any . . . way," Geoff started to say, thought better of it and stood up to refill his glass. Back on the sofa with another half-full tumbler, he took a gulp. "Anyway, because I helped, Al Loretto is cutting me in for a percentage."

"Darling," Pam said evenly. "Don't you think that's dangerous?"

Geoff's expression darkened. "What d'ya mean?"

"It sounds dodgy . . . well, it's blackmail, actually."

He screwed up his face. Pam took a gulp of wine, eyeing her husband over the rim of the glass. Her mind was racing. She had quickly put two and two together. The camera scam had netted someone big.

"Geoff, I know what you're talking about. And I know Al Loretto is more than a businessman."

"Oh?" He gave her a nasty look. "You do, do you?" He pulled himself up.

"Sit down, Geoff!" Pam snapped and emptied her glass.

"No. I won't sit down! Who the hell do you think you're talking too?

Pam stared him out.

He refused to acknowledge her for several moments, twirled the contents of the tumbler, then slowly sat down.

"What's got into you? I know about the brothels. I know you've upset Loretto. But you won't let it go, will you? Now you tell me you're blackmailing someone?"

"Not just anyone," Geoff spat. "Only Ken Boston!"

Pam glared at him. "Are you *insane*? You've become obsessed with money."

Hewes closed his eyes for a moment, took a deep breath. "I'm obsessed? Obsessed! Of course I'm obsessed, you stupid bitch! How do you think I find the money for the private schools? How do I pay for your clothes, your fancy shoes, your $2,000 handbags . . . the holidays in Phuket?"

"I work."

"*Hah*!" he spat.

"Geoff, I . . ."

He was up again, his whiskey tumbler flying through the air, its contents spraying across the floor as it went. It shot past Pam's right ear missing her by an inch. Before she had time to recover, Geoff was round the coffee table.

She managed to half-rise, half-slide along the sofa, but her husband was too fast for her. He was on her in a second. "You fucking ungrateful bitch!" he yelled and slammed a fist into the side of her face, sending her sprawling. She pulled up a cushion to protect her face and curled up in a ball. Geoff's fists rained down. "Bitch . . . Stupid, stupid bitch!"

There was a noise from the doorway. It cut through Pam's muffled cries and Geoff's profanity. He spun round. Their seven-year-old daughter, Sophia, was standing across the room, screaming. Next to her stood her nine-year-old brother, Sam, his face ashen.

Chapter 119

GEOFF STRAIGHTENED AND walked across the room to the doorway. The children shrank back in terror and he felt a momentary pang of guilt and hurt. Then his anger welled up again. He heard Pam pulling herself up from the sofa and he grabbed the children, shoving them into the hall.

"Come on, kids, we're going away for a little while."

"But Mommy!" Sam protested, jerking back toward the room.

Geoff ignored the boy. "Mommy needs some time on her own," he said, maneuvering the kids across the hall.

Pam reached the doorway. "WHAT ARE YOU . . . ?" she was yelling. "WHERE . . . ?"

Geoff and the children were at the front door. He yanked it open and herded them out. Pam was across the hall in seconds, but the door was closing. She reached out for the gap. Her husband pulled on the handle, hard, trapping his wife's fingers.

They could hear Pam's scream of pain from outside and both kids started to cry uncontrollably. Geoff had his car keys in his pocket. He clicked the remote and pushed the children into the backseat of the Audi. Sam was protesting. He went to hit his father as Sophia scrambled across the seat to the far door.

"Don't," Geoff Hewes snapped. Then more gently . . . "Look, Mommy's okay, but we have to go away."

Sophia stared at him, shaking with terror. Geoff slammed shut the backdoor and stepped away.

He heard a crunch on the gravel of the driveway, turned and swayed.

The baseball bat seemed to come out of the darkness from nowhere. Geoff saw it complete the last few inches of its journey as it smashed into his forehead sending him crashing onto the hood of his car.

He heard the children squeal and felt a second smack to his left temple. He couldn't move, just lay there as the blows kept coming. He heard his own skull crack open, caught the spray of blood out of the corner of his eye. A terrible tremor of pain shot down his spine. He gasped and the smell of blood flooded his shattered nose, the taste of it in his mouth.

And then he died.

Chapter 120

JUSTINE AND I were almost at the end of Simeon Street, about to turn right from Military Road, when I saw a large figure running from the driveway of No. 20.

Pulling into the street, I parked at the curb and yanked on the handbrake. We both heard screams and jumped out of the car, sprinted ten yards along the sidewalk toward the Hewes' house and turned onto the gravel.

The driveway was like a scene from a *Saw* movie. Geoff Hewes lay face up, the side of his head smashed in. He was clearly dead, his blood spattered all over the front of the car. Two young children were in the back screeching hysterically.

We ran to the rear doors. The kids couldn't move, couldn't stop screaming. I managed to pull Sam out and told him to go to the house. The boy was spasming with terror.

I whirled back to the car and saw Justine on the other side, opening the rear door and cupping the little girl under her knees and shoulders, lifting her out. I took her from Justine and we headed for the house.

It was only then that I heard whimpering from the hall. The door was open a crack. Still cradling Sophia, I opened the door with my foot and lowered the little girl to the step. I saw Pam sitting inside, rocking, her broken fingers out in front of her, tears streaming down her bruised face.

The two kids ran into the house, almost falling onto their mother. Pam tried to hold them, but her hands were smashed up.

"What in God's name's happened?" Justine exclaimed, running over to the injured woman.

I reached for my cell.

Pam could barely speak. Her children clung to her, terror in their faces, eyes wide, tear-streaked cheeks.

"Daddy's dead!" Sam cried.

"*What?*" Pam stared at the boy, then up at me.

"We need to get you an ambulance, Pam." I stabbed 000.

"Craig? What's happened?" Pam croaked.

I ignored her. "Emergency . . . Simeon Street. Number 20. One fatality and a seriously injured woman . . . Yes." I glanced over to Pam and saw the horror in her eyes. Justine had an arm about her shoulder. "Yes," I said again. "Get here quick!"

Pam was trying to pull herself up. Justine helped her.

"Listen to me." I took a step forward and turned Pam's face to mine. "Geoff's dead, Pam. I have no idea what –"

"NO!" she screamed. "NO!" Pulling away, she glanced at the kids for a second, staggered to the front door and out onto the driveway.

Even in the subdued light from the street she could make out Geoff's misshapen head and contorted body, the blood. She fell onto him where he lay on the hood, her own physical pain suddenly numbed. Then she pushed her head down into his abdomen and began to wail.

Chapter 121

IT WAS 10 pm and Darlene was alone in Private HQ. She kept unsociable hours, always had. She'd been one of those students who worked during the night and slept until 3 pm.

She walked over to a large metal bench dominating the center of the lab. Above her hung a powerful light bleaching the work surface. On the counter lay remnants of Julie O'Connor's papers salvaged from the apartment in Sandsville.

She had already spent several hours sifting through the material, sorting it into three piles. Useless ashes, vaguely useful scraps and a small heap of material that might be of some practical use.

This last pile included about a dozen pages of a scrapbook. She glanced through these, turning the pages carefully with latex gloves. It was a peculiar mess. Many of the surviving pages contained pictures of Julie holding babies. Then there were pictures of babies cut from magazines, ads for prams, baby clothes, toiletries.

A few pages on she saw a crude drawing of a nursery. On the following pages, names. A long list, two columns to a page. At the top of the left column, Julie had written "GIRLS". Topping the right column was the word "BOYS". Under these headings were dozens of names, alphabetized, some crossed out and written over, many misspelled.

A set of double pages from the scrapbook had separated from the rest. She saw familiar names. One said: "WHORE NUMBER THREE. ELSPETH LAMPARD," the other: "WHORE NUMBER FOUR. YASMIN TRENT." Beneath this, details of the murders from Julie O'Connor's perspective.

With great care, she leafed through, then stopped suddenly.

On the brightly lit counter lay another double page that had slipped away from the others. She could see three words: "WHORE NUMBER FIVE." Next to that a deep brown scorch mark.

Chapter 122

JULIE WALKED FROM the train station, south along Seymour Avenue and then right into Sebastian Road. She followed this route six days a week, but always early each morning – this way at 7 am – retracing her steps to the station twelve hours later. Today was different. She was walking toward SupaMart at 10.10 pm and she looked like a middle-aged, mustachioed man.

The street was quiet, a residential haven basking in a balmy summer's evening. Ahead, Julie could see the SUPAMART sign lit up above the front window of the store.

She strode straight past the entrance, the rectangle of glass fronting the shop, then down a broad alleyway toward the parking lot at the rear. Hanging a left, she found the darkened doorway into the back of SupaMart. The door was bolted and padlocked.

Julie slotted a key into the padlock, turned it, found a second key for the lower Yale, twisted that, pushed, and the door swung inwards.

She was in a corridor, flicked on the light and a florescent strip spattered into life. Concrete floor, concrete walls, concrete ceiling. She pulled the door closed, took three paces along the passage, stopped at another door bearing a sign: STOREROOM 1.

It was unlocked, the light on. It was filled with stock for the shelves in the store. At 6 am tomorrow, a three-person team would arrive to take the goods out onto the shop floor. Later tomorrow, a truck would arrive to replenish this stock. It was a cycle, a rhythm.

There was a concealed cupboard at the back of the third shelf up from the floor. She had spotted it weeks ago when she was sent to the storeroom to get some detergent. She yanked on the handle. Inside, a few items she'd put there two days ago – clothes, a sleeping bag, a thermos, some basic toiletries.

Julie gathered the things up, unfurled the sleeping bag on to the floor and lay on it. She was used to sleeping rough. After walking out on her evil mother, she'd lived on the streets for four years. She'd been raped twice, had her skull fractured as she slept in a park and almost died on the operating table. No, unlike the stupid, soft bitches she delighted in killing, she knew Julie Ann O'Connor was as tough as iron.

She leaned back against the wall and pulled out her notebook. At the top of a double page close to the back, a name. Beneath this an address followed by a list of people – the woman's family and friends. Then a collection of phone numbers. Last, some notes, a set of things she thought might one day be useful information about the woman she'd targeted: "Favorite restaurants", "Gym address, number", "Habits."

Under "Habits", she'd written: 'This whore likes to run. She runs and she runs . . . silly bitch. She runs around Parsley Bay, a couple of miles from her house. Always the same time – early riser, this babe . . . 6 am. Easy!"

Chapter 123

I LEFT JUSTINE to look after everyone. An ambulance was on its way.

I walked out into the hot night. I'd seen someone run from the driveway as we'd pulled up no more than six or seven minutes ago. There might still be a chance of finding him.

I headed off in the direction the man had run and started to jog along the tree-lined road. I stopped at the end of the street. "This is ridiculous," I said to myself, glanced up and saw a young couple just a dozen yards away. The woman looked distressed. Her partner was on his phone. He looked agitated. I walked over to them slowly. The man turned off his cell.

"What's up?" I asked gently and looked with concern at the woman. She was rubbing her left arm and had a bruise to her right cheek.

"Some madman with a baseball bat came charging along the road toward us. I've just called the cops."

"He hit you?"

She shook her head, the tracks of dried tears on her cheeks.

"Just barged her out of the way," the guy spat. "She smacked her head on the wall . . . there." He pointed to his left. "Bastard . . . if I ever get my . . ."

"Which way did he go?"

The man gave an odd look. "That way . . . Tyson Road . . ."

I sped off without another word.

There was no one about. I dashed past neat suburban homes, white fences, flowerbeds, gate posts. To my right, an unbroken line of cars stood tucked into the curb. Then I stopped abruptly.

Ahead lay a small patch of grass, a kids' playground, the swings motionless, the slide empty in the moonlight. I could just make out a large shape sitting on a park bench.

I approached slowly.

The man was sitting hunched up, his head in his hands. At his feet lay a bloodied baseball bat. He was sobbing loudly, heard me approach, lifted his head, recognized me.

"Craig," the man said between gasps. He was in a bad way.

"Patrick!" It was the bouncer from The Cloverleaf who'd had his life ruined by Hewes. "What happened?"

He didn't reply, just kept sobbing. I couldn't see his face.

"Patrick?"

"I killed him, Craig. I killed him in front of his kids! I didn't know they would be there. But once I started I couldn't . . . Oh Christ!"

I heard the wail of police cars. They screeched to a stop on the road a few yards away.

"It's over now, Patrick," I said and sat down on the bench beside him.

Chapter 124

"HEY, JOHNNY," DARLENE said, looking up from her microscope as her colleague knocked on the open door of the lab.

"What are you up to?" he asked.

"What are *you* up to? It's gone eleven."

"I was bored. Thought I'd come in to do some work. What a sad life I lead!"

Darlene gave him a crooked smile. "So what does that say about me?"

"I judge not!" Johnny had his palms up. "What're you working on?"

She pulled back from the scope. "Take a look."

He peered into the eyepiece. "Means nothing to me."

"And not much more to me," Darlene remarked. "It's part of Julie O'Connor's scrapbook, but it's so badly charred I can't make out the words. I'm getting really pissed with it to be honest."

"Not surprised." Johnny paced over to Darlene's desk. He saw the small pile of invites Software Sam had left yesterday.

"I heard about these," he said, picking up the tickets. "Micky Stevens' party . . . right? Craig mentioned them."

Darlene nodded. "Yeah, that guy . . . friend of Micky's dropped them in. With all the stuff going on here I'd forgotten."

Johnny stared down at the invitations. "It's tonight." He stared into Darlene's eyes.

"Oh, no. I've got . . ."

"Darlene? What is wrong with you?" He walked over, the invitations in his right hand.

"Johnny Ishmah," Darlene said, beaming. "You're not asking me out on a date, are you?"

He flushed red.

"Oh my God! You're blushing!" Darlene said, hand to mouth. "How . . ."

"Don't say cute!"

"Alright . . . *not* cute!"

He smiled. "So, then? What do you think?"

Darlene looked down at the sample under the scope, then back up, shrugged. "What the hell?"

Chapter 125

DARLENE DROVE A '70s VW Beetle she'd lovingly restored. Johnny often reflected on the eccentricities of the woman. She looked like a young Elle Macpherson but loved nothing more than messing around with blood and body parts during the week, only to get her hands black with grease at the weekends. He'd always found it a heady mixture, but knew she was way, way out of his league.

The car chugged through the exit gate of the garage. The security guy smiled and gave her a shy wave.

"Sweet bloke," she said, turning to Johnny. "Insisted he come back to work as soon as he could. Only had a few days off after suffering concussion."

It was 11.32 pm and the sidewalks of the CBD were abuzz. They passed a club on George Street called The Ivy, a line out the door stretching two blocks.

Johnny leaned in toward the radio – an original sixties collectable. Pointed to the machine. She nodded and Johnny nudged down the "On" switch. Classical music flowed from the speaker.

"You ever been to anything like this before?" he asked, picking up the invitations.

Darlene shrugged. "Long time ago."

Johnny knew she'd been a model for almost a year after graduating from university. She didn't like to talk about it much. He assumed it hadn't been a positive experience.

"How do you change channels on this thing?"

"Don't like Monteverdi? . . . The dial."

Johnny slowly turned the knob. He passed through a jazz station, the ABC late program. Then some pop music came on. He went past it, backtracked, tuned it.

"Unreal!" He turned to Darlene.

"What?'

"Only Micky Stevens' new single! Heard a snatch of it earlier today."

"Coincidences do happen." Darlene turned off George Street. They both fell silent for a few moments, listening to Micky's new song.

She hung a right into Castlereagh Street and looked round at Johnny. "Pretty catchy tune . . . What's up?"

He was pale, staring at the radio. Held up a hand. "Sssh! Listen!"

The music swelled, Micky repeated the chorus: *"I just wanna die at midnight in your arms. Like Jimi and Janis and Kurt Cobain too . . . Club 27 charms."*

"What's the time?"

"11.40."

"Darlene! Put your foot down!"

Chapter 126

THEY DIDN'T NEED to wait in line, showed the invites to a huge bouncer at the head of the line. He peered at the papers, stared Darlene and Johnny up and down, nodded to the double doors. As Darlene walked in, she took a closer look at Micky's invitations. In the top right of each she saw the letters: "VIP."

It was a huge club. Music throbbed from powerful speakers. Lights swept and flashed. One vast wall was covered with an early Pink Floydesque display of psychedelic colors.

It was packed. They forced their way across the main floor of the club. Where the hell was Micky?

They reached the bar, leaned in, trying to attract the attention of the barman.

Johnny glanced around, saw Chris Martin from Coldplay talking to Russell Crowe. At the other end of the bar half of INXS shared a joke with Michael Bublé

Darlene wasn't paying much attention. She caught the eye of the bar tender. She was good at doing that.

"Hello, darlin'," he oozed. "What can I interest you in?"

She switched on the charm. "I'm a close friend of Micky's."

"Of course you are, sweetheart!"

She flashed her invite and the guy changed his tone.

"Okay. Cool. So, what do you want, honey?"

"Where's Micky right now?'

The man shrugged. "How should I know?"

"I *really* would like to know," she hissed. "And I *really* think Micky would like me to know too. Get me?"

He straightened. "Upstairs in his suite. 212. Second floor, far end . . . I'd use the stairs, the heads are taking the elevator straight to the washrooms on second." And he tapped his nose.

Chapter 127

MICKY'S SUITE LOOKED like the set of *Satyricon* . . . precisely what would be expected of a rock star on his twenty-seventh birthday. Scantily clad, kohl-eyed women tottered around clasping champagne glasses, a dealer sat in one corner looking pleased with himself, a female dwarf in a tutu carried around a tray heaped with cocaine.

Micky and Katia held court surrounded by admirers. He strummed an acoustic guitar and sang one of his lesser known songs. A spliff dangled from the corner of his mouth.

Hemi filled an armchair close to where the bedroom flowed into a vast lounge. He'd positioned himself there deliberately so he could follow the action. He was drinking his usual sparkling mineral water and nobody spoke to him.

Micky was on the last repeat chorus of his song when he saw Hemi roll forward and collapse to the carpet in a wobbly groaning heap. He stopped strumming immediately, turned to Katia. She hadn't seen the big man crumple, but heard the sound of him reaching the floor. She was first up and across the room. Micky came round the end of the bed still holding his guitar.

Katia crouched beside Hemi and managed to roll him over. He was out cold and began to snore. She raised her head to Micky, and burst out laughing. The rock star looked concerned for a moment but then found it very funny. "Too much sparkling water, Hemi," he mumbled.

Katia stood up and came round to hug Micky. "Let's get outta here."

He looked down at her, eyes swimming. "But it's my party."

"I want to take you somewhere quiet and lick you all over."

Micky giggled stupidly. "Well, that's an offer I ain't gonna refuse . . . am I?"

"Graham's room is empty. He's banned everyone . . ."

"Graham's?" Micky suddenly looked scared.

"Don't worry . . . He's downstairs schmoozing. I got the key earlier from reception . . . I wanted us to see in your birthday together . . . just you and me. I want to protect you. No one can touch you 'til after midnight."

Chapter 128

THEY STUMBLED ALONG the corridor giggling. Reaching the door, Katia slipped the key into the lock, opened the door slowly, pulled Micky inside. Graham Parker was getting up from the end of the bed, a bottle of Bourbon in his hand. He looked smashed, had a split lip and a line of Steri-strips across his cheek.

"Ah!" Katia said.

"Don't mind me," Parker slurred.

Micky began to jabber incoherently pointing at Parker.

"What's he saying?"

Katia shushed Micky and guided him to the bed.

Parker looked at the bottle and frowned, turned it upside down. "Damn!"

"I'll get you something." Katia left Micky sitting up on the bed, his head back on a mountain of pillows. He was gazing at Parker warily. A few moments later, she was walking back from the drinks cabinet with a bottle in one hand, a tumbler almost full to the brim with amber liquid. She handed the tumbler to Parker. He made a grab for the bottle. "Ah ah!" she tutted and took it over to Micky.

Parker pulled himself into an armchair, took a liberal gulp.

"I've got a story," Katia announced. Parker looked at her blearily.

"Oh, I like stories," Micky said, swigging from the bottle.

"There was a pope. I can't remember which one. It was a long time ago, maybe in the tenth century, sometime like that. Anyway, he wasn't a very popular pope and so he decided to go on a tour of all the Papal Dominions to try to buy the favor of his flock with indulgences. He reached Verona on Mid-Summer Day and was dispensing his promises and his money to the people of the city when a woman who was known to be a witch stood up and yelled to the crowd that the pope would die on October 2 that year, just over two months later."

Micky was looking at her rapt as a child being read a bed-time story. Parker had his eyes closed, chin on chest.

"They arrested the woman of course, burned her at the stake in front of the pope. But even though the witch was dead, the pope was terrified by her curse. He returned to Rome imme-diately and tried to put the memory of what had happened in Verona out of his mind. But it was no good. As October 2 approached the pope became more and more agitated. On October 1 he gave strict instructions to his staff and to the car-dinals and locked himself in his private chambers. He would see no one and he would not eat or drink anything until 12.01 the morning of the third.

"The pope's servants followed his every wish and as the clock struck midnight and the second of the month passed into the third the room was unlocked. The elated pope sprung from his bed, walked to the servant, tripped, smashed his head against the leg of a table and died instantly."

Micky looked horrified and was just about to ask something when Parker tumbled to the floor.

"Shit!" the rock star exclaimed. "Another one!" He turned to see that Katia had taken off her pink silk ribbon necklace and had the sharp tip of the tiny sword at his jugular.

Chapter 129

THE STAIRS STOOD at the far side of the dance floor packed with heaving, sweating bodies.

"Must be a back way," Johnny yelled into Darlene's ear.

She glanced at her watch. It was 11.55 pm. "No time." She made for the edge of the crowd, forcing her way between the revelers and the wall of the dance floor. It was almost impossible to move.

Johnny took out his Private ID and squeezed past her. Under the pulsating light show he looked like a plainclothes cop holding up his badge. The sea of humanity parted before him.

He reached the stairs and Darlene almost fell over him. "Neat trick," she said.

The first floor was dimly lit, the noise from below still incredibly loud. A red carpet led along a corridor between a dozen rooms. They ran for the second flight of stairs.

It was quieter, no one around. Then they heard a sound – laughter, a girl squealing. Darlene glanced at her watch: 11.58.

On the far wall a sign: "Suites 208–215", an arrow left. Darlene turned on her heel, headed off, Johnny close behind.

The door to 212 stood ajar. They slowed, turned in and

almost fell over a couple of girls rolling around on the floor kissing passionately.

Johnny and Darlene saw Hemi lying on the floor, arms and legs akimbo.

"That's not good," Darlene said, pointing at the massive Maori. Johnny went up to the first person who'd listen to him and could string two words together, and asked where Micky was. Darlene ran through the bedroom into the lounge and on to the second bedroom. The bed was a tangle of limbs, groans and moans audible above the music coming from a beat-box in the corner.

After checking Micky wasn't one of the bodies on the bed she did a one-eighty, charged back into the main bedroom.

"Anything?" she asked Johnny.

"Nope. That lot down the corridor . . . the druggies in the washroom, the bar tender mentioned. Maybe they know something."

"Or Micky's with them."

They tore along the plush carpet, careered around a corner, pulling up just short of an elderly Asian maid pushing a cart filled with toiletries. She was wearing earplugs.

"Whoa!" she shrieked and pulled out the earplugs, grimacing at the noise.

"Sorry," Darlene said. "Can you help? We're looking for Micky Stevens."

"Who?"

"The pop star?"

"Never 'eard of him," the maid said irritably. "Just can't stand this awful noise." She paused. "Oh, I know who you mean! It's his party . . . right?"

Darlene nodded.

"He's got Suite 212. Terrible mess he always makes."

"He's not there."

"I saw him only a few minutes ago. He went off with a girl."

Johnny stepped forward. "Tall, skinny, black hair?"

The maid nodded. "They went that way. The older man . . . his boss."

"Micky's manager?"

"Whatever you call him . . . his room is down there . . . 215."

Chapter 130

THEY RAN AT full pelt along the corridor. The door to 215 was locked. Johnny whipped a penknife from his pocket. Darlene stood aside as he levered up a blade and slid it into the lock. He twisted it right, left, back, then left again. They heard a click and the door opened.

Katia was on the bed crouching over Micky, her black eyes almost supernaturally huge. The rock star looked petrified, rigid, eyeing the tiny but deadly sword at his throat.

It took Darlene and Johnny a second to absorb it all. They saw Micky's manager, Graham Parker, unconscious on the floor.

"What's happening?" Johnny asked, trying to keep his voice as calm as he could.

"Yeah . . . what *is* happening?" Micky slurred. He had sobered up out of sheer terror, but his voice hadn't caught up.

Katia blew the singer a kiss. "Dear Micky," she said softly. "You see . . . just like all pop stars, you could never keep your cock in your pants, could you?"

"What?"

"You probably don't even remember her, do you?"

"Remember who, Katia?"

"In 2010 Fun Park played a gig in Moscow. You must remember that!"

"Yeah."

"After the show you met a young girl."

"I've met a lot of . . ."

"Don't!" Katia yelped and moved her hand forward a fraction.

Micky's fists clenched. "Agh!"

"Oh stop being a baby!"

Micky took a couple of deep breaths. He was sweating profusely. "You bitch!"

She blew him another kiss and smiled sweetly. "I mention the girl because . . ."

"What fucking girl?" Micky turned his eyes to Johnny and Darlene and gave them an imploring look.

"That girl was my sister, Anais. You got her pregnant."

"What! I didn't . . ."

"You didn't what, Micky? Didn't screw her? 'Cos I know you did."

"I had no idea . . ."

"She wrote to you. She tried to contact you. Never a single reply. You discarded her, simply brushed her off." Katia was staring down at the singer, her face contorted, eyes ablaze. Johnny and Darlene knew they could do nothing.

"Katia," Micky pleaded. "Please . . . I didn't know. No one told me. Maybe I can help now . . ."

"She's dead, Micky. Died having a backstreet abortion."

There was a stillness in the room. No one spoke.

"I'm so sorry," Micky began.

"Sorry?"

"I didn't know . . ."

"Anais suffered so much." A tear slithered down Katia's cheek.

Micky moved in the bed and placed his hands gently on Katia's cheeks, wiped away the tears. He looked into her eyes. "I really am . . ."

For a second, Katia began to respond, closed her eyes, went to kiss the pop star. But then she jolted, eyes snapped open. She shoved him back, the tiny dagger at his vein again.

"I could have killed you anytime, Micky, but I wanted you to *suffer*. I instilled in your mind the idea of you joining Club 27 a few months ago – you've been too stoned to remember that. And, I could also blame it all on Parker. I made you think that too."

Time was running out . . . both Johnny and Darlene sensed it. Katia had suddenly gone frighteningly calm. She leaned back slightly. They could see her tighten her grip on the miniature sword.

There was a movement from behind the woman. Darlene and Johnny managed to stay still, to show no reaction.

Katia flicked them a glance. "I have to kill him, you see," she said, now way too calm. "An eye for an eye . . . and I loved Anais."

She went to push her hand forward and Graham Parker's fist swung round. Katia reacted fast, ducked and shot her hand out away from Micky's throat, running the tiny blade across Parker's face. He yelped, fell back, hands to his face, blood gushing between his fingers.

Katia was off the bed, ramming straight into Darlene,

knocking her into Johnny with surprising force. Johnny grabbed for Katia as he tumbled, but she sidestepped him and was through the door out into the hall.

Chapter 131

"DARLENE, STAY HERE. Call 000." Johnny snapped, turned and headed after Katia.

She'd vanished, but there weren't that many places she could run to. Johnny turned a corner and saw the woman slam open the door to Micky's suite. He heard screams from the room and ran after her.

She was like a storm trooper plowing through the party sending people flying left and right. She turned, saw Johnny no more than ten feet behind her and lashed out. A woman fell to the carpet, smashing her head on a chair leg. Katia almost tripped over Hemi who had been left to sleep on the floor.

For a second she didn't seem to know what to do. Then she reached for a champagne bottle, smashed it on a table, gripping it in her right hand. She spun round. Half the people were so stoned they moved like zombies. A few looked petrified. Katia grabbed the closest girl to hand, a naked waif with cocaine powdered over her tiny breasts. The kid screamed as she was pulled back and Katia held the jagged spikes of the shattered champagne bottle to the girl's slender neck.

"Get back!" Katia bellowed as Johnny approached.

Someone killed the music and the place fell silent.

"What are you doing, Katia?" Johnny said, taking a step toward her.

The woman was wreathed in sweat, her eyes black and wild, hair stuck to her exquisite face.

"This isn't you, Katia."

"Get back I said. NOW!"

"Katia." Johnny stopped and crouched down a few feet in front of her. Across the room a woman began to sob.

"This is a young kid," he said, flicked his eyes toward the terrified girl. "Just like your sister . . . Just like Anais."

"You don't know anything about Anais," she spat.

Johnny had his hands up. "I know she suffered. You said so yourself."

Katia screamed suddenly. "Shut up! I don't want to hear it." She went to move her hand to cut the girl's face to shreds. Johnny dived forward, grabbed the Russian woman's hand with his left and smashed his right fist into her gut.

She lost grip on the bottle, the girl slumped to one side and Katia groaned but kept on her feet, stumbling backwards. Johnny rushed forward, smacked her across the face, hard. She flew across the room like a swatted insect, slammed into a cabinet of glass shelves bringing the whole lot down on top of her, shards cascading all around her still body.

Chapter 132

THE COPS WERE called and Micky Stevens' twenty-seventh birthday party came to an inglorious close. Katia was taken into custody. Micky went with Graham Parker in the ambulance to St Vincent's Hospital.

It wasn't until 3.30 that Darlene pulled away in her Beetle to take Johnny to the station in the CBD. He had five minutes to catch the first morning train home.

"Fantastic work tonight, Johnny," Darlene said as they walked toward the ticket machine. "We make a great team," and she pecked him on the cheek.

He blushed.

"You're doing it again, dude!" Darlene laughed.

He turned and went for the stairs down to the platform, raising his hand as a wave goodbye, his back to her, a big smile on his face.

Darlene strode to her VW parked just outside the station and sat behind the wheel staring silently at the tall, shadowy towers, the leafy, deserted avenue ahead running toward the bridge. She hadn't felt so alive for a long time. Sleep was absolutely out of the question.

Chapter 133

EVERYTHING IN THE lab was as Darlene had left it over four hours earlier. On the central counter lay the collection of singed papers and piles of crispy, black remnants from Julie O'Connor's scrapbook. A few feet above it hung the microscope.

She slipped on her lab coat, took her glasses from the right pocket and stared into the eyepiece, pulling over the last page she'd viewed earlier, the words "WHORE NUMBER FIVE". The name wiped by fire, the entire page brown.

"Superficial burn though," Darlene noted to herself, "which makes it all the more frustrating. If only . . ." Her mind was racing. She could try solvents. "No . . . too dangerous," she said to herself. "Might destroy the thing entirely. Ultraviolet?" she whispered. "What about ultraviolet?"

She pulled up a chair and sat down, hand to chin. Sighed heavily. "No . . . wouldn't work . . . wrong sort of disruption of the paper fibers."

All these processes involved "peeling away" the upper layer of flame damage, she thought. If she could do that she could see what was underneath. But no, there was no way . . .

She froze. "Yes!" Pushing back the chair, she got to her feet, suddenly feeling a little giddy. "Easy girl . . . ! But you *are* a genius, Darlene Cooper." She smiled as she strode across the room to the store cupboard. *"You are a bloody genius!"*

Chapter 134

IT WAS CALLED a "Saser" and two months earlier, when Darlene was giving Craig a wish-list of equipment for the lab, she'd almost crossed it off. She was thanking all that was holy she had kept the Saser on the list. Even with a price tag of ten grand, tonight it could prove to be worth every cent.

For that money, the machine didn't look much. It wasn't even very large, just a couple of shiny buttons on the front. It looked just like a small photocopier.

Appearances were deceptive. The Saser was an amazing invention, and there were maybe only half a dozen in the world.

She found it on the second shelf on the right of the store-room. It was quite light, easy to lift down. She put it on the counter below the overhead microscope, plugged it in and watched a small screen light up.

She pulled over her chair and started programming the device. She remembered the spec. A Saser, she recalled, was, according to the technical review she'd read in *Forensics Now* magazine, a little like an X-ray machine. But – and this was its

USP – it didn't see *right* through things to show bones of the body or the contents of a suitcase like an airport scanner. A Saser could be finely adjusted to penetrate beneath the surface to any predetermined depth. In skilled hands, it could reveal layer upon layer of any object. It was exactly what she needed now.

She lifted the lid and picked up the final pages of Julie O'Connor's scrapbook.

The contents appeared on the screen. The pages were covered with scorches, almost all the writing wrecked. Darlene adjusted a few parameters and pushed the "Scan" button.

The Saser made a hissing sound. She studied the screen. The image appeared almost identical to the original – just small patches of scorched paper cleared. She could trace the lines of a few letters that had been invisible.

She altered the penetration depth and upped the resolution, pushed "Scan" again.

A new image appeared.

"That's better!" she said, stunned by the quality. The picture had sharpened dramatically. She could see numbers, letters, whole words. She scrolled up. The top of the page looked better, but still not enough to show what she was after – the damn name.

Darlene adjusted the parameters a third time, her mind racing, numbers and quotients running through her brain. She had to get the depth right or she would overshoot, go straight through.

She pulled back on the resolution and doubled the depth of penetration to one five-hundredth of a millimeter, pushed the "Scan" button again.

The wait was agonizing. Darlene's eyes were glued to the screen. She could hear her own heart thumping.

As she read two words at the top of the page, Darlene felt the hairs on the back of her neck rise.

GRETA . . . THOROGOOD.

Chapter 135

JULIE HAD SET her phone to wake her at 4.30. It went off dutifully on time, but she was already awake. She hadn't slept . . . too lost in wonderful thoughts, thoughts of blood, rolled-up banknotes, revenge . . . sweet, sweet revenge. She got up, changed into fresh clothes, threw the wig, moustache and men's things into a plastic bag.

It was still dark as she tugged open the door onto the parking lot at the rear of SupaMart. Totally deserted, of course. Just two cars left from the previous night. She tossed the plastic bag into a nearby dumpster.

It was three miles from here to where the silly bitch went jogging every morning. 6 am. Parsley Beach. "How typical," Julie said aloud. "Just when she goes out *running*, I'm on the frigging train from Sandsville to serve stupid bitches like her."

She turned onto Sebastian Road and just kept walking, the anger building with each step. She could feel the long knife through the lining of her jacket, and her smile broadened as she contemplated what she would do to Greta Thorogood.

Chapter 136

WHEN MY PHONE rang, I was in a deep sleep, floated up to wakefulness, confused, reached for the phone, and eventually recognized Darlene's voice.

I glanced at the clock. It said 5.42. "Don't you ever sleep, Darlene?" I groaned.

"Sorry, Craig. But I think you'll wanna hear this."

I was out the door in five, cell phone to my ear as I pressed the remote for the car.

Greta's cell just rang and rang and finally went to voicemail. I left a message. "Greta. It's Craig. If you get this message at home, stay where you are. Got that? Stay put and call me back. I'm heading over to your place right now."

I searched for the Thorogoods' home number as I pulled onto Military Road and headed toward the bridge, found it, punched the preset. No one picked up. I disconnected, tried again. Waited, waited . . . still nothing.

The traffic was beginning to build. I put my foot down, bugger the cameras, and if I got stopped? Well then I got stopped.

I sped left onto Warringah Freeway, the black colossus of Sydney Harbour Bridge in the distance, the towers of North

Sydney to my right, a much larger collection of skyscrapers directly ahead over the bridge.

Three minutes later, I was on the Cahill Expressway. I shot down the off-ramp, weaving between slower cars, ignoring the blaring horns, ignoring the speedometer. I tore down onto New South Head Road and just went for it. I saw two cameras go off, but I didn't care. Slowing, I pulled into Stockton Boulevard, the Thorogoods' house a little way down on the right.

Lights were on. I tried the home number again as I stepped out of the car and ran along the sidewalk. No response. I reached the doorbell, leaned on it. Nothing. Tried again. Banged on the huge hardwood door.

The door opened and I almost fell into the hall. Brett was standing barefoot in a bathrobe, hair wet, bewildered.

"What the . . . ?"

"Where's Greta?"

"What do you . . . ?"

"Where is Greta?" I yelled.

"She's out on her run . . . Why?"

"Your wife's the next victim."

"WHAT!" His expression changed to one of horror. "How can you . . . ?"

"Just do, Brett. Where does she run?"

"Parsley Bay, about three miles away," he said, his voice cracking with shock.

"I know it."

"Always the same route – along the beach, up through the reserve, along to the parking lot. CHRIST! . . . Look, GO, Craig! GO NOW! I've got squads all over the Eastern Suburbs. I'll get a team there immediately."

Chapter 137

ONE OF THE greatest pleasures in life, Greta thought as she closed the door of her BMW and turned to the path down to the beach. It was already seventy degrees plus and she loved the summer.

She ran down the path and two minutes later she was on the sand, the sun casting a fresh morning glow all around. The ocean was so perfect it looked like it'd been Photoshopped.

She found her rhythm and ran close to the water where the sand was harder. To her right, a line of palms. No one around, rarely was. That was one of the things she loved most about this spot, it gave her half an hour of blissful solitude. When she got home she'd have to sort out the kids' breakfast, pack the bags ready for school. Then see Brett off on the driveway, get the children in the car and do the mile-long drive to the drop-off.

Later, as usual, she would meet friends for lunch at Tony's or Oasis. Then it would be the mad dash to school – the 3.30 pick-up. Back home, dinner for the kids. Later, after the children were in bed it would be dinner for her and Brett, a glass of wine . . . thank God! Then, into bed and Brett no doubt getting amorous.

She ran on, focusing on her rhythm, her pace, the ocean, the scent of freedom. The temporary bliss.

She didn't notice Julie O'Connor just a few yards away concealed in the palm trees watching her, smiling.

Chapter 138

I SCREECHED OFF down Bexham Boulevard and back out onto New South Head Road. I knew Parsley Beach – it was in Vaucluse. A beautiful spot, panoramic view.

Averaging ninety miles an hour, it took a little over two minutes to reach the turn-off. I saw another speed camera flash as I shot past, but I couldn't give a damn. I swung a hard left off the main highway onto a smaller road, followed the curves, descended a steep hill, and almost overshot the parking lot. I knew the path down to the beach lay on the far side of the scrap of sandy ground. This morning, only one car was parked there – Greta's BMW 320i convertible.

I ran across the open space and down the first steps of the path that led through the reserve. I could hear the crashing of waves directly ahead.

I took the steps slowly, glancing around, sniffing the air. Julie O'Connor could be anywhere. I shoved away the dread, thought I might already be too late.

There was a bend in the path. I gripped the wooden handrail on one side as the descent became steep. Stopped, listened. Nothing but the sound of birds, waves, the breeze rustling the eucalyptus.

I glimpsed sand, a flash of blue water. The beach was less than a hundred feet ahead down the sloping, curving stairway.

A tight bend. I held the rail with both hands, eased down two steps, and there was Greta. She'd just reached the first steps up from the beach.

I was about to call to her when I saw movement to her right. Julie O'Connor surged from the undergrowth with shocking speed.

"Greta!"

She looked up, saw me, began to smile, and the O'Connor bitch was on her.

I felt my stomach flip, and for a second I froze.

Julie grabbed her around the neck, pulling her back. Greta stared at me, eyes wide, and screamed.

I took half a dozen steps toward them.

"YOU BETTER STOP!" Julie shouted.

I kept going.

"STOP . . . ! I've got a very, very big knife 'ere. And the tip of it is just touching this whore's spine."

Greta screamed again.

"Oh, shut the fuck up!" O'Connor hissed in Greta's ear, then turned back to me.

"Let her go."

Julie O'Connor laughed. "Oh, yeah! . . . Right! We have girl business to discuss. Don't we?" She twisted Greta's face round, her fingers digging into her cheeks.

I took another step forward. They were only thirty feet away now.

"STOP! I SAID STOP!"

I walked down two more steps.

"I TOLD YOU TO FUCKING STOP!"

Greta convulsed.

"Oh dear, there's blood on her lovely running top!"

Greta's face had drained. She was panting, eyes like black dishes.

I stopped. Put my hands up. Caught a glimpse of movement behind Greta and O'Connor. My cousin had appeared ten steps behind them, two officers with him, guns drawn.

"Look, can we talk?" I said.

Julie laughed again, a nasty rasp. "Why would I wanna talk? I have this bitch under my control. She's *mine* . . . She's mine. I can do what I want with her. Make her beg, make her squirm. She's a whore . . . right? She gives it up for Brett. Mr. Big Policeman. She gives it up and she gets her Chanel, her Prada, her holidays on Hamilton Island. Two kids, and her husband might screw around on the quiet, but it's a deal . . . right? What has this stupid bitch ever done for herself?"

"She's a human being, Julie."

Chapter 139

"THE KNIFE'S IN a bit further," O'Connor bragged. She looked down. "Oh yeah . . . more blood." She grinned.

Mark rushed forward.

Greta fell to one side, groaning as she hit the sandy path. I saw Julie swing to her left, her knife slicing the air, a hateful look on her face as she slipped off the path.

"You go round the top," Mark said to me, quietly. "I'll take the path." He turned to his men. "Nichols . . . go back down to the beach and round. Taylor, stay with Mrs. Thorogood."

I could see Greta wasn't badly hurt, so I ran up the steps. Mark's plan was a good one. Between us, we'd have the woman, I was sure of it.

Ten seconds later and I was at the top step, the parking lot ahead of me. I ran onto the sandy rectangle, skirted the edge, found the next path down to the beach and headed onto it. I guessed Mark would be about fifty yards below on an adjacent path.

I took the steps down two at a time, the stair treads even. Turned right, then left, another tight left. Drew up in the sand.

Mark was coming toward me along a sandy path. I caught a

movement to my left. The O'Connor woman charged through the bush and smacked into him, knocking him off balance. He stumbled to his left, pistol flying from his hand.

Julie O'Connor was on him in a second, her right hand raised, the horrifying blade over Mark's face.

I didn't pause to think, just rushed forward and grabbed the woman by the shoulders. I was stunned by how powerful she was. Using all my strength I managed to yank her away, but I was sent sprawling onto my back. She was incredibly agile and got to her feet before me. I propelled myself upright, watched as she came for me. Mark began to pull up, but he was slow. Julie lunged at me, growling like an animal. I misjudged her thrust and felt a screech of pain rip through my abdomen.

I dropped to my knees and saw the point of the woman's bloodied knife coming toward my face, heard the crack of a gun going off and felt a heavy weight slamming down on top of me.

Chapter 140

I OPENED MY eyes and saw a man's face. It took the shape of my cousin Mark's. I felt an instant stab of déjà vu. Slowly, my senses returned. I could feel the coolness of cotton sheets. The room was lit with natural light, curtains pulled back across a window in the opposite wall.

Everything came to me in a rush.

"You were very lucky."

"I feel like I've been here before," I managed to say.

Mark smiled. That's when the vision of the past shattered.

"What's the damage this time?" I said flatly, giving my cousin a baffled look.

"Oh, perforated intestine . . . and she just nicked your spleen."

I lifted the sheet and saw a bandage across my abdomen. "I got off light," I said cautiously.

"I got off lighter, Craig . . . Thanks to you. And you were unarmed!"

"You shitting me?"

Mark grinned and looked down at his feet. "I don't want to go out and choose curtains with you, Craig, but to be honest . . . I'm worn out with this constant war. God. It was all a long time ago. We've both lost . . ." He trailed off and looked into my face.

I sensed the numbing effect of painkillers. "How long have I been out?"

He glanced at his watch. "Thirty-five, thirty-six hours."

I slowly pulled myself up in the bed. "What's happened?"

"Julie O'Connor's under armed guard in intensive care."

"And Greta?"

"She's fine. In shock, but unharmed. Nasty cut in her back. She was here earlier – but you were still out. You're her hero!"

I produced a small laugh. "Ow! Christ!"

"Only hurts when you laugh right, Craig?"

"It was a close one."

"Sure was." He looked at me seriously. "But it's over . . . right?" And he fixed me with his eyes.

I nodded and lay back on the pillows. "So look . . . the O'Connor woman . . . she was driven by pure jealousy, yeah?"

"Only partly. Seems there was more to it than that. One of my guys found out something very interesting this morning. Three months ago, Julie O'Connor was the victim of a botched operation – a tuboplasty or something like that. It was to . . . I dunno . . . unblock her Fallopian tubes or some shit. Guess who the gynecologist was?"

"Cameron Granger . . . Of course!"

"Your girl Darlene's managed to get a lot of background stuff from the woman's scrapbook. O'Connor was desperate to have children and when the op went wrong it went spectacularly wrong!"

"She was infertile?"

"Totally. Her life fell apart. She was already living on the breadline in Sandsville. Her boyfriend, Bruce Frimmel, left her. She killed him. It gave her the taste for doing it some more, I guess. And it was all made worse because of where she worked. In her scrapbook she refers to the Bellevue Hill women as 'whores'. She thought they were little more than prostitutes – leading lavish lives thanks to rich husbands."

"That would explain the money inserted in the victims – a symbolic gesture."

"Not just money, Craig. *Fake money* . . . for what she saw as fake women, fake wives."

"Isn't it amazing though?" I said. "The killer takes it out on other women. She didn't try to kill the person who caused all the trouble in the first place, Dr. Granger."

"Seen it before. O'Connor displaced the blame. That's why I said earlier it was exaggerated by the place she worked in. Deep down, repressed for years, she *was* envious of the women she saw each day in Bellevue Hill. Being messed up by Granger pushed her over the edge."

"We'll probably never know what the original spark could have been."

"Actually, we do. That girl of yours, Darlene, is shit hot. She found out Julie was traumatized in childhood. There was a file on her at St. Joseph's Psychiatric Hospital. Julie spent some time there almost ten years ago – she'd been living on the streets, raped, mugged. According to the reports, she claimed her mother had tortured her as a child. The authorities tried to check the story but the woman, Sheila O'Connor, had moved abroad."

"So she was seeking some twisted revenge?"

"I guess."

I took a deep breath and gazed across to the window. "And Cameron Granger got away with it."

"Well, not altogether. He lost his wife."

I nodded, sighed heavily.

"And," Mark went on, "one of my sergeants – Howard Tindle . . . a good kid – he sniffed a rat."

I raised an eyebrow.

"The hospital Granger works in closed ranks, protected the bastard. They covered up his malpractice with O'Connor. They assumed she was too naive and too dumb to do anything about it. And, in a way, she was. But the truth will come out now. Granger's finished."

"Good," I said with genuine feeling.

Chapter 141

IN A WAY, history was repeating itself.

It was the day after I was released from hospital. I was in my car taking Justine to the airport, driving along the same road I'd traveled three years ago. There was a beautiful woman beside me, but no child in the back. And I was a very different person.

The airport was packed. Justine checked in and I walked with her to the Departure Zone, the scanners and security guys just a few feet away.

"It's been eventful," I said.

"Can't deny that, Craig."

"You've been a great help. If ever you feel like a break from the LA office . . ."

"I might seriously consider that."

"Wish Jack my best, yeah?"

"I will."

She walked through passport control. I watched her turn and wave and I thought . . . "Jack Morgan, you are one lucky guy."

Chapter 142

I WALKED INTO the conference room at Private HQ and the team applauded me. Hadn't expected that.

I surveyed the gathering – Johnny, Mary, Darlene and Colette – the core of my life and my work.

"Thanks," I said rather weakly. "Not sure why I deserve it . . ."

"I think we all deserve a pat on the back, actually," Johnny said.

"It's been one hell of a first week!" I replied. "So, how have things wound up?"

"Geoff Hewes was buried yesterday afternoon," Mary began. "Pam Hewes is back home with her kids. I called in to see if there was anything . . . Of course it'll take her months to recover fully."

I nodded. "And what about Graham Parker?"

"Seventeen stitches and a very rock 'n' roll scar. Micky's fine. Spent a night in hospital after his party, but no permanent harm done. He's rehearsing for a big tour. Out of gratitude, he's helping Parker settle his gambling debts. Katia is being deported."

"But what about the song you told me about? The one describing his own death. Why did he even write that?"

Johnny shrugged. "I think it was purely an artistic gesture. He felt helpless, controlled by 'the suits'. He's a sensitive guy, but that sensitivity had slipped into paranoia. His phenomenal drug intake couldn't have helped!"

"And what about Hemi?"

"He's up and running . . . well waddling."

We all laughed.

"He's mighty pissed though . . . as you would imagine!" Johnny added.

"I heard you bumped into Al Loretto's boy, Jerry."

"Yeah, I did. He was helpful in making me realize what a mess Parker had gotten himself into."

"And you've heard nothing from his dad?"

"The cameras have gone again from the brothels, apparently. Loretto got his way in the end, of course."

"And I reckon if the bouncer hadn't got to Geoff Hewes first," Mary commented, "Loretto wouldn't have given him another chance."

"They were lining up for the guy!"

"Word got out about the lovely Ken Boston," Darlene commented. "He's resigned."

I raised an eyebrow. "What about the Ho family, Mary?"

"Dai was under observation in hospital. He was severely traumatized. His father has booked him in for plastic surgery. The police here are liaising with the Hong Kong authorities. They're after the big boss, Fong Sum, but I'm pretty sure they're wasting their time."

"Untouchable?"

"For the moment. Ho is just relieved his son was saved. He now wants to have the case of his wife's murder reopened. He's convinced twelve years ago a bent cop was in the pocket of the Sydney Triads and buried evidence. He's sure the Triads killed Jiao. He wants to prove it *and* to identify those involved."

"Good luck to him!" I said leaning back in my chair. "Well, sounds like we've had a few positive results. Not bad for our first week!"

"And why shouldn't we have?" Darlene asked.

I smiled. "Yeah, you're right. Why shouldn't we have?"

"Oh, there are these, though," Johnny added and pushed a small pile of papers toward me across the conference table.

I glanced at the top one. The words: "Roads and Maritime Services" printed in the top right corner . . . speeding tickets.

I lifted my eyes and saw the entire team grinning at me.

"Looks like I might have to call in a favor," I laughed.

A holiday you'll never forget...

SECOND HONEYMOON

Coming July 2013

Turn the page for a sneak preview

CHAPTER 1

ETHAN BRESLOW COULDN'T stop smiling as he reached for the bottle of Perrier-Jouët Champagne chilling in the ice bucket next to the bed. He'd never been happier in his whole life. He'd never believed it was possible to be this happy.

"What's the world record for not wearing clothes on your honeymoon?" he said jokingly, his chiseled six-foot-two frame barely covered by a sheet.

"I don't know for sure. It's my first honeymoon and all," said his bride, Abigail, propping herself up on the pillow next to him. She was still catching her breath from their most daring lovemaking yet. "But at the rate we're going," she added, "I definitely overpacked."

The two laughed as Ethan poured more Champagne. Handing Abigail her glass, he stared deep into her soft blue eyes. She was so beautiful and—damn the cliché—was even more so on the inside. He'd never met anyone as kind and compassionate. With two simple words she'd made him the luckiest guy on the planet. *Do you take this man to be your lawfully wedded husband?*

I do.

Ethan raised his Champagne for a toast, the bubbles catching a ray of Caribbean sunshine through the curtains. "Here's to Abby, the greatest girl in the world," he said.

"You're not so terrible yourself. Even though you call me a girl."

They clinked glasses, sipping in silence while soaking everything in from their beachfront bungalow at the Governor's Club in Turks and Caicos. It was all so perfect—the fragrant aroma of wild cotton flowers that lingered under their king-size canopy bed, the gentle island breeze drifting through open French doors on the patio.

Back on a different sort of island—Manhattan—the tabloids had spilled untold barrels of ink on stories about their relationship. Ethan Breslow, scion of the Breslow venture-capital-and-LBO empire, onetime bad boy of the New York party circuit, had finally grown up, thanks to a down-to-earth pediatrician named Abigail Michaels.

Before he'd met her, Ethan had been a notorious dabbler. Women. Drugs. Even careers. He tried to open a nightclub in SoHo, tried to launch a wine magazine, tried to make a documentary film about Amy Winehouse. But his heart was never in it. Not any of it. Deep down, where it really counted, he had no idea what he wanted to do with his life. He was lost.

Then he'd found Abby.

She was loads of fun, and very funny, too, but she was

also focused. Her dedication to children genuinely touched him, inspired him. Ethan cleaned up his act, got accepted at Columbia Law School, and graduated. After his very first week working for the Children's Defense Fund, he got down on one knee before Abby and proposed.

Now here they were, newly married, and trying to have children of their own. *Really* trying. That was becoming a joke between them. Not since John and Yoko had a couple spent so much time in bed together.

Ethan swallowed the last sip of Perrier-Jouët. "So what do you think?" he asked. "Do we give the DO NOT DISTURB sign a break and venture out for a little stroll on the beach? Maybe grab some lunch?"

Abby nudged even closer to him, her long, chestnut-brown hair draping across his chest. "We could stay right here and order room service again," she said. "Maybe *after* we work up a little more of an appetite."

That gave Ethan an interesting idea.

"Come with me," he said, sliding out of the canopy bed.

"Where are we going?" asked Abigail. She was smiling, intrigued.

Ethan grabbed the ice bucket, tucking it under his arm.

"You'll see," he said.

CHAPTER 2

ABBY WASN'T SURE what to think at first. Standing there naked with Ethan in the master bathroom, she placed a hand on her hip as if to say, *You're joking, right? Sex in a sauna?*

Ethan put just the right spin on it.

"Think of it as one of your hot yoga classes," he said. "Only better."

That pretty much sealed the deal. Abby loved her hot yoga classes back in Manhattan. Nothing made her feel better after a long day at work.

Except maybe this. Yes, this had great potential. Something they could giggle about for years, a real honeymoon memory. Or, at the very least, a tremendous calorie burner!

"After you, my darling," said Ethan, opening the sauna door with good-humored gallantry. The Governor's Club was known for having spectacular master bathrooms, complete with six-head marble showers and Japanese soaking tubs.

Ethan promptly covered the bench along the back wall with a towel. As Abby lay down, he cranked up the heat, then ladled some water on the lava rocks in the corner. The sauna sizzled with steam.

Kneeling on the cedar floor before Abby, he reached into the ice bucket. A little foreplay couldn't hurt.

Placing an ice cube between his lips, he leaned over and began slowly tracing the length of her body with his mouth. The cube just barely grazed her skin, from the angle of her neck past the curve of her breasts and all the way down to her toes, which now curled with pleasure.

"That's... *wonderful*," Abby whispered, her eyes closed.

She could feel the full force of the sauna's heat now, the sweat beginning to push through her pores. It felt exhilarating. She was wet all over.

"I want you inside me," she said.

But as she opened her eyes, Abigail suddenly sprung up from the bench. She was staring over Ethan's shoulder, mortified.

"What is it?" he asked.

"There's someone out there! Ethan, I just saw somebody."

Ethan turned to look at the door and its small glass window, barely bigger than an index card. He didn't see anything—or anyone. "Are you sure?" he asked.

Abby nodded. "I'm sure," she said. "Someone walked by. *I'm positive.*"

"Was it a man or a woman?"

"I couldn't tell."

"It was probably just the maid," said Ethan.

"But we've still got the DO NOT DISTURB sign on the door."

"I'm sure she knocked first and we didn't hear her." He smiled. "Given how long that sign's been out there she was probably wondering if we were still alive in here."

Abby calmed down a bit. Ethan was probably right. Still. "Can you go check to make sure?" she asked.

"Of course," he said. For a laugh, he picked up the ice bucket and put it in front of his crotch. "How do I look?"

"Very funny," said Abigail, cracking a smile. She handed him the towel from the bench.

"I'll be back in a jiff," he said, wrapping the towel around his waist.

He grabbed the door handle and pulled it toward him. Nothing happened.

"It's stuck. Abby, it won't open."

CHAPTER 3

"WHAT DO YOU mean the door won't open?"

In a split second, the smile had disappeared from Abby's face.

Ethan pulled harder on the handle, but the sauna door wouldn't budge. "It's like it's locked," he said. Only they both knew there was no lock on the door. "It must be jammed."

He pressed his face against the glass of the little window for a better view.

"Do you see anyone?" Abigail asked.

"No. No one."

Making a fist, he pounded on the door and shouted. "Hey, is anyone out there?"

There was no response. Silence. An annoying silence. An eerie silence.

"So much for it being the maid," said Abby. Then it

dawned on her. "Do you think we're being robbed and they've locked us in here?"

"Maybe," said Ethan. He couldn't rule it out. Of course, as the son of a billionaire, he was less concerned about being robbed than being locked in a sauna.

"What do we do?" asked Abby. She was starting to get scared. He could see it in her eyes, and that frightened him.

"The first thing we do is turn off the heat," he answered, wiping the sweat from his forehead. He hit the Off button on the control panel. He then grabbed the ladle sitting by the lava rocks and held it up to show Abby. "This is the second thing we do."

Ethan wedged the ladle's wooden handle into the door-jamb as though it were a crowbar, leaning on it with all his weight.

"It's working!" she said.

The door shifted on its hinges, slowly beginning to move. With a little more muscle Ethan would be able to—*snap!*

The handle splintered like a matchstick, sending Ethan flying headfirst into the wall. When he turned around, Abby said, "You're bleeding!"

There was a gash above his right eye, a trickle of red on his cheek. Then a stream. As a doctor, Abby had seen blood in almost every conceivable way and always knew what to do. But this was different. This wasn't her office or a hospital; there were no gauze pads or bandages. She had nothing. And this was *Ethan* who was bleeding.

"Hey, it's fine," he said in an effort to reassure her. "Everything's going to be okay. We'll figure it out."

She wasn't convinced. What had been hot and sexy was

now just hot. Brutally hot. Every time she breathed in, she could feel the sauna's heat singeing the inside of her lungs.

"Are you sure the sauna's off?" she asked.

Actually, Ethan wasn't sure at all. If anything, the room was beginning to feel hotter. *How could that be?*

He didn't care. His ace in the hole was the pipe in the corner, the emergency shutoff valve.

Standing on the bench, he turned the valve perpendicular to the pipe. A loud hiss followed. Even louder was Abby's sigh of relief.

Not only had the heat stopped, there was actually cool air blowing in from the ceiling vent.

"There," said Ethan. "With any luck, we've triggered an alarm somewhere. Even if we didn't, we'll be okay. We've got plenty of water. Eventually, they'll find us."

But the words were barely out of his mouth when they both wrinkled their noses, sniffing the air.

"What's that smell?"

"I don't know," said Ethan. Whatever it was, there was something not right about it.

Abby coughed first, her hands desperately reaching up around her neck. Her throat was closing; she couldn't breathe.

Ethan tried to help her, but seconds later he couldn't breathe, either.

It was happening so fast. They looked at each other, eyes red and tearing, their bodies twisted in agony. It couldn't get worse than this.

But it did.

Ethan and Abby fell to their knees, gasping, when they

saw a pair of eyes through the small window of the sauna door.

"Help!" Ethan barely managed, his hand outstretched. "Please, help!"

But the eyes just kept staring. Unblinking and unfeeling. Ethan and Abby finally realized what was happening. It was a murderer—a murderer who was watching them die.

CHAPTER 4

IF I'VE SAID it once, I've said it a thousand times. *Things aren't always as they appear.*

Take the room I was sitting in, for instance. To look at the elegant furniture, plush Persian rugs, and gilt-framed artwork adorning the walls, you would have thought I'd just walked into some designer show house out in the burbs.

Definitely not some guy's office on the Lower East Side of Manhattan.

Then there was the guy sitting across from me.

If he had been any more laid-back his chair would have tipped over. He was wearing jeans, a polo shirt, and a pair of brown Teva sandals. In a million years you'd never have guessed he was a shrink.

Up until a week ago, I seemed pretty laid-back, too. You'd never have known that I was on the verge of trashing a somewhat promising eleven-year career at the FBI. I was hiding it well. At least that's what I thought.

But my boss, Frank Walsh, thought otherwise. Of course, that's putting it mildly. Frank basically had me in a verbal headlock, screaming at me in his raspy, two-pack-a-day voice until I cried uncle. *You have to see a shrink, John.*

So that's why I agreed to meet with the very relaxed Dr. Adam Kline in his office disguised as a living room. He specialized in treating people suffering from "deep emotional stress due to personal loss or trauma."

People like me, John O'Hara.

All I knew for sure was that if this guy didn't ultimately give me a clean bill of mental health, I would be toast at the Bureau. Kaput. Sacked. The sayonara special.

But that wasn't really the problem.

The problem was, *I didn't give a shit.*

"So, you're Dr. Grief, huh?" I said, settling into an armchair that clearly was supposed to make me forget that I was actually "on the couch."

Dr. Kline nodded with a slight smile, as if he expected nothing less than my cracking wise right from the get-go. "And from what I hear, you're Agent Time Bomb," he shot back. "Shall we get started?"

CHAPTER 5

THE GUY CERTAINLY didn't waste any time.

"How long ago did your wife die, John?" Dr. Kline asked, jumping right in.

I noticed there was no pen or notepad in his lap. Nothing was being written down. He was simply listening. Actually, I kind of liked that approach.

"She was killed about two years ago."

"How did it happen?"

I looked at him, a bit confused. "You didn't read any of this in my file?"

"I read all of it. Three times," he answered. "I want to hear it from you, though."

Part of me wanted to leap out of my chair and pop the guy with a right hook for trying to make me relive the single worst day of my life. But another part of me—the part that knew better—understood he wasn't asking me to do something that I hadn't already been doing on my own. Every day, no less. I couldn't let it go.

I couldn't let *Susan* go.

Susan and I had both been FBI special agents, although when we first met and married, I was an undercover police officer with the NYPD. I became an agent a few years later and was assigned to a completely different section from Susan's, the Counterterrorism Division. A few exceptions notwithstanding, that's really the only way the Bureau allows for married couples.

Susan gave birth to two beautiful boys, and for a while everything was great. Then everything wasn't. After eight years, we divorced. I'll spare you the reasons, especially because there wasn't one big enough to keep us apart.

Ironically, it wasn't until I worked on a case involving a black widow serial killer who nearly poisoned me to death that we both realized it. Susan and I reconciled, and along with John Jr. and Max, we were a family again. Until one afternoon roughly two years ago.

I proceeded to tell Dr. Kline how Susan was driving home from the supermarket when another car ran a stop sign and plowed into her side at over sixty miles an hour. The posted speed limit on the road was thirty. Susan died instantly, while the other driver barely had a scratch on him. What's more, the son of a bitch was drunk at the time of the accident.

A drunk *lawyer,* as it turned out.

By refusing the Breathalyzer and opting instead to have his blood drawn at a hospital, he was able to buy himself a couple of hours—enough time to allow his blood alcohol level to dip under the legal limit. He was charged with vehicular manslaughter and received the minimum sentence.

Was that justice? You tell me. He got to see his kids again while I had to sit mine down and explain that they were never going to see their mother again.

Dr. Kline remained quiet for a few seconds after I finished. His face gave nothing away. "What was she buying?" he finally asked.

"Excuse me?"

"What was Susan buying at the supermarket?"

"I heard you," I said. "I just can't believe that's the first question you're asking after everything I told you. How is that important?"

"I didn't say it was."

"Butter," I blurted out. "Susan was going to bake cookies for the boys, but she didn't have any butter. Pretty ironic, don't you think?"

"How so?"

"Never mind."

"No, go ahead," said Dr. Kline. "Tell me."

"She was an FBI agent; she could've died on the job many times over," I said.

Then it was as if some switch inside me had been flipped on. Or maybe off. I couldn't control myself; the words spilled angrily out of my mouth.

"But no, it's some drunk asshole who plows into her on the way back from the supermarket!"

I was suddenly out of breath, as though I'd just run a marathon. "There. Are you satisfied?"

Dr. Kline shook his head. "No, I'm not, John. What I am is concerned," he said calmly. "Do you know why?"

Of course I did. It was why the Bureau had suspended me. It was why my boss, Frank Walsh, insisted on my coming here to get my head examined.

Stephen McMillan, the drunk lawyer who killed Susan, was being released from prison in less than a week.

"You think I'm going to kill him, don't you?"

Kline shrugged, deflecting the question. "Let's just say people who care very much for you are worried about what you might be planning. So, tell me, John…are they worried for a good reason? Are you planning revenge?"

CHAPTER 6

RIVERSIDE, CONNECTICUT, IS about an hour's drive from midtown Manhattan. Channeling my inner Mario Andretti, I drove it in forty minutes flat. All I wanted to do was get home and hug my boys.

"Jeez, Dad, you trying to crush me or something?" chirped Max, who was throwing a baseball against a pitchback on our front lawn when I pulled in. For a ten-year-old, the kid could really rifle it—all fatherly bias aside, of course.

I finally unwrapped my arms from around him. "So are you all packed?" I asked.

School had been out for a week. Max and his older brother, John Jr., were heading off to sleepaway camp the next morning for a month.

Max nodded. "Yeah. Grandma helped me get everything

together. She even wrote my name in all my underwear with a Sharpie. Weird. *Whatever*."

I would've expected nothing less from Grandma Judy. "Are she and Grandpa here?"

"No. They're out shopping for dinner," said Max. "Grandpa wanted steaks for our last night all together."

When Susan died, her parents, Judy and Marshall Holt, insisted on moving up from Florida, where they'd retired. They said it would be impossible for me to raise the boys alone while I was still working at the Bureau, and they were right. Also, I think they knew that being around Max and John Jr. would help—if only a little bit—ease the pain of having lost their daughter, their only child.

They'd been nothing short of incredible since the day they arrived, and while I could never fully express my gratitude for their time, love, and sacrifice, the least I could do was treat them to a four-week Mediterranean cruise while the boys were off at camp. I was just glad I paid for it while I was still getting a paycheck from the Bureau. Not that I would've changed my mind. It's that Marshall and Judy would've never accepted the trip. That's the kind of people they are.

"Where's your brother?" I asked Max.

"Where else?" he answered with an eye roll underneath his Yankees cap. "On his computer. The geekazoid."

Max went back to striking out imaginary Red Sox batters while I headed inside the house and upstairs to John Jr.'s room. Naturally, the door was closed.

"Knock, knock," I announced, walking right in.

John Jr. was indeed sitting at his desk, in front of his computer. He immediately threw up his hands at the sight of me.

"C'mon, Dad, can't you knock for real?" he said with a groan. "Haven't you ever heard of the right to privacy?"

I chuckled. "You're thirteen, dude. Talk to me when you can shave."

He rubbed the peach fuzz on his chin, smiling. "It might be happening sooner than you think," he said.

He was right. My older boy was growing up fast. Too fast, maybe.

John Jr. was eleven when he lost his mother, a very tricky age. Unlike Max, J.J. was old enough to feel everything an adult would feel—the full pain and anguish, the overwhelming sense of loss. But he was still just a kid. That's what made it so unfair. The grieving forced him to mature in ways no kid should have to endure.

"What are you working on?" I asked.

"Updating my Facebook page," he answered. "They won't let us do it at camp."

Yes, I know. That's one of the reasons why you're going, sport. No video games, cell phones, or laptops allowed. Only fresh air and Mother Nature.

I walked behind him and shot a peek at his MacBook. He instantly flipped out, slapping his palms against the screen. "Dad, this is personal!"

I never wanted to be a parent who spied on his kid or secretly logged on to his computer to make sure he wasn't saying or doing things he wasn't supposed to. But I also knew that there was nothing "personal" about the Internet.

"Once you post something online, anyone in the world could be looking at it," I said.

"So?"

"So you need to be careful, that's all."

"I am," he said. He was looking away.

It was moments like these when I really missed Susan. She'd know just what to say and, equally important, what not to say.

"John, look at me for a second."

Slowly, he did.

"I trust you," I said. "The thing is, you have to trust me, too. I'm only trying to help you."

He nodded. "Dad, I know all about the creeps and stalkers out there. I don't give out any personal information or stuff like that."

"Good," I said. And that was that.

Or so I thought. Walking out of J.J.'s room, I had no idea, no clue at all, that I was just about to crack one of the biggest and craziest cases of my career.

And as fast as you can say "Dinner is served," it was all about to begin.

JAMES
PATTERSON

**To find out more about James Patterson
and his bestselling books, go to
www.jamespatterson.co.uk**

Also by James Patterson

ALEX CROSS NOVELS

Along Came a Spider • Kiss the Girls • Jack and Jill • Cat and Mouse •
Pop Goes the Weasel • Roses are Red • Violets are Blue • Four Blind
Mice • The Big Bad Wolf • London Bridges • Mary, Mary • Cross •
Double Cross • Cross Country • Alex Cross's Trial (*with Richard
DiLallo*) • I, Alex Cross • Cross Fire • Kill Alex Cross •
Merry Christmas, Alex Cross • Alex Cross, Run

THE WOMEN'S MURDER CLUB SERIES

1st to Die • 2nd Chance (*with Andrew Gross*) •
3rd Degree (*with Andrew Gross*) • 4th of July (*with Maxine Paetro*) •
The 5th Horseman (*with Maxine Paetro*) • The 6th Target
(*with Maxine Paetro*) • 7th Heaven (*with Maxine Paetro*) •
8th Confession (*with Maxine Paetro*) • 9th Judgement
(*with Maxine Paetro*) • 10th Anniversary (*with Maxine Paetro*) •
11th Hour (*with Maxine Paetro*) • 12th of Never (*with Maxine Paetro*)

DETECTIVE MICHAEL BENNETT SERIES

Step on a Crack (*with Michael Ledwidge*) • Run for Your Life
(*with Michael Ledwidge*) • Worst Case (*with Michael Ledwidge*) •
Tick Tock (*with Michael Ledwidge*) • I, Michael Bennett
(*with Michael Ledwidge*)

STAND-ALONE THRILLERS

Sail (*with Howard Roughan*) • Swimsuit (*with Maxine Paetro*) •
Don't Blink (*with Howard Roughan*) • Postcard Killers (*with Liza
Marklund*) • Toys (*with Neil McMahon*) • Now You See Her (*with
Michael Ledwidge*) • Kill Me If You Can (*with Marshall Karp*) •
Guilty Wives (*with David Ellis*) • Zoo (*with Michael Ledwidge*) •
NYPD Red (*with Marshall Karp*) • Second Honeymoon
(*with Howard Roughan, to be published July 2013*)

NON-FICTION

Torn Apart (*with Hal and Cory Friedman*) •
The Murder of King Tut (*with Martin Dugard*)

ROMANCE

Sundays at Tiffany's (*with Gabrielle Charbonnet*) •
The Christmas Wedding (*with Richard DiLallo*)

FAMILY OF PAGE-TURNERS

MAXIMUM RIDE SERIES

The Angel Experiment • School's Out Forever •
Saving the World and Other Extreme Sports •
The Final Warning • Max • Fang • Angel • Nevermore

DANIEL X SERIES

The Dangerous Days of Daniel X (*with Michael Ledwidge*) •
Watch the Skies (*with Ned Rust*) •
Demons and Druids (*with Adam Sadler*) •
Game Over (*with Ned Rust*) •
Armageddon (*with Chris Grabenstein*)

WITCH & WIZARD SERIES

Witch & Wizard (*with Gabrielle Charbonnet*) •
The Gift (*with Ned Rust*) • The Fire (*with Jill Dembowski*) •
The Kiss (*with Jill Dembowski*)

MIDDLE SCHOOL NOVELS

Middle School: The Worst Years of My Life (*with Chris Tebbetts*) •
Middle School: Get Me Out of Here! (*with Chris Tebbetts*) •
Middle School: My Brother Is a Big, Fat Liar (*with Lisa Papademetriou*)
• Middle School: How I Survived Bullies, Broccoli
and Snake Hill (*with Chris Tebbetts, to be published June 2013*)

I FUNNY

I Funny (*with Chris Grabenstein*)

CONFESSIONS SERIES

Confessions of a Murder Suspect (*with Maxine Paetro*)

GRAPHIC NOVELS

Daniel X: Alien Hunter (*with Leopoldo Gout*)
Maximum Ride: Manga Vol. 1–6 (*with NaRae Lee*)

For more information about James Patterson's novels, visit
www.jamespatterson.co.uk

Or become a fan on Facebook

I'm proud to support the National Literacy Trust, an independent charity that changes lives through literacy.

Did you know that millions of people in the UK struggle to read and write? This means children are less likely to succeed at school and less likely to develop into confident and happy teenagers. Literacy difficulties will limit their opportunities throughout adult life.

The National Literacy Trust passionately believes that everyone has a right to the reading, writing, speaking and listening skills they need to fulfil their own and, ultimately, the nation's potential.

My own son didn't use to enjoy reading, which was why I started writing children's books – reading for pleasure is an essential way to encourage children to pick up a book. The National Literacy Trust is dedicated to delivering exciting initiatives to encourage people to read and to help raise literacy levels. To find out more about the great work that they do, visit their website at www.literacytrust.org.uk.

James Patterson